To the Ever After

by

Julia Harrison

From the Other Side

To the Ever After

Cover Art by *Lisa Dawn MacDonald*

The Wild Rose Press, Inc.
PO Box 708
Adams Basin, NY 14410-0708
Visit us at www.thewildrosepress.com

Publishing History
First Edition, 2026
Trade Paperback Print ISBN 978-1-5092-6428-5
Digital ISBN 978-1-5092-6429-2

From the Other Side
Published in the United States of America

Dedication

To the strongest people I know, my children,

Dane, Maddi, Kobi, and JJ.

Chapter 1

It was the rain that started it. In an effort to rouse me from a fitful slumber, the torrential downpour pelting angrily at the window prodded at my sleeping brain, searching for a way in.

There are times when reality accidentally slips into a space it doesn't belong. When the outside world, its sounds especially, trespass beyond the line of consciousness and intermingle what is real with what is not. It steers dreams in a direction they were never meant to go and makes the journey from asleep to awake hard and filled with confusion.

There was no rain in my dream world. In truth there were no dreams at all, just a lightless silence, and not the comforting kind. But the rainstorm was heavy. Heavy enough to infiltrate my unconsciousness and lead my brain down a corridor of memories to relive moments past. It pried open a steel trap door that I lacked the energy to close.

Before I was aware enough to escape, it ushered me back to the last heavy rainstorm I had experienced. And to him.

Dark, dense clouds descended, pushing through the stifling humidity like an angry linebacker to announce the arrival of the storm that had been threatening for days. We had tracked the group of four Sygans through the quiet streets of town and out toward the sprawling rural farmlands of Hunterdon County. It was late afternoon when we finally caught up with them.

The farther west we traveled, the damper and heavier the air became. The humidity that had encased us created an almost visible shroud of vapor that sat slick on our skin and made our breathing heavy and fast.

The mass of nervous anxiety that weighed heavy in my stomach had nothing to do with the chase. It started weeks ago and had grown with each passing day. Every attempt I made to make Aamon see reason had failed. He refused to acknowledge the red flags I saw so clearly. The hunt forced my body into autopilot, but my mind was elsewhere, distracted by my inability to convince him.

My frustration was on a low boil, and it had nothing to do with the unseasonal temperatures or the rogue Sygans, once human entities and residents of Daeon's darkness. They ventured often onto Earth's plane and rarely without cause. Whether working alone or in gangs, their objective was always the same, to steal human souls at passing. To entrap them within a glass vessel called an orb. Valuable collateral with which to trade in the black markets of Daeon.

My every attempt to suppress my annoyance only acted to further ignite it. Efforts that were meant to bring calm somehow converted my anger into a seething, combustible force. The high atmospheric pressure drove up the Fahrenheit and with it the volatility of my barely restrained fury.

It made as much sense as the summer storm in fall, and I was running out of time. Where were the words I needed to reach him? My frustration was as much with myself as it was with Aamon. We had never struggled with communication, to such an extreme that words were rarely necessary. Yet try as I might, I could not find the right words to express the growing panic that Aamon's interactions with Griffin caused.

Griffin hadn't done anything terrible since his return. But there was something about him that just wasn't…right. I couldn't put my finger on it. But I had to get Aamon far away from Griffin and their fake, budding bromance as quickly as possible.

With a thunderous clap, the skies opened. The rain fell heavily, pelting with such force that each drop rebounded sharply as it struck the ground. The open meadows, sparse trees, and farmland crops offered no protection from the downpour. Within seconds, we were soaked. But the speed of our footsteps never slowed and neither did the dialogue between us.

"I'm not stupid, Aamon. I understand your rationale to a certain degree. But not inciting an argument is one thing. Developing a friendship is on a whole other level of crazy, one that I can't comprehend."

Aggravation was my driving force. As it increased, so did my pace. We were close. I could feel the energy from our prey. A surge of adrenaline coursed through my system. My heart rate accelerated in response and propelled me forward even faster. Whatever speed I set, Aamon matched flawlessly. Our feet pounded the earth beneath us mercilessly as we closed quickly on the Sygans.

Maybe I had needed a little dose of violence to soothe the furnace of frustration that cooked me from the inside out that day.

"You don't need to understand it. You just need to trust me, and frankly, your lack of faith in me is a little insulting." Aamon's voice remained steady.

"You're disappointed at my inability to master your level of conniving?" I snapped.

"You'd do well to work on your poker face. Not everything has to be on the surface. It's a matter of tactics," he answered, choosing to ignore my obvious sarcasm. All the while his eyes remained fixed firmly ahead.

I wasn't trying to incite an argument, but the subject continued to gnaw at me. It itched like an irritating scab, a scab I couldn't help but pick at. A scab that caused me to misdirect my contempt.

The issue was all mine, but just because I could acknowledge such a fact didn't help to alleviate its symptoms. Once in motion, I simply could not stop, not until I had rid myself of every little needle of doubt and unease. The whole façade was cringeworthy, but it was more than just that.

There was something about wearing a mask of two faces that made me feel like a coward. Aamon was right. I had no poker face. I was too much of an open book and in the past had foolishly taken great pride in just that. Even recognizing that my *what you see is what you get* attitude would ultimately lead nowhere good, like bringing about a pointless argument with the one person I was trying to protect, I still struggled to break free from it.

I was letting my gut and my ego lead me instead of my head. My pride was unquestionably my absolute worst enemy.

The Sygans sensed us as we closed in. Aware that their attempts to outrun us had failed, they slowed and circled around, sliding on the drenched grass, as they prepared for a fight.

Without pause, we attacked. Our moves flowed in synchronicity without direct thought or attention. We were always a second quicker, always a step ahead of the enemy. The task at hand was important, but the execution was carried out without effort. I for one was entirely more focused on our argument.

"I don't trust him, and yes, I know I sound like a broken record, but that's only because I don't feel like you hear me."

Aamon dodged to the left, avoiding the fist of Sygan number one who swung wildly in his direction. "I hear you," he responded, raising his arm above his head and driving his elbow into the Sygan's crown before he had time to regain his balance.

"Then you're not taking me seriously," I retorted, as I backhanded Sygan number two with such force that his feet lifted from the ground. He sailed through the air and landed unceremoniously at Aamon's feet. Aamon lifted one leg and brought his foot down sharply, crushing the creature's skull without so much as a glance in its direction.

"I am taking you seriously—*down!*"

I ducked in response as the axe thrown by Sygan number three sailed over my head. With his eyes riveted on mine, Aamon extended one arm and caught the flying weapon. He flipped it over and tossed it to me as I stood.

"So why the fuck are you acting like he's your friend?" I snapped, as I spun with the axe extended and sliced through the gut of Sygan number three as he barreled toward us. "Keeping your friends close and your enemies closer does *not* equate to socializing with them. He is not your fucking friend."

"Alyssa, what would you rather I do? I've done this dance before. I'm sorry that you see it as a weakness. It's not. It's no more than a stupid fucking game, but a game you have to play to win. I'm using my head instead of my gut for once."

My ego took the slap, and for a moment my anger flared, defensive and wounded. "And I'm not!" I snarled.

The thunder that had continually rumbled from somewhere in the distance suddenly bellowed loudly just above our heads. The storm clouds darkened the already dimly lit sky, brightened sporadically by lightning flashes that danced within. Their angry fingers poked and prodded manically, desperate to find a way out.

The steady beat of the raindrops continued. Fired with force, they pricked exposed flesh like tiny thorns, adding to my irritation.

"I tell him to fuck off, and we're all in danger. And I don't mean me or you, I mean anyone associated with us who does not possess the power to walk away from a fight with him." Aamon's tone remained controlled, but each word was delivered with emphasis.

Well, that was the dig that I deserved.

He could have gone in for his pound of flesh and named my mom and son, Kasey, outright. I would have, and lord knows I would have deserved it. But he didn't. Even in an argument when I was being completely irrational and unreasonable, he still tried to protect me.

Behind Aamon, Sygan number four appeared, screaming profanities as he ran toward us. Aamon's focus remained fixed firmly on me as he waited until the very last moment to sidestep the creature. With lightning speed, he swung out his arm to clothesline it. The Sygan struck Aamon's rigid arm and crashed to the ground before being kicked roughly in my direction.

Channeling a serious amount of angst, I punched the Sygan hard as he tried to struggle to his feet, knocking him to the rain-soaked ground. I raised my foot over his face and smashed it down. One blow was enough to incapacitate him, but I continued to pelt his head with my blows, pulverizing what was once a skull. The brutality, although unnecessary, acted as an excellent outlet for my frustration.

I turned to Aamon, who eyed me with a hint of amusement.

I should have apologized. My intent was just that, but he stopped me. As a white flash cracked like a whip across the sky, he pulled me roughly toward him and silenced the words that sat on my tongue with his kiss. Saving me from the humility I deserved. His lips connected with mine and held me to him with a magnetic force. His breath scorched my throat like hot whiskey, and his fingers burned through the damp layer of sweat on my skin.

It was only supposed to be a kiss, but when he tried to pull back, I weaved my fingers through his hair and drew him closer. He pulled back a little and raised one eyebrow questioningly. Again, I pulled him in tight, and with heavy breaths I murmured in his ear.

His chest expanded as he inhaled sharply, and a low growl rumbled from deep within him. He snatched me from my feet abruptly, cupping my behind in his huge hands. Breathlessly I again whispered in his ear, explicit in what I wanted and how I wanted it, demands that rained down between a hundred tiny teasing kisses. With me still wrapped around him, Aamon strode forward three steps. He stopped when he reached the foot of a large tree. Its gnarled roots dipped and rose beneath the wet earth on which it stood. He pinned me against its rugged, drenched bark and ripped at my clothing like a wild animal.

He tore away my shirt and squeezed my naked breasts. Sucking them hard, his teeth grazed my nipples and made me cry out in ecstasy. Without letting my feet touch the ground, he pulled away my pants singlehandedly, running his hand between my thighs. Two fingers slipped inside of me while his thumb kept up a continuous rhythm, increasing in speed and pressure, pushing me to my limit.

"I want to feel you inside of me," I begged.

And as the storm raged relentlessly around us, he fucked me hard, giving me exactly what I had cried out for. The hot and frenzied spin cycle washed away my anger and my doubts. When we finished, we remained locked in a twisted embrace, naked bodies pushed firmly together in the steady stream of rain.

Satisfied and spent, I rested my forehead against his and placed one hand softly on his face. I pulled back just a little, just enough to study him closely. His sultry dark gaze held mine and pushed away my immediate fears of judgment. My thumb grazed the warm skin of his cheek, wiping away the raindrops that ran from his drenched hair and hung from his thick eyelashes that framed unblinking eyes.

Even free of my human constraints, I continued to fight a battle with myself. Every time, I got caught in a moment that allowed me to resist my inhibitions and gave me the courage to bare my soul. Imperfections, vulnerabilities, and all.

"How perverse is it that thirty seconds after killing,

I'm begging you to fuck me?" I laughed, my eyes downcast.

He cupped his finger beneath my chin and lifted my head, staring at me intently with a small reassuring smile before he leisurely leaned in and planted a kiss, slow and soft on my lips. "Some may say perverse. I say pretty fucking hot," he responded, shooting me a look that made me want to do it all over again.

"Should I be concerned?"

"Lady, there is no circumstance, no location, no time ever that I don't want you. If that's something to be concerned about…well, I'm all right with that."

With a laugh, I reached for my discarded clothes, pulling on sodden jeans and attempting to fashion a tie-front top from the remnants of my shirt. I leaned against the tree trunk as I watched him dress. Feasted my eyes on the ripples of his abdominal muscles as he stretched his arms overhead and tugged a soaked T-shirt over his head, the saturated material clinging tight to his body and making my heart rate quicken.

He caught me eyeing him and flashed an uncustomary boyish smile before he abruptly disappeared, his image snatched from me by own consciousness.

Betrayed by my own mind as it booted me sharply from my memory corridor back into a much colder, much harsher reality. I was so mad at it for allowing me to walk step-by-step through it all. For awakening memories of what I no longer had, for wafting what had been right before me, just out of reach. It was a cruel reminder of what was lost.

I swallowed back sobs as I rolled from my bed and padded softly to the restroom to splash cold water on my face and attempt to regulate my breathing. I reached for the faucet and froze at the footsteps that echoed down the hallway, as if any sound or movement would disclose my thoughts and alert him to my dreams and innermost reflections.

The footsteps paused outside of the bedroom door. Instinctively, I pressed my palm against the bathroom door, as fear crept through me with the thought that he might enter my bedroom, leaving only the wedge of wood between us. A piece of wood I was convinced would not be sufficient to protect my wandering mind from him.

I waited with bated breath until eventually the footsteps started again and carried him away. I fought down a wave of nausea and pulled my palm stiffly from the door. Looking down, I focused hard on both hands, willing the shaking to stop. I clutched them tightly together when the power of my will failed me.

I turned my back to the door and leaned carefully against it before sliding softly down to the floor. I pulled my knees to my chest and wrapped my arms around them tightly.

The flashbacks would start soon. I would be powerless to stop them. Instead I would have to endure them and make every effort to conceal their existence. They could last for hours, days, weeks, and maybe even months.

I fucking hate this…

Stop!

I could not allow my thoughts to run away with me. I fought the same internal battle on a regular basis, left with no alternative but to drag my emotions kicking and screaming into the inner recesses of my head. To bury them deep within the darkness before I walked away without a single glance back.

With my head bowed, I stood. I took a deep breath and reached for the door handle, careful to make every effort to avoid my reflection in the bathroom mirror.

There were many things I could not face; and my reflection came pretty far up that long list. To look at myself, to see what I had become would undoubtedly break me. Breaking was a luxury outside of my budget.

With a click, I snapped off the light and returned silently to my bed.

Chapter 2

Hindsight is a great thing. It is said often and by many, and for good reason.

There is a certain way that things are supposed to happen. A clearly mapped path of logical standing.

When you're on the outside looking in, those obvious choices seem simple and straightforward. But the view from the inside is often quite contradictory. If the outside is a calm and clear day's walk in the park, the inside is an hour or two into a category five hurricane. A roaring, swirling turmoil in which vision of any degree is minimal and any cohesive thoughts are swept into oblivion before they have begun. There is no clarity. There is no path. There is just blind panic and an impending sense of doom.

And then there's the ending.

There's always supposed to be happy ever after. Once trials and tribulation have been overcome, and overwhelming odds have been beaten, there can only ever be a happy ever after, right?

But that is not always the case.

Regardless of what life you are living.

Life after death is not quite what I'd anticipated. In truth, it wasn't something I ever really thought about when I was alive. I wasn't religious or spiritual. The only truth I knew was that death was an end.

My life had barely begun when it was snatched

away, and I was cast into an existence far different from anything I could have imagined. There was no definitive end, not for me. No Heaven. No Hell. No above or below.

There are three planes of existence, each aligned with the other. Earth sits between Laeon, a plane of light, and Daeon, a plane of darkness. The inhabitants of each can and do travel between them. Living beings are almost entirely oblivious to them, the good and the bad.

One of the most basic instincts possessed by the living is self-preservation. This is what prevents them from crossing over each plane. That dark alley that makes the hairs on the back of your neck stand up, the hole in the crawl space that generates the fight or flight response, that part of the forest devoid of singing birds and chirping bugs. The secluded beach or sunny pasture that fills your heart with an inexplicable sense of contentment and peace, all glimpses of the interweaving of two planes. Some will briefly enter one or the other, usually purely by accident, but never for long, and rarely will they return the same person they were when they entered.

Good versus evil is an age-old concept, one derived from a truth that has, over time, become a twisted and convoluted version of its former self. Good and evil absolutely exist, but human beings are not born with a predisposition for either. Rather, our souls consist of elements of both. Every being has a balance of both good and evil within. Laws, cultural norms, and social constructs manipulate us into a desire to attain a label of good. To be perceived as righteous and of high moral standing, and why? Because we are always answerable to a higher power. Anything that deviates from this has dire consequences. If no legal or social ramifications materialize, then the belief is that the cosmos, as a whole, will transpire against you. Like there is a vengeful universe examining our every move in the hope of detecting any digressions to warrant inflicting some karmic damnation upon the perpetrator of such wrongdoing.

In actuality, all living creatures possess unadulterated free will. They just don't know how to use it or even believe that they have it. It's almost too big a concept to comprehend. Life experiences, especially traumatic ones, can impact one's persona, but not to the degree that is assumed.

Every now and again we catch sight of our darker instincts, some even embrace it. Not every crime is committed out of necessity, not every abuser was once abused, not every serial killer suffered a traumatic head injury. Nurturing our narcissistic impulses, inflicting mental or physical torture for pleasure, annihilating an entire race in the name of ideology, are all perfect examples.

Regardless, the living do possess the ability to decide where their souls end up after death. Life is such a small part of existence. Don't get me wrong, although we are born with both good and evil elements, what you strive for during life does either lighten or darken your soul.

The bad that you may have done, and by that, I mean actual bad, not rules inflicted by fictitious religions, but actions that cause direct pain and suffering to others without any justification, can be redeemed prior to death. You have right up to the moment of crossing to choose your path. There is no God or gods who sit in judgment, who dole out post-life punishments for sins committed during life. For most they make their choice and pass to their next existence. But for some, like me, Earth remains their home.

Just for a little while I had it all. I had friends that became family. They saved me, supported me, and taught me. I had love. I had a place, and I had a purpose. And at the center of it all was Griffin. A leader. A brother. A hero. But behind every hero, regardless of the fairytale, lies a truth webbed in darkness. And that darkness can only remain suppressed for so long.

Nothing lasts forever, and betrayal is a bitter pill to swallow. Secrets and lies sullied what was once so pure, pushing me beyond a line I ever thought I would cross. There were two sides; aren't there always? Sometimes I think I chose my side. Sometimes I think it chose me.

I embraced my darkness. I embraced my power, and for the first time in any of my lives, I was free. I found peace. And so much more. I found Aamon.

But for Griffin it was the final straw.

He broke. He lost himself, and we all became his collateral damage. Even segregated from the ones I once considered family I harbored no hate. Well, not much, at least. All was not lost for Griffin. Still he had a chance to atone.

Griffin should have recuperated just as he had previously. Served his period of darkness detox in Laeon and bounced back all Zen and serenity-roided up. He should have stepped back into his somewhat-controlling pious leadership role. Should have returned merrily to his three musketeers and resumed his soul-saving heroics. Should have left me to wallow in my pit of lust-fueled darkness as it sucked away the final remnants of my soul, according to some at least.

There are many things he should have done, many things that were damn well handed to him on a silver platter, but none of which he did.

Despite the best hopes and intentions of everyone, Laeon failed him. Or maybe he failed Laeon. Rehab can't be enforced, can it? The road to recovery begins with a desire to heal, to recover, to start again. A desire Griffin had lost somewhere along the way.

And so, just a few short weeks after he left this plane, he returned.

Not better.

Worse. Much worse.

Last time his damage was visible.

This time it was concealed.

All he had gained was the ability to mask the cracks and crevices. To collude against what was real. To brandish a well-crafted mask which effectively disguised who he had truly become.

Now I recognize how terrifying those first steps into the abyss were. Now I recognize the red flags that waved manically. Now I recognize the magnitude of the shift that happened right before us, and the catastrophic consequences of remaining within the scope of what would become ground zero. Now I recognize the ignorance which led me unaware, providing blinkers against the ever-expanding cataclysm.

Like I said, hindsight is a great thing.

Chapter 3

The knock on the door came as a surprise. Noah usually let me know ahead of time if he intended to visit. I wasn't bothered, though. The company was appreciated.

Noah, Steven, and Amelia were Earth-bound beings. Like me, they had remained firmly on this plane following their deaths. Once upon a time they were my saviors, my family. That was until circumstances turned them into my enemies. We were rebuilding bridges, an act that for some came easily, for others, not so much.

I opened the door and stepped back for him to enter. "I didn't know you were coming over."

I froze. There was no warm smile, no exuberant hug or loud quip characteristic of Noah. He remained rooted to the spot, his muscles tensed, his face taut. Despite opening his mouth, no sound came out.

A cold wave of fear washed over me. "What's wrong?"

He gulped and shifted his weight. I peered through the doorway to glance quickly up and down the empty corridor outside of the condo.

"He's back." His voice was barely more than a whisper.

It took a minute for my brain to fully engage. I almost laughed at what had to be an elaborate joke. My eyes searched desperately for Noah's and any hint of amusement. His expression remined flat and cold.

I tried to swallow, but my cotton-dry mouth wouldn't allow it.

"When?" I croaked surprising myself. The question I really wanted to ask was "How so soon?" but something stopped me. Just because I needed to know didn't mean I wanted to know.

Noah shifted again. His fingers twitched as they hung by his sides, searching for something to do. I shook my head and tried to calm my racing mind as I gestured for him to enter. He shuffled forward just slightly. Just enough for his eyes to sweep around the large open plan condo.

"I'm home alone. Surely you know that already," I snapped in a tone harsher than intended.

Noah's shoulders slumped slightly. He stuffed his hands into his pockets and stepped inside. With empathic powers to sense the energies of all beings, Noah knew from streets away that Aamon wasn't home.

I repeated my question as we took a seat opposite each other at the long dark wooden table that dominated the dining area of the sprawling open space.

"A few days," he admitted.

Days!

My eyes stared expectantly into his as I gestured for more information.

"He seems okay. Quiet. Apologetic. Remorseful."

"This is too soon," I murmured. I glanced up at Noah. "Don't you think this is too soon?"

His arms rested on the table. He turned his palms upward and gave a small shrug. "It's sooner then I'd expected, but he seems…normal."

He was holding back.

"What are you not telling me?" I asked slowly.

"There isn't anything I'm not telling you. I wanted to let you know and to make sure we can continue to move forward. We're in a good place, and I don't want anyone to ruin that."

I leaned forward and placed my hand over his on the table. "He won't ruin anything," I assured him.

Noah cleared his throat nervously. His eyes flickered down to the table. "He wants to arrange a meeting." His voice was so low it was barely audible.

The absurdity of such a notion made me laugh, a short sharp ugly sound. Wide-eyed, I gazed at Noah as I asked, "With who?"

Noah raised an eyebrow. I pulled my hand back sharply.

"Oh, fuck off. I know you're not suggesting me!"

"You and Aamon actually." Noah studied me carefully, his lips clenched tightly together.

I shook my head as I snarled, "And how do you think that's going to go?"

Noah sighed heavily. He ran both hands through his hair and slumped farther down in his seat.

"My days of playing Switzerland are long gone. And there's no fucking way I'm getting between Aamon and Griffin again. My mediator days are also a thing of the past. You need to be aware of that."

"This isn't my suggestion. Quite the opposite." Noah's voice trailed away.

"You were assigned the role of messenger," I concluded.

I stood up too quickly. The scrape of my chair across the floor echoed loudly.

A small frown flitted across Noah's brow. "You

want me to leave?"

"I just need to get my head straight. I can't give you an answer right now," I stammered.

He stood slowly, his eyes on mine. "I didn't expect one."

I crossed my arms and glanced toward the door. Noah's face fell. Guilt prodded at my already overloaded mind. "I'm not mad at you, and like I said, this won't come between us. It's just a lot." I tried to sound sincere but failed miserably. Barely healed scars had suddenly become exposed. They ached and throbbed as the butterfly stitches that held them together were callously torn away. It was unavoidable. Noah was as much a victim as I, yet the fragile bridge we had taken weeks to construct started to sway. Regardless of his efforts, his loyalty still lay with Griffin. The first bricks of the wall between us laid by the side he'd taken.

Silently, he left. As the door closed, my nerves imploded, impervious to my every attempt to calm them.

Aamon returned late that evening, as expected. While I waited for him, what had started as a small knot of anxiety had grown steadily in size and weight, transforming into a heavy rock of dread and guilt.

I had nothing to feel guilty about, nor could I rationally justify any feelings of anxiety, yet every attempt to talk myself down had failed. The overwhelming emotional turmoil left me pacing almost manically around the condo.

I could feel him as he approached. Forcing myself to be still, I gripped the back of one of the dining chairs as I attempted to regulate my breathing. It didn't work. Aamon burst into the room and rushed to my side. His intense dark eyes bore into mine as he demanded to know what was wrong.

"He's back," I responded as I studied his reaction. Aamon's face remained impassive. He raised one eyebrow but said nothing.

I tried again, confused by his lack of response. "Griffin is back."

"Did something happen?" Aamon asked.

"Well, no," I admitted, "but shouldn't we be concerned?"

"Why? What do you think he's going to do?"

I shrugged, genuinely baffled by his blasé attitude but just as confused by my own reaction to the situation. Aamon pulled me close, wrapped his warm arms around me, and lowered his head to murmur softly in my ear. "I don't believe he is stupid enough to just turn up here, and besides, he is no threat to you, Alyssa. Your power is far greater than his. You have nothing to be worried about. Chances are it will be a while before any of our paths cross again."

Aamon kissed my head and made his way into the bedroom to change. I followed him.

"We live in the same damn town," I pointed out.

"And how much time do we actually spend on this plane?" he called out from the next room.

I trailed after him, pausing just inside the doorway.

"That's the thing. Noah came by today." I studied Aamon carefully for a reaction.

"Let me guess. Sent by Griffin?" Aamon smothered a laugh as he unbuttoned his shirt, "See, I told you he wasn't stupid enough to knock on this door."

"Yes. He sent him to arrange a meeting with both of us. We're just going to tell him to go fuck himself, right?"

Aamon paused, bare chested, shirt in hand with a furrowed brow. Seconds slipped by before he sat without a response on the edge of the bed and proceeded to remove his boots. The silence between us was charged. The anxiety ball that had contracted started to expand again.

"Aamon." My voice sounded stronger than I felt.

He looked up at me, removed his socks, and threw me a small smile.

"Maybe it's not a bad idea." He shrugged as he stood, unzipped his pants, stepped out of them, and retrieved them from the floor without breaking eye contact. He moved carefully forward, calculating my response as he closed in. The reaction of my body betrayed my mind as desire rolled in heated waves throughout me. I took a step back. He stopped.

Aamon tossed his pants onto the bed and slowly raised his hands in an act of surrender. "I think we need to know exactly where he is, mentally. I'm not suggesting this to alarm you—quite the opposite. I think it's the best way to alleviate your fears."

I exhaled slowly, and he stepped carefully toward me. His eyes seared mine as he reassured me, "I would never let anyone, or anything, hurt you."

A flash of guilt again sliced through me. But I finally realized its origin. It was guilt born of my own actions, or lack of actions, to protect Aamon. I had let him down, and he had continued to support me regardless, his loyalty never wavering. I wasn't afraid of Griffin directly; I was afraid of letting Aamon down for a second time. Of inadvertently doing or saying something that would leave him feeling anything but what he actually was to me, my absolute everything.

That guilt prevented me from arguing with him. It prevented me from further voicing my concerns. An action, or lack of action, which set forth a chain of events that would end in utter catastrophe.

We spent the remainder of the evening as we spent most of our time back then. In a bubble. What we did was irrelevant. We did it together, and that is what fulfilled my heart and soul.

Arrangements between Noah and Aamon were made. My silence implied a shared belief that the decision to meet was a good one, another misconception cast by my own hand.

I hadn't wanted to meet with him. I had barely gotten over our last encounter. I hadn't expected him to return so soon. I was unprepared, and this made me angry at myself for my foolishness.

In his absence, I had fought hard not to think about him, conditioned myself to avoid anything Griffin-related. The possible consequences of the actions I'd taken to persuade him to remain in Laeon, the plane of light and healing, haunted me and sent me down a rabbit hole of panic and dread. Therefore, I fought hard to abide by the *out of sight out of mind* rule that seemed to work so well for others.

But he was back, and his return had pushed me so far down that dreaded burrow I felt sure I was in danger of entering another realm. Would he return thinking he'd find peace, friendship, possibly even something more with me? A sane and rational person would not, but Griffin hadn't demonstrated anything close to sanity in his final few weeks on Earth.

I had no idea how long Laeon would take to work its magic on him, but I was damn sure he'd need more time than a few measly weeks given the fragile state he had been in.

Then there was Aamon to consider. Placing the two of them within the same vicinity had the potential to be disastrous, like mixing combustibles. It was not a situation I relished the thought of being in.

The only thing worse than complying and attending the proposed meeting was remaining absent. I would drive myself crazy with my amazing ability to catastrophize. Plus, I was the only being in existence who held at least the smallest degree of control over either of them.

I had run a million scenarios through my head, and not one of them ended positively. Yet just a few days later, there I was, back at the industrial estate, trying to convince my feet to partake in the complex endeavor of walking. I didn't want to return, but I was still furious at myself for experiencing anxiety.

"You don't have to go through with this. You can hang out here with Birsha," Aamon had offered with a half smile. I had insisted on bringing backup just in case, and Birsha played neutral well.

"Yes, I do," I'd retorted through gritted teeth.

Aamon watched me carefully with narrowed eyes as he asked, "Who are you mad at?"

He really didn't get it. There was no such thing as potential danger to Aamon. He retained control of any situation he was flung into. Human traits such as inexplicable anxiety, or fear that could at least in part be deemed rational, were beyond his comprehension.

"Him, Laeon, Amelia, myself." I squinted up at the building before me, rolling my shoulders like I was preparing for a fight.

"Amelia?" he queried, as a bemused look played across his features.

"Leave my grudge alone," I snapped. Finally gaining some control over my extremities, I stepped forward to yank roughly on the door.

As we rounded the seventh floor, the wide rolling door opened, and Noah stepped across the threshold to greet us. Seeing just two of us in the hallway, he looked past us expectantly. "He's welcome to join you," he offered, his face straight.

"He's good where he is, thanks," Aamon answered, his voice strained. I glanced at him. Was he pissed that Birsha had joined us? Had my insistence damaged his ego? Was he concerned that the others may incorrectly assume he felt threatened by Griffin, or by them? My paranoia was on overdrive.

Aamon leaned casually against the door frame and extended his arm for me to enter first. My eyes met his, and again a small smile flickered across his lips. He wasn't mad, his only concern was for me. I breathed a sigh of relief. Today I was not strong. Today I needed his support, and as always, I had it.

Stepping into the loft was supposed to be uncomfortable, possibly even painful. A bitter reminder of the contention and hurt I'd experienced the last time I'd been there. But to my dismay, it still felt like home, the refuge of safety it had been during the first few months after my death.

The unexpected feeling tugged at my conscience, like it somehow betrayed Aamon.

Steven and Amelia stood on opposite sides of the room, Amelia positioned against the lower-level bookshelves and Steven against the wall between the window and large fireplace. Griffin sat in the middle of the room, on the sofa that faced the doorway. His shoulders were slumped, and his gaze was fixed firmly on the floor. As we entered, he stood and glanced up briefly without fully lifting his head.

I paused, unsure of what to do. To say the situation was awkward was an understatement.

Aamon strode forward, slightly to my side but a couple of feet ahead. His face was expressionless, but his dark eyes glinted as he studied Griffin.

"Thank you for agreeing to meet with me." Griffin's voice was low and controlled. Only when he finished speaking did he raise his head, just slightly, just enough to try to make eye contact with me. I looked away, focusing on the wide window and the city views in the distance.

We sat, joined by Noah and Steven. Amelia maintained her distant position, and for that I was thankful.

Griffin cleared his throat. "I'm not going to sit here and insult anyone by trying to excuse my behavior. I was wrong in everything that I did. My loss of control was down to my own actions, and I am the only one to blame."

He shifted in his seat. His eyes moved between all of us. "I have no to right to ask for forgiveness, and so I won't. I wouldn't hold it against you if you told me to go to hell. It's what I deserve, and I don't mean that in a pitying sense. I was an utter bastard who hurt the people closest to me, and for that I'm sorry."

His face creased, and he took a deep shaky breath. My gaze remained fixed on the window, the only glances I snatched came when he turned in Amelia's direction, the furthest point from my line of sight.

"I take full responsibility and will work hard to fix what I destroyed. If I could take it all back, I would."

Aamon remained relaxed. His right ankle rested on his left thigh. One of his arms spread out along the back of the couch, the other rested behind me. He maintained his silence throughout, shifting every now and again, his features stoic as he stared unblinking at Griffin while he spoke. Careful to avoid eye contact, I scrutinized everything I could about Griffin. The tone of his voice, the pace of his probably well-rehearsed words, every movement, every blink, the speed and depth of each breath, and the energy he emitted. I examined him like a specimen beneath a microscope, looking for anything that could lay credence to my suspicions and anxiety.

I got nothing.

He sounded sincere. He asked for nothing from us. Not even forgiveness.

And worse than that he sounded different. He sounded like the old him, the one I'd trusted. The one who'd protected me so long ago.

He said his piece, and no response was necessary. Aamon and I stood up to leave. Steven stepped forward, grabbed my hand, and pulled me into an embrace. His long arms held me in a hug that I happily returned.

"I miss you, don't be a stranger," he whispered in my ear. Noah, clearly taking his cue from Steven, also stepped forward. He offered his hand to Aamon, a handshake that Aamon accepted, then swept me into his arms, in true overly dramatic Noah style of course.

Across the room, Amelia shifted awkwardly. She threw half a smile in our direction but thankfully retained her position.

Griffin stood; and my heart skipped a beat. In response he shoved his hands in his pockets, a clear sign that my fear was unnecessary. He had no intention of pushing his luck with me. Aamon took a step toward me, slid his hand around my waist, and in doing so steadied my breath as he gently veered me to the door.

I almost made it. I almost exited without looking directly at him.

Almost.

"I'm sorry." His whisper was so low I thought for a moment that I had imagined it. I glanced at him. His bronzed eyes blazed as he stared at me. They were so much darker than I remembered. A pained look twisted his features, incinerating the last strands of my resolve with ease. In that moment, I no longer hated him.

Chapter 4

Griffin's return motivated us all to work a little harder to rebuild the relationships that had been left in tatters. I wasn't one to quit, but as the days turned into weeks it became harder and harder to ignore the changes in Griffin.

His behaviors depended upon who he was with. Meek and mild in Aamon's presence. Disrespectful and inappropriate when he was not. He didn't touch me. He didn't directly say anything damning. But he would stand too close. Stare too hard. Allow his eyes to rest on the intimate parts of my body for too long. At first I dismissed it, putting it down to paranoia. But as Griffin's behavior continued to raise red flags, I became less able to maintain my silence. Each concern I raised added to the mounting tension between Amelia, Noah, and me. They accused me of causing trouble, of looking for problems where they didn't exist and of villainizing Griffin, who in their eyes was the eternal victim.

Slowly but steadily the cracks deepened into crevices. The final straw came when I attempted to make amends with Amelia.

Noah's efforts to hold us together were relentless. The argument I'd had with Amelia had been nasty, but for Noah's sake I was willing to move past it. I traveled from the condo to the loft as dusk fell on a picture-perfect fall evening. The crisp air rich with the aromatic scents of cedar and golden aspen was intoxicating. A breathtaking sunset had transformed the sky into a canvas of amber and red, which quelled my irritation and filled me with nostalgia.

Noah had assured me Amelia would be the only one home and unaware of my intended visit. I let myself in and scanned the first level, which sat quiet and empty. The steady thrum of water drew me up to the next level. Amelia's door sat open, the room beyond it dark. A single shaft of light shone from the partially open bathroom door. I turned to leave, intending to wait for her downstairs when I felt it.

There was something else there, an energy within the darkness of her room.

I paused. The hairs on my arms and neck stood on end as I edged closer to the open door to investigate. The light from the bathroom silhouetted the figure of a man, watching, waiting in the shadows, his gaze fixated on the bathroom.

I froze. As my eyes adjusted to the darkness my brain scrambled to make sense of the scene before me. Completely naked, he surveyed her. Inside the steamy shower cubicle, with her back to the doorway, she was oblivious to her audience as she lathered and rinsed her body. A rhythmic melody played from the shower radio that she hummed along in time to.

I recoiled in horror when I realized what her watcher was doing. I stepped back slowly to avoid detection and backed up against the wall outside of her room. With one hand across my mouth, I peered through the sliver of space between the door and the doorframe.

This wasn't the body of stranger. I gagged at the familiarity of the thick neck and broad shoulders, at the toned arm and large hand that gripped his erect penis and pumped furiously as he masturbated.

Caught between wanting to rescue Amelia from the perverse and sickening show and desperate to flee far away myself, I stumbled as I stepped back. His footsteps were unrushed as he moved steadily toward the doorway, his hand still working unperturbed by the interruption. I gasped and pressed myself closer to the wall inching down the hallway. Icy cold fear weaved its way through my veins, quickened by my accelerated heartbeat.

Without hesitation, he strode out of Amelia's room and sauntered up to me, completely indifferent to his lack of clothing and what he knew I'd just caught him doing.

He stopped inches from me. My breath caught in my throat, and my cheeks burned. I tried to move away, recoiling in horror as he placed one palm flat against the wall next to my head and thrust himself hard against my stomach. He lowered his lips close enough to brush against my ear and whispered, "Wanna lend a hand, Alyssa, or maybe a mouth? Aamon simply raves about the magic of your tongue when you suck him off."

I balked; burning fury replaced the fear as it coursed through my veins, my eyes burned into his, and with a growl, I shoved him hard away from me.

He simply laughed and strolled coolly down the corridor.

Before I could stop myself, I fled and only stopped when the chilly air of late fall stung my face. Away from the sickeningly depraved scene, I was able to catch my breath and gather my thoughts. There was no question in my mind of what I needed to do. With a groan, I sprinted back into the building and crashed into Amelia's bedroom. She was bundled in a robe perched on the edge of her bed towel-drying her hair. She let out a small shriek.

"Christ almighty, have you ever heard of knocking?"

Desert-dry breaths rasped against my chest as I fought to inhale properly. Amelia jumped up from the bed, her face a mix of alarm and confusion.

"What's wrong?" she barked dropping the towel to the floor.

I shook my head and gasped, "I came to speak to you. But there was someone here, in your room."

Wide-eyed, she spun to survey the room as she hissed, "Who and where?"

I grabbed at her arm. "He's gone now. But Amelia, he was watching you shower."

Instinctively she clutched at her robe, tugging it tighter across her chest. "What the fuck? Where did he go? Are you saying someone just wandered in here? Was he human? Was he a Sygan?" She begged for answers. Her questions tumbled quickly one after the other, leaving me no time to respond.

"No." My voice quivered. "Nobody wandered in. It was Griffin." I glanced behind me toward the bedroom door, afraid he would casually saunter back in. I pushed the door closed quietly and walked to the dresser opposite the bed, leaning my still-trembling body against it.

Amelias face paled, and she sank to the bed. Her eyes narrowed as she continued to question me. "Griffin was watching me shower?"

The doubt etched across her face sent my heart beat racing again. "He wasn't just watching you, Amelia. He was jacking off to you as you showered."

She sat upright sharply. The last of her concern and fear melted quickly away.

"You don't believe me?" I exclaimed, choking back a sob.

She opened her mouth, then closed it again, folded her arms across her chest, and tilted her head slightly to one side.

"Amelia! Why would I lie about something as…fucked up as that?"

"I have no idea. Why would you even be here in the first place?" she asked with a biting tone.

"I came to apologize."

"And then just happened to catch Griffin doing something that has the potential to alienate him from us all?" She mused softly.

The color drained from my face, my once-flushed skin was now cold and my voice barely a whisper as I muttered, "You have got to be kidding me!"

She stared blankly at me, her face set.

"I think you should leave."

I pushed myself upright from the dresser, pointed toward the door and cried, "Why don't you go ask him yourself? He's that psychotic he'll probably tell you the truth."

Amelia gave a small laugh. "Right, yeah, he's the psychotic one."

"Amelia, please, I'm scared for your safety. You should leave, come stay with me or something," I stammered, fighting back tears of frustration.

"I'll get right on that," she responded dryly as she stood and swept toward the door. She jerked it open and with a small nod in the direction of the hallway added, "You need to leave now."

I swiped away angrily at the tears I could no longer hold back as I charged from her room.

"It was great seeing you, Alyssa, but maybe keep your bullshit and gaslighting for your Sygans next time," she spat.

I turned back to her, desperate for her to see the truth. "Amelia, he's broken. I know you see it too. Why the hell are you so quick to dismiss me?"

"We saw this coming."

"What?" I shook my head. "I don't understand. Saw what coming?"

She gestured toward me. "All of this. Your twisted need for vengeance. Your goal to turn everyone against him."

We.

My shoulders slumped as I exhaled sharply. I'd been played. This was exactly what Griffin wanted. He'd set me up, and I'd fallen for it as had Amelia.

"He's lying," I murmured, defeated.

"That's exactly what he said you'd say. You are not the person I used to know, Alyssa, and your act doesn't work on me. I'll tolerate you for Griffin's sake, even though I know he'd be better off without you. I won't be the one to put him through any more heartbreak. But tolerate you is all I'll ever be able to do," she hissed before slamming the door shut in my face.

Humiliated and alone, I got out of there as quickly as I could. I returned to an empty condo, with no idea where Aamon was or what time he would return. I crawled into bed and cried softly into my pillow, hating everyone and everything, including myself.

Chapter 5

When Aamon returned in the early hours, I shared with him what I had witnessed, the experiences I'd had, and it made him angry, yet he still excused Griffin's behavior.

"How do you know she wasn't aware of him? Maybe they were role-playing. Maybe they're fucking. You and Amelia will never see eye to eye. I don't know why you'd waste your time pretending just to appease Noah."

I shook my head. "Fine. Dismiss that part all you want. But what about what he said to me?"

Aamon face darkened, and a low growl escaped him. "That's a matter I'll take up with him personally."

"Do you believe me?" I whispered.

Aamon's face fell. "What?" He pulled me into an embrace. "Of course I do. Never doubt that."

I pulled away.

"Then explain it to me," I begged. "You claim to trust me and my instincts. You admit to witnessing disconcerting behaviors from Griffin too, yet you spend almost every day with him."

"I don't do it to upset you. I do it to protect you. He's coming apart, but there's more to it than that, and the only way I'm going to get any answers is to get him to trust me."

It was almost like the more he distrusted Griffin, the

closer in he stepped. I understood his search for answers, but in my opinion, he was going the wrong way about it.

Frustrated and angry, I pushed back on Aamon's attempts to placate me, stomping into the bedroom and slamming the door.

The following day I awoke at dawn, and Aamon had already left.

Stubborn and irritated, I refused to sit around and wait for him. I dressed quickly and left the condo, eager for the distraction of a hunt. But the streets were quiet. The absence of any rogue Sygan activity should have been a cause for concern, but my mind was distracted by so many other things. After only a few hours of patrol beneath the dark rainy skies of early November, I admitted defeat and skulked home.

I was not okay. But my day was about to get worse.

Griffin, now a frequent visitor to the condo, was there when I arrived home. Drenched from the downpour, I walked through the condo, darkened by the thunderous black storm clouds that filled the sky outside. I pulled off my sodden boots by the door and squelched my way across the living area, removing saturated clothing as I went. I got all the way to the bedroom door before I realized he was there. Seated in the corner by the window, he watched me in silence. With hooded eyes his stare lingered over the most intimate parts of my body, making me feel far more exposed than I was.

I couldn't speak. Shock extinguished my temper. The intrusion of my safe space left me vulnerable and weak. With a snarl, I dashed into the bedroom, swinging the door shut sharply behind me.

Securely locked in the bathroom, I removed the rest of my clothing. Beneath the steaming shower, I scrubbed and rescrubbed at flesh defiled by his leering gaze. Tears fell quickly, and when my legs eventually gave way, I sank to the floor and curled into a ball, sobbing beneath the steady stream of scorching water.

When I stepped from the shower, my skin was as red as my bloodshot eyes. I still didn't feel clean, but knowing he could still be close made me desperate to dress. I glanced around the bathroom. Dirty wet clothes filled the hamper, leaving me nothing clean or dry to put on. In my hurry to bathe I hadn't taken a change of clothing in with me. The thought of leaving the bathroom with only a towel wrapped around me made me balk. Tears threatened to fall again. This was my home. My bathroom that I was afraid to leave. My bedroom I was afraid to enter.

The tears that fell this time were ones of fury. Wrapped in the biggest towel the bathroom had to offer, my hand hovered by the door. Every muscle tensed, my jaw clenched, and my arms became taut. My fingers, rigid claws of steel, gripped and squeezed the door handle as I pulled it open.

My room was empty. Tentatively I edged forward, one hand an iron grip that held my towel firmly in place. Two steps to the side and I was in the sprawling closet where I snatched up underwear and sweats before I darted back into the bathroom and the safety of a locked door. I dressed quickly, feeling a thousand eyes on me despite being completely alone.

I prayed for Aamon's return. For Griffin to have left, with or without him. Again I had to force myself from the bathroom. Only to become confined to the bedroom.

Griffin had been in there.

His scent hung in the air. Concentrated pockets of

his essence lingered outside of the bathroom door, on my side of the bed, and by the drawers that held my underwear. I gagged. I couldn't even curl up on my own bed without feeling violated.

Backed into the far corner of the room, I sank to the floor. With my knees pulled tightly to my chest, I became a ball that rocked forward and backward. Tiny, jerked movements that failed to comfort screaming nerves.

That's how Aamon found me. Cocooned far from reality, his touch tipped me into sensory overload. With my fight response triggered, I attacked him, clawing and screaming as adrenaline and cortisol shot through my body. My dilated eyes took moments to register that the being who had entered my room, who had reached forward to embrace me, who my body perceived as a threat was not Griffin, but Aamon.

His panic and fear did nothing to bring me down. Desperate to protect me he fought back, refusing to release me despite the blows I rained down on him. The smell of his blood as it trickled from his mouth snapped me back to reality. I dissolved into sobs as he cradled me against his chest.

"I'm sorry. I didn't know it was you," I croaked between gasps. I could barely hear above the rush of blood that bellowed through my ear drums.

"What happened?" he demanded.

"I thought you were Griffin."

Aamon became still. His arms turned to stone.

I squirmed free and pulled myself up on shaky legs. Crossing my arms tightly across my chest, I avoided his stare as I hissed through gritted teeth, "Has he gone?"

Aamon shot to his feet, his fists balled tightly, and his black eyes flashed. "What the fuck did he do?"

"Don't you feel him?" I snapped. "In here, in my fucking home. By my fucking underwear and my side of the bed." I gestured wildly around the room. "Do you know how fucking violating that is?"

I stormed into the closet to snatch down a duffle bag from the high shelf. Aamon followed me, his face pale. "What are you doing?"

I pushed past him to throw the bag on the bed before stalking back into the closet to grab jeans and sweatshirts, a jacket and dry boots.

"I'm leaving. I can't do this anymore."

"What! No, stop." Aamon grabbed at the clothes fighting them from my arms and flinging them to the closet floor.

Again, I pushed past him. "Fucking keep it. I don't need it," I screamed as I stormed empty-handed toward the bedroom door.

"Alyssa! What the fuck is happening? Are you leaving me? I don't understand." The terror in his voice made me pause. Inhaling deeply, I turned slowly back to him. His eyes were wide, and his shoulders slumped. He held his hands in front of his body as he begged me. "Please, please don't leave."

I looked away. The last of my resolve began to crumble. He rushed to me, grasped my hands, and sank to his knees before me. "I'm sorry, you have to believe me. Baby, this is the last thing I wanted. I was trying to protect you."

I snapped my eyes to his. "You shut me out," I whispered.

He trailed tiny kisses across my knuckles. "That wasn't my intention. Tell me what I can do to fix this. I can't lose you, you're my everything."

"Let me in."

He nodded. "I love you."

"I love you too."

Chapter 6

Aamon stayed close to home for the next few days, and for the first time in a long time, he was truly present. The knot of anxiety in my chest began to loosen. I had him back.

I awoke in the early hours of the morning with an inexplicable ball of anxiety that felt like a boulder in my stomach. Careful not to wake Aamon until I could understand myself what was going on, I crept from our bed and into the living area. Every effort I made to either understand or rid myself of the feeling had failed and as the hours ticked by my anxiety grew in intensity until I could take pacing the apartment no more.

I had to get out.

I ducked into the bedroom to grab clothing as my energy intensified to an almost palpable level, emanating from me like a noxious chemical cloud. Like a corporeal entity, it wound through the air between me and a half-sleeping Aamon and jabbed him into consciousness.

Immediately alarmed, he leapt from the bed, startling me and eviscerating the last of my already frayed nerves.

I gasped.

In an instant he was by my side. "What is it?"

"I don't know," I stammered. "It's…there's something not right. I need to get out."

He darted into the closet and reappeared pulling a

shirt over his lean torso with one hand. In his other, he grasped boots. Striding toward the doorway he urged me to follow my instincts. "Let's go."

Aamon tugged on his boots as he crossed the condo to the front door. With no explanation needed, we left. To him, where I went and for what purpose was irrelevant. All that mattered was that I did not go alone.

I didn't pause. I didn't try to figure out in which direction I should head, I just moved. My vigorous power walk was aimed in no particular direction, but my speed and desperation increased with each step until I either ran or risked whatever had taken refuge deep within me rupturing and ripping me apart from the inside out.

There may have been no conscious effort to head in any particular direction, but of course even if the details alluded me, there was always a purpose to my intuition psyching itself into a frenzy. My heart sank as the route I instinctively took started to lead us to a familiar destination. The heaviness added even more weight to my overextended gut, driving my run to increase in speed and desperation.

I should have known. There were only two people whose imminent danger could possibly invoke such a reaction, and just a few short hours ago, one had been peacefully asleep inches from me.

I flinched at the all-too-familiar flash of blue lights that cast blinding beams through the darkness and greeted us before we'd even rounded the corner at the end of the street. Yellow tape cordoned off my mom's house and drive. Two squad cars sat on the same curbside from which I'd taken my last breath, and there was a flurry of activity from uniformed officers. A black pickup was parked at the end of the driveway, Police K9 Unit emblazoned in white along its side.

Within the house, every light was illuminated. The front door sat agape, radiating a bright orange glow across the porch and front lawn. I didn't stop my sprint until I reached the open doorway, where I skidded to a stop so abruptly I had to grab the frame to anchor myself from the momentum of the movement.

With my heart on the cusp of exploding, I stepped inside, and like a freight train it hit me. Every twirling, winding, powerful wisp of energy expelled by family and strangers alike converged upon me sharply.

The weighted mass of anxiety I carried internally and the oppressive pressure of what rained down upon me externally came within milliseconds of a collision. Like angry beasts with only a membrane to separate them, they reacted to each other aggressively. With my breaking point long gone, I struggled to breathe as my knees buckled. Aamon, who never left my side, swept me up in one fluid movement moments before I hit the floor.

He half carried, half dragged me into the kitchen and into the midst of many conversations between uniformed police, detectives, and liaison officers. I didn't need to hear the details; I knew all that I needed to know at that moment. Kasey was missing. Vanished from his bed in the dead of night.

Slumped against the wall, I looked at Aamon. His eyes probed mine intently, and deep within the darkest well, I saw the briefest flash of something unfamiliar. I saw fear.

No sooner was it there than it was gone.

The kitchen had become a living entity. It was filled

with constant movement, sound, and a pulsating aura. Police radios crackled, photos lay sprawled across the breakfast counter, and the people that filled the space formed small huddles that assessed, questioned, and theorized. Never still for more than a few brief moments, each person flowed between loosely arranged groups, participants in an intricate routine that constantly shifted and swayed. Every sound and every movement carried with it an undertone of panic. Masked by many, but present to me.

I stood with my back pushed against the wall, overwhelmed to the point of suffocation. I could just about make out my mother. She was hunched over the small table in the breakfast area, located at the opposite end of the long room, surrounded by professionals, answering repetitive questions and reiterating the evening's timeline between sobs.

Her pain made my heart ache. It made me question how much a person could lose before their cracks became irreparable, before their level of broken became too much to ever return from. Guilt stabbed at my already bleeding heart, piercing it with a cold, hard blade. I had been the first to leave her. Utterly against my will and at no fault of my own, and yet I still carried an obscene amount of remorse for an action beyond my control.

Right there in the kitchen, slap bang in the middle of the main hub of activity, I was still an outsider looking in. It didn't matter how physically close I got. As long as I remained unseen, unheard, and unfelt, I would always be on the outside. Ever shielded by an invisible and impenetrable glass box.

A dark vortex of hopelessness started to open up

beneath my feet. I was losing my mind, and the realization made me almost thankful for the possibility of escaping an existence filled with any more pain.

"Get back on the clock," Aamon barked as he jerked my shoulder sharply. It was exactly what I needed. His words delivered a sharp metaphoric slap to break me from my hysteria and replaced the anxious ball of fear with a fury so potent and absolute it seemed inextinguishable.

We moved quickly. We swept the exterior of the house, then headed away from the small community. When we reached the freeway, Aamon stopped.

"It's not ideal and the last thing I want is to be away from you, but we should separate."

"It makes sense. We can cover more ground," I agreed, my voice much steadier than it should have been.

"Start heading west. Aim for openings for Daeon first. I'll have backup join you."

I froze. My breath became caught in my throat as panic rose like hot bile. "You think a Sygan did this?"

Aamon placed his hands on my shoulders. His intense gaze captured mine and held it calmly. "I'm addressing the worst-case scenario first. It's just a process of elimination."

As my body started to tremble, my brain started to race.

"We need someone to check Laeon's doorways. I mean, I can do it. I think maybe I should do it. But if I need to check Daeon first, and there's so many, I don't know how much time or how long—"

"Hey, hey. Look at me." Aamon squeezed my shoulders, recentering my focus. "You stick to Daeon. That's all you need to focus on right now. Noah and

Steven can move through Laeon far quicker than you, and they're more familiar with it."

Yes. Noah and Steven.

"I should call them," I croaked.

I started to walk backward, stepping away from Aamon, and in the direction I was to go.

"I'll do it," Aamon assured me. "You just focus on Daeon Okay?"

"Okay," I called after him as he sprinted in the opposite direction.

I covered the first two of Daeon's gateways before Birsha and a Sygan whose name I instantaneously forgot joined me. Birsha squeezed my arm. "We're going to find him, Mama. I promise you."

Tears pricked at my eyes, but I refused to allow them to fall. I was absolutely due a breakdown, but not yet. Not until my baby was safe.

We checked the remaining entrances, one more in that vicinity right in the center of town, and another farther west just beyond the falls where the Passaic River ran through the Great Piece Meadows nature reserve.

Our path crossed often with others who, under Aamon's command, had joined the mission.

Entering each gateway, we tracked through Daeon in a desperate search for any wisp of a human essence. We found nothing.

"How the hell can he have just vanished?" the nameless Sygan hissed to Birsha. I kept my eyes trained forward and my pace steady.

Birsha snarled in response, "He hasn't. We are going to find him, and until we do shut the fuck up and focus on your job."

When we had covered ground beyond a reasonable

distance west, we changed our trajectory and tracked north. We ran into Amelia and Griffin by Ringwood State Park where the New Jersey border meets New York. I hadn't considered them willing to join our efforts. In truth, I hadn't really considered them at all, but all past transgressions and animosities were on hold. And rightly so. This wasn't about me and them. A child was missing.

Together, the five of us headed back to Paterson and to Aamon's condo where I had been informed all parties were reconvening at dawn, which was now barely more than an hour away.

I prayed as I traveled. Even the knowledge that no almighty God existed didn't stop me. I prayed for Kasey's safety. I prayed that he had somehow accidentally wandered into Laeon, drawn the way Magda had said children often are. Any other alternative was too horrific to bear.

Daylight had filtered away the dark clouds of the evening by the time we arrived back at the condo.

Bodies filled the large lobby of the building. All eyes were on Zagan who barked out orders allocating shifts, partners, and zones to the gathered Sygans. Pushing our way through the crowds, we hit the stairs in a manic sprint to the upper floor of the complex.

Aamon stood in the center of our home. He was addressing the small group that had congregated there when we entered. He paused, but I stood back against the wall, willing him to continue. Most of the Sygans there I recognized. Seraphina, Eli, Gill. Noah and Steven were also there, their bodies tense as they took direction from Aamon.

Nothing.

Despite the impressive numbers and the scope of the wide-scaled and frenzied search, all efforts had failed to locate Kasey. My heart sank.

"We've covered good ground, but we've barely begun. The surface checks of Daeon and Laeon were insufficient. Teams have been deployed in all key areas. The search perimeter has been extended another two hundred miles. I don't care what rock you have to kick over, find this kid," Aamon demanded.

I rocked on my feet. The room around me blurred, and I pressed myself hard into the wall. Anxiety was everywhere. It pulsed with the heart of a living entity, and its epicenter was Aamon. It was more than just a byproduct of his concern for me.

The crew started to file out. I grabbed Steven's arm as he and Noah passed by. He turned and pulled me into a hug. "I'm okay," I murmured. Words to convince myself more than him. Noah drew a shaky breath. I glanced at him.

"What is it?"

"I do think we'll find him." He nodded, his eyes wide.

"But?"

"But. Laeon isn't like Daeon. It's power to conceal is more…efficient. There's nothing to track," he admitted softly.

Steven tugged at my ice-cold hand. "If he's there, we'll find him," he reassured me. "We just have no way of knowing if he did pass through there or not. It's not going to be a quick process."

I nodded.

They left.

One by one, everyone left the condo until only

Aamon and I remained. I looked at him, awaiting instruction. Instead he pulled me close, and I cracked just a little.

The briefest of sobs was all I could allow myself. Pulling back, I swiped at my tears. "Where do I go? Should we work together or separately now?" I glanced around. Birsha and Mister Nameless had left already. I was clueless as to whether that was intentional or not.

"I need you to stay here," Aamon whispered.

My head whipped up to face him. "What the hell are you talking about?" I swung one arm toward the door. "I need to be out there. I need to find my child."

"I need a functioning command center. Zagan can't do it alone," he reasoned.

I balked. "You want me to stay here with *Zagan?*"

Aamon shook his head. "No. I want you up here." He gestured around the condo. "Zagan will remain in the lobby dealing with the masses as they check in." He grasped both of my hands and gently squeezed them. "Baby, I need you here, controlling the communication between the key players."

I started to shake my head, started to pull back.

"When we find him, I'm going to need to get him to you as quickly as possible. Think about who his potential rescuer may be."

I paused.

"I can't do that if you're somewhere out of range."

He was right. The most resourceful place for me was right there.

"What about you?" I asked.

Gently he kissed the top of my head. "I need to be on the ground. But I'll check in often, okay?"

Again I nodded, afraid at what might escape my

mouth if I tried to speak. Aamon left. I was alone.

As the hours ticked by, my desperation grew. I paced a thousand miles. Took check-in calls, then paced a thousand more. At some point in the late afternoon, whilst I sat at the dining table, exhaustion tightened its grip. I rested my head on the table, my forehead cradled by my arm, and was pulled into a restless nap. Somewhere between states of consciousness was the clock. Its cold face leered over me, and its incessant ticks reverberated throughout every nerve ending. It existed somewhere in the world between sleep and waking, not truly a part of either realm.

It was a bitter reminder that I did not need. A reminder that wherever he was, Kasey was running out of time. As the evening crept toward us, Aamon returned with Griffin, Gill, and Birsha. The theory of Kasey's whereabouts had started to shift.

"He isn't on Earth. I'm sure," Aamon said.

"How can you be sure?" I asked. We stood in the kitchen. The others were scattered around us eating from takeout containers that lined the granite countertop.

"We've covered a vast area. Even the trackers can't locate a trace," Griffin answered, a few feet away perched on a bar stool against the breakfast bar.

I kept my attention fixed firmly on Aamon. "How and why would he have passed between planes? It doesn't make any sense."

With nothing positive and time quickly becoming the biggest enemy, I was struggling to keep it together.

Aamon reached out to take my hand. "He wouldn't have wandered into Daeon," he assured me.

Griffin glanced between the two of us. His eyes skirted swiftly over our clasped hands. "I agree. But it's definitely plausible he sought out Laeon."

Aamon's grip tightened. The muscles in his jaw did too.

I looked at Griffin. "What do you mean?"

He glanced down at his now empty plate and shrugged. "I mean, I'm just saying. You visited him a lot, exposed him to an energy he could have associated with the energy from Laeon."

I blinked. Each cell of blood that flowed through my veins iced over.

I did this?

I couldn't breathe. Invisible steel hands encased my diaphragm and prevented me from inhaling. Across the room, Birsha leapt to his feet. He shoved the table as he rose, his plate clattered, and a half-full takeout coffee cup tumbled to its side. Its contents formed a creamy white puddle on the dark wood table.

Griffin glanced at Aamon and paled. Aamon said nothing. He didn't need to. His eyes blazed, and his shoulders hunched His hand that was free from mine curled into a fist, and a low growl emanated from his chest.

"What the fuck is wrong with you?" Birsha hissed as he moved toward Griffin.

Griffin raised both hands. "If we have any chance of finding him, we need to assess the facts. That's all I was doing."

"Maybe you should wait for us in the lobby," Gill spat.

Griffin stood. He glanced at Aamon, who remained rigid, his stare unwavering at Griffin.

"I just want to find Kasey," he whispered before he turned and left.

"Fuck Griffin and his accusations. He has no idea what he's talking about," Birsha reassured me.

Aamon relaxed his stance. He turned to me. "He knows exactly what he's doing. I should have known better than to let him help."

I shook my head. "I can rise above his insinuations. Kasey is far more important, and if Griffin's of any value, then you should use him."

Aamon's lips brushed mine. He reached for his jacket and strode toward the door. Birsha and Gill quickly followed. Again, I was alone.

The only thoughts I was able to form were in respect of finding him. I begged and pleaded with the universe to give me back my baby. I promised anything and everything in return. Whether it was the universe, or some unknown powers that be, something or someone somewhere heard my pleas and listened to them. But there was a price to pay. I had bargained with anything and everything, and my everything is exactly what they took.

I cleaned. I paced. I conducted regular check-ins, and shortly before dawn, I felt their approach. I waited as the door opened, and bodies shuffled through. Anxiously, my eyes searched for Aamon. Desperate to find him, I overlooked the shared expression of each person that filed through the doorway. Noah and Steven, Zagan and Eli, Gil and Mister Nameless.

No Aamon.

The nervous energy was stronger. The tension palpable. Neither of which helped to quell the rising panic that threatened to engulf me. My eyes swept over the group. I opened my mouth to speak when footsteps from the hallway caught my attention. I stepped forward, expecting Aamon to round the corner.

I gasped and stepped backward.

A bruised and beaten Griffin stood rigidly in the doorway. A river of deep red tracked down his left cheek that left a trail of glistening drops on the floor. His knuckles, dark purple and mottled, trembled, and his chest heaved as his breaths came shakily and fast. His red-rimmed eyes refused to meet mine. His voice broke as he croaked, "He's gone."

My legs buckled.

"Kasey…" I gasped.

"No," Zagan replied softly. "Kasey is safe. Birsha took him home."

I frowned. That wasn't the arrangement. I was to be called when Kasey was found. I glanced at Steven. "He's okay," he promised me.

I shook my head. What the fuck did Griffin mean?

The realization hit me with the speed of a fighter jet and the power of an apocalyptic storm. The volcano of anguish that erupted from my chest morphed into a scream I could not stop. I lashed out at the hands that tried to calm me.

"I tried to save him," Griffin pleaded.

"I don't believe you!" I screamed with bloody murder as I lunged for him. Hands and arms built a net of protection for him. Or maybe it was for me. "*Get out*," I shrieked with what was left of my voice before I fell deep into the void of darkness.

It completed a numbness that had started the moment I'd laid eyes on Griffin. The metallic scent of the blood splatter that marked his skin, his clothing, and the claret-stained floor. The sight of each of his war wounds, the raspy sounds of his labored breaths, and the shock and despair that emanated from him like solar flashes that had just for a moment concealed the cold harsh truth.

Enveloped by an inky black and disassociated beyond functioning, I disconnected to such a degree that my body, gripped in shock's iron-clenched fist, was rendered incapable of carrying out its most basic of functions. Even my lungs required specific and direct instruction from my brain to release each inhale of breath.

I remember just one thing before I slipped. In one desperate attempt to save myself, I cast a wide net, searching for Aamon's energy, which was always locatable regardless of which plane he was on. But the net returned as empty as the void. I watched powerless as the last vestiges of him disintegrated before me, disappearing like specks of dust in the wind.

Time passed.

Of how much I was unsure. When I opened my eyes I was on my bed, our bed. Once again alone.

People came and went. Birsha more than most, wanting to speak with me. Wanting to explain in detail what had happened, but I was already too far gone. Tumbling through a tunnel of derealization, unable to decipher what was real from what was not.

When I was able to move, I went to Kasey. My poor traumatized baby. I sat silently beside him night after night, unable to form a thought or action outside of a desperate search for any semblance of Aamon between this world and the next. Again and again, I cast out an empathic net but pulled back nothing remotely related to him.

He was gone.

Chapter 7

One thousand three hundred forty-one hours since that moment. Fifty-six days. Eight weeks and at least a thousand breakdowns since he disappeared.

Self-loathing is the worst. I knew. I absolutely knew. I resented those around me for not believing me. I was angry with everyone and furious at myself. I would never feel like I had done enough. How could I? Had I done more, the outcome could have been different. Instead, I found myself tethered to a reality that was stuck on repeat. An endless cycle of watching and waiting, constantly surrounded by fear. Fear for the what-ifs and for the what was to be.

Eight weeks have passed since I lost him. Eleven weeks have passed since I did what I should have done in the first place. Trusting my intuition, breaking my silence, and making myself the villain in everyone's story.

Calculating the time passed is dangerous and fills me with confusion. Just yesterday, fall was creeping its way in, but now we're in the dead of winter and about to enter a new year. Yet another painful reminder of the ever-increasing distance between him and me.

As my hands gripped the sink, I fought down nausea. The dull morning had done nothing to alleviate the queasiness that started the night before. I scrunched my eyes to avoid catching a glimpse of my image in the mirror. Given the amount of time I spent locked in the restroom, I really should consider removing the damn thing. I leaned over the ceramic bath and twisted the hot water faucet, immediately soothed by the steady thrum of the water as it filled the tub.

My truth was buried deep. Any recollection of moments passed placed the real me in danger. But every now and again I needed to feel him, his breath on my cheek, his huge arms encasing me, and the heat from his eyes as they burned through the deepest darkest recesses of my soul.

The previous night's dream dragged me backward. It thrust me uncontrollably through a waterslide of memories, a dark and lonely tunnel filled with flashing images of past events that delivered me right back to the beginning. Quickly, I slipped out of my clothes and into the steaming water. I drew in a deep breath and summoned up the nerve to tiptoe back, to revisit a segment of the circumstances that broke me into a thousand pieces.

In the battle against Kerwin and his Sygans last summer, I had won. Kasey and my mom had survived. Aamon and I had remained strong.

My relationship with Amelia seemed irreparable, but with Noah and Steven I was hopeful.

Those first days had been hard, but I remembered them with fondness. Physically and mentally battered and bruised, I had allowed myself to slip into a state of dependency for the first time in any of my existences. Aamon took care of me. He was the only elixir with the ability to heal me, and he did so efficiently.

He helped me to become acquainted with myself. I hadn't completely lost who I was. It was more like I had added to her. I was still me, but a newer version. I still had a lot to learn about myself, but I was no longer afraid of who I was and that in large part was down to Aamon.

I closed my eyes and sank deeper into the steel tub, seeking comfort from the warmth of both the water and my memories.

My sanctuary.

In my mind I was back at Aamon's condo, bathing with him, leaning back against his broad chest as his arms encased me. As my mind carried me from room to room, I saw us in a million different ways. Snapshots of moments past were viewable for only seconds before they were stolen away by invisible hands.

I savored every second of every image. In the bedroom as we slept, our limbs twisted and entangled like vines. In the living room as we slow danced together in the dead of night. The only light in the darkened room provided by the fire, the shadows cast out by its flames flickered and swayed along with us. In the kitchen as we cooked, seated at the dining table as we ate and strategized together.

Each memory emitted an aura of warmth like a sepia halo. In each scene, I was surrounded by him in every tangible and intangible way. I tried desperately to hold us there, locked within those moments. But even in my mind, time refused to be stilled, pushing me unwillingly and sequentially forward, into the hours and days that followed.

It was ironic that my present was frozen, yet my memories were a casualty of time.

And then there he was, the other one, Griffin. Again. Infiltrating my happy place, demanding my attention as always.

Bastard.

The feeling I'd had when he first returned seemed alien to me now, because right then in that moment, I didn't hate him.

The memory of his eyes, so piercing, so intense, caused me to jump. My body shifted suddenly in the now-tepid water of the bath. The liquid sloshed against the sides and splashed onto the tiled floor beneath it. I shuddered, a reaction that was only partially due to the drop in the water's temperature.

Shakily, I stepped from the tub and wrapped towels tightly around myself. I rubbed my shivering body dry and quickly pulled on clothes, taking care, as always, to avoid my reflection as I hurried from the bathroom. Without a backward glance, I flicked off the light and left behind damp towels, puddles, and memories of an existence so far from the present that I'd start to believe it belonged to another lifetime.

Chapter 8

Maybe it was beginning a new year without Aamon that prompted my slide down memory lane. The thought of losing even the smallest of memories had become almost as painful as losing him in the first place, an insane notion, until you realized that recollections of past events are literally all that death left you.

It wasn't that I didn't want to have such memories, or that the desire to submerge myself in them entirely wasn't there. It was that doing so right now made the task of fooling myself that much harder. A task that was necessary to get through each minute, each hour, and each day.

I padded softly from my bedroom, one of only two in this newly renovated unit and styled in a similar fashion to the original loft, which was situated two floors down.

Griffin looked up from his seat in the open plan lounge and placed his book to one side. He rose as I descended the six stairs that separated the sleeping and living areas, his urbane demeanor ever present.

"I heard you up in the night. How are you feeling?" His burnt amber eyes were filled with concern that seemed genuine.

I breathed a small sigh of relief. "I had trouble sleeping," I admitted as I edged toward the kitchen and the pot of freshly brewed coffee.

He followed me closely; I kept my back to him as I moved toward the counter on the far side of the small kitchen. I reached for a mug and carefully filled it from the steaming pot, my gaze fixed on the window above the sink. His movements caught me off guard as he snaked his arm around my waist, turned me toward him, and pulled me in close. I remained still, allowed his embrace, and focused on keeping each breath steady.

If I pulled back even slightly, he would get angry. That version of him I could not handle pre-caffeine.

He kissed the top of my head; his thumb traced the pattern of my spine down to my waistband. I tensed. He paused, but held on for just one more moment, pushing the boundaries as he always did. I waited, knowing eventually he would let me go. I just had to be patient. I just had to stay calm.

He had referred to this place as my home. More recently, the *my* had transitioned into *our*.

Griffin, Noah, Steven, and Amelia had always lived in the renovated industrial building situated on the outskirts of New Jersey's Patterson County. The old mill district consisted primarily of disused factories, abandoned mills, and warehouses which had sat empty and forgotten for years.

Despite his earlier assurances that the space had been created for me and only situated in the same building for my own protection, it had over time become a shared residence. His relocation had been gradual. What had started off as a few days had transitioned into him moving in full time. It didn't matter what he called it; I was under no illusion. This was very much his home, and he was the only one who got to call the shots.

I hadn't wanted to move there. In the weeks that

followed Aamon's death, I had pushed back hard against everyone who tried to help me. I needed to grieve alone and hated everyone, including myself.

It was Noah and Steven who had convinced me in the end. Each citing a list of different reasons except for one, and that was for Kasey's sake above my own.

Once there, it was Griffin who had robbed me of the strength to leave, who reminded me often that my reckless and selfish actions had placed not only Aamon but Kasey in danger. It was the general consensus that I couldn't be trusted not to do the same again. In Griffin's opinion, I needed him, Kasey needed him, and as he reminded me over and over, he had a promise to fulfill to Aamon. After all, Aamon had sacrificed his life to save Kasey. Following his dying wishes was the very least that *we* could do.

I was broken beyond the ability to function, and like a wolf on the hurt he took complete advantage of that, raining guilt upon what was left of me, extinguishing the final tiny sparks of any fight I had left within.

I was thrown onto a carousel of grief, guilt, and fear that spun at nauseating speeds. It stole away any semblance of control. Of course it was all my fault. I was the one to blame for everything. The fact that others were still there, willing to support and help me, was something I should be eternally grateful for. The setting was constructed impeccably, realistically crafted, and threaded carefully. Lies interwoven with the truth, to create a flawless method of control.

But I had a secret.

I knew.

Griffin was concealing something. Some guilt he harbored. Only those who are truly guilty put so much effort into convincing others that they alone are in the wrong, deflecting their culpability and highlighting someone else's error.

It was the only thing that kept me alive. The only thing that stopped me from doing what I'd tried to do once before. I glanced down at my arm. A fine silver line scarred my flesh from wrist to elbow. It's harder to die the second time around. Only a weapon forged on an alternative plane to Earth held the power for such a task. My weapon of choice had been a dagger, and I'd almost succeeded, almost.

Keep your friends close but your enemies closer, Aamon's words citing an age-old adage.

Griffin had constructed this façade for a reason, and I was hell bent on getting to the bottom of whatever it was that he was trying to accomplish. But for now, my knowledge was useless. Therefore, like so many other things, it remained hidden, buried deep alongside memories, emotions, and every facet of the truth.

Like most mornings, we made our way down to the main loft, to Noah and Steven, and of course Amelia.

Amelia barely acknowledged me as she greeted Griffin warmly. His kiss lingered on her cheek and his hands, which were wrapped around her, fell to a hover just below her waistline. The words he whispered made her blush, yet throughout the entire exchange his eyes remained fixed firmly on mine.

I turned away, thankful as Steven entered from the kitchen. A small frown flitted across his face as he passed Griffin and Amelia still locked in an embrace. Keeping his eyes forward, he strode toward me, ignoring the unnecessary sneer Griffin cast him. He stood in front of me, strategically positioned to block their little performance from my view. I gave a small smile of relief.

"How are you feeling today? You look tired."

"I'm sleeping better," I offered weakly.

"Did you eat?"

I shook my head. The thought of food made me nauseated.

Amelia broke away from Griffin and sauntered into the kitchen. I crossed my arms as Griffin made his way over to where we stood, the contention he emanated reaching us before he did.

"And what are we talking about over here?" He leaned between us, a mockery of interest.

Steven shoved his hands into his pockets. His jaw line clenched slightly. "Just chit-chatting. Would you like breakfast?"

A vile smirk spread across Griffin's face. "Sharing secrets?" he asked.

"Not at all, Griff. I was asking how she'd slept was all." Steven's voice remained low and steady. His hands remained stuffed deeply in his pockets.

Griffin rocked back on his heels. His eyes narrowed as he studied Steven. "I didn't think picturing her in bed was your thing. Considering switching sides, are we?"

Steven flinched but remained silent. Each morning was the same. A subliminal battleground where Griffin constantly prodded and poked at boundaries, hungry for a reaction.

Disregarding the palpable tension, Noah bounded down the staircase, providing a temporary release for Steven and me from Griffin's twisted game. I watched Noah closely. He seemed completely unaware of the friction between Steven and Griffin.

As Noah discussed tactics and tracking with Griffin, Steven moved toward the sofa. Grateful for the distraction Noah provided, I followed him. Fresh flowers, tastefully arranged in a large vase, sat in the center of the coffee table. The air was filled with the scent of garden roses, lilies, and snapdragons. I smiled at Steven and nodded at the bouquet. "Date night treats?"

His cheeks flushed a little, and a wide grin spread across his face. "The prelude to a belated Christmas night out," he replied.

"Not tonight, I trust?" Griffin's caustic tone shot through the air causing us both to flinch. His eyes swung from Steven to glare at Noah.

"It was..." he stammered, confusion etched across his face as he stepped back slightly from Griffin.

"But we have an extremely important patrol tonight, Noah," Griffin snapped, his cold stare frozen on Noah.

Important patrol?

A cursory glance around the room confirmed I was not the only one hearing this information for the first time.

Griffin released Noah and turned his attention to Steven, like this whole scenario had somehow been orchestrated by him.

"No, no, it's not a problem," Noah quickly interjected. "Entirely my fault, and of course I'll be there, Griff."

Griffin's eyes remained on Steven, his head tilted slightly to one side as he challenged him. "Steven, will that be a problem?"

My stomach coiled, and my cheeks flushed, humiliated for him. Steven's face darkened, and his lips formed a tight line, but with a strained voice, he responded, "Of course not. No problem at all, Griffin."

I stood up just as Amelia came out of the kitchen carrying two steaming mugs, she handed one to Griffin. "There's a patrol tonight?"

Griffin accepted the coffee and turned toward me, a smug smile plastered across his features. "And which one of you lovely ladies will be joining us?" He gestured between Amelia and me.

Just why! Why was he so intent on instigating conflict within the group?

I shrugged and turned away. My nonchalance would infuriate him, but I was still stinging from his treatment of Steven. Of course, Amelia couldn't resist the opportunity to exacerbate the situation.

"I'd offer to join you. In fact, it would be my pleasure, but I think you need to keep her close by, lest she go crawling back to her beloved Sygans."

"Ahh, of course, the bastard Sygans," I mocked.

"They are bastards! But then you'd know that more than most given you were fucking one of them," Amelia retorted with a sneer.

With an eye roll, I gestured toward her precious Griffin. "You do remember he was one of them?"

She stepped forward, her face contorted in anger, her knuckles pale as she gripped the mug tightly. "You don't deserve him; you don't deserve any of us!"

Noah reached out quickly, prying the hot cup from Amelia's hand. She released it but kept her stare on me.

I took a step toward her, my fists clenched. She'd chosen the wrong day to provoke me. I glowered at her. If she wanted to try her hand at playing dirty, let her. She was way out of her depth. Not to mention my fury at the stinging insult she'd thrown. Was she really that delusional to think I'd have any interest in *Griffin*? Of course, that wouldn't stop me from playing on her obvious insecurities.

"Aww, Amelia, do I detect a note of jealousy? Are you afraid one of our beds is going unused?" I taunted.

"Like that would surprise me from a fucking whore!" Amelia took another step forward, closing the gap and putting us no more than a couple of feet apart.

Griffin stood between us; a small smile tugged at the corners of his mouth as he surveyed the scene with anticipation. He was enjoying every moment.

Before either one of us could exchange blows, Steven leapt between us. With both arms extended, he pushed us in separate directions and demanded we stop.

Griffin's smile disappeared. "Who the fuck asked you to intervene?" he growled as he squared up to Steven.

"You want them to start beating the crap out of each other?" Steven asked incredulously.

I stepped in front of Steven and placed my hand on Griffin's tensed arm. "It's done. Let's go," I begged, trying to ignore the arrogant smirk he threw in Steven's direction as he swaggered from the loft.

I remained silent as we made our way upstairs. It was a silence that would be short-lived. The air between us was charged, and Griffin's mood had shifted yet again. As soon as we entered the upper unit, he turned on me.

"Why the fuck do you defend him?" he growled, his face close to mine and his fists clenched.

I took a shaky breath and kept my voice low and steady as I replied, "I didn't take anyone's side. I was just trying to defuse the situation."

"Defuse the situation," he mimicked. "You mean you were trying to manipulate me. After everything I've done for you, everything I've given you. I stood by you and for what? For you to humiliate me?" he bellowed.

Furiously, he paced forward and backward, continuing his rant. "Oh, so it was coincidental that he'd arranged an elaborate evening on the same day as our patrol. Wake up, Alyssa. Even you can't be that blind to what he's doing."

"What is it you think he's doing?" I asked, truly perplexed.

"He is trying to sabotage my relationship with Noah. He is trying to break up our family!" Griffin hissed.

"That isn't the case," I insisted softly, careful not to allow my words to sound like an accusation. "He wouldn't do that; nobody tries to intentionally upset you, Griffin."

Griffin sneered at me. "You see him try to belittle me, see him trying to distance Noah from me. Next will be Amelia, and then you." He paused, his face softened as he stepped toward me, his eyes wide as he pleaded, "I already lost my brother." His voice cracked as he continued, "How much more do I have to lose?"

Was he serious? He fucking hated Aamon, and the feeling was mutual!

My insides turned to icy steel, and I fought against the urge to gag. I drew in a breath. Griffin studied me carefully as he stepped closer.

"Am I going to lose you too?' he whispered, making my stomach lurch.

The knock at the door came with impeccable timing, answering my prayers as it pulled his attention away from me, for the time being at least.

"Come in," I quickly called out, relieved when a subdued Noah entered.

"Hey, buddy." Griffin strode over to Noah and greeted him with a warm hug and a wide smile. His ability to swing between moods was nothing short of terrifying. "Are we ready to go?' Griffin glanced between us; I painted what I hoped resembled a smile across my face as I nodded.

There was nothing unique or remotely important about our patrol that stretched into the evening, far later than necessary. A point that neither Noah nor I had the inclination to bring up with Griffin. It was easier to deal with Griffin if he was under the assumption that he had won. I stole the occasional look in Noah's direction, trying to ascertain if he was aware that he'd been played, but Noah remained a closed book, refusing to give anything away.

Later that evening, I excused myself from Griffin's company as soon as was reasonably possible. Contemplating the empty nothingness that sleep provided filled me with dread. I had lost the ability to remain focused enough to read, and memories from that morning's soak had left me too depleted to even consider running a bath.

If I paced, Griffin would hear me, possibly take it upon himself to investigate. So instead, I sat in silence and waited for the expected click of the front door latch as Griffin left, the same way he did most nights.

I didn't question where he went. I didn't care to. Sometimes I could still sense him close by, often in the bottom floor training room or socializing with Amelia.

Being around him was exhausting and chaotic. His trauma-induced personality swings were erratic and hard to understand. He could switch between being psychotically angry, to gentle and caring in a heartbeat.

The click came late that night. I waited. Silently counting away the minutes that put distance between us and swept away the eggshells that accompanied Griffin wherever he went.

As soon as I could, I crept from the loft and went to the only place on Earth capable of comforting me. The farther from Griffin I traveled, the easier it became to breathe.

My mother's house was still my safe space. It was the only place left that offered comfort. Even though I had avoided it when I needed it the most.

After I lost Aamon, I had tried to keep a decent distance between myself and the living. The guilt of what happened to Kasey weighed heavily on my soul. It pulled me into a trench of depression and constricted my ability to form a clear thought.

My part in Aamon's demise was beyond my scope of comprehension. It was simply too painful to even consider. Each time it was thrown in my face, I learned to shut down. I couldn't control what others chose to say, but I had gotten pretty good at controlling what I allowed myself to hear.

There was a pattern in Griffin's behavior. When I did something that displeased him, when I spent too much time alone, or when I started to withdraw from him in any respect, he would suddenly focus his time and attention on Kasey and my mom. He would drop casual remarks about their day, make small comments about where they had been or interactions he had witnessed, all seemingly innocent of course, but there was something malignant about his method of exploitation. He used

Kasey and my mom to condition my behavior and my attitude. Above all else, he used them to silence and restrain me.

Distancing myself from Kasey didn't protect him from Griffin; denying myself access to him became a pointless sacrifice. I resumed my visits only when Griffin left at night and often spent hours there, watching and listening, activities I'd become accustomed to. On the evenings I didn't make it back before Griffin, I would find him fake sleeping on the couch or in bed with his door wide open. His slumber too still and too quiet to be real. The morning after any late returns, the coffee pot would sit empty.

Griffin ensured that guilt and I never separated. Each time he became irrationally annoyed, he would remind me that I was the source of dissension within the group. Each time Amelia made a bitchy comment or instigated an argument, I would be reminded of how, at the root of everything, I was the one to blame.

It hadn't been that way in the beginning.

Chapter 9

With an overwhelming sense of relief, I arrived at my mom's house. Finally, I had the space to think straight, a stark contrast to the blinding suffocation of the loft.

Even in the dead of night the dimly lit two-story structure cocooned me in safety, lightening my heavy heart just a little. I swept the perimeter, assessing for any trace elements left behind by Griffin, or Sygans, or any other potential threat. Satisfied with the security, I relaxed, pausing briefly in the back yard below Kasey's bedroom window. His essence lingered lightly in the air, and it served as a fast-acting sedative for my anxiety.

Circling back to the front of the house, I considered my options. Collateral damage was unavoidable during conflict, the victims of which were always the weakest, the helpless, and the innocent. Inevitably it became a gamble between whoever is the most vulnerable and victory.

Like hell would Kasey and my mom become pawns in Griffin's power struggle. Standing against him could place them in a potentially precarious situation. Their fragility again had become my vulnerability, weakening me back to almost human form and forcing me to keep my darkness locked deep within the recesses of my being. Maybe.

Question marks littered my brain like confetti.

I jogged softly up the porch steps. The rattan furniture was new, bigger than the last set with beige cushions and a throw. Its modular design looked out of place on the classic fifties-style porch. I liked it but missed the older wicker versions. Anything new reminded me of a future I had no part in.

A fine covering of frost had crystallized every surface with an intricate design of silver and white that glistened in the moonlight. Sounds of the evening filled the crisp January air. Small creatures foraged amongst the frozen twigs and evergreen foliage and scurried quickly to avoid a hunting nighthawk, and in the distance, vehicles traveling up and down the highway created a soft background hum that harmonized with the static buzz from the street lights. Snuggled in against the puffy cushions, I contemplated how I'd ended up it such a shitty situation.

Strength and power are useless if they can't be used. The only rationale for my continued submissive behavior was to protect my mom and Kasey. To shelter them from danger. Initially, I'd tried to keep a healthy distance between them and anything that wasn't a regular part of life, but despite my best efforts my approach simply had not worked.

Kasey had always been my constant. From the very first days following my death, I found solace and comfort just being around him. He was a healing force in my life, and after. Staying close to him was something my heart and my gut implored me to do.

I learned the hard way that if something contradicts what your heart and gut tell you, if a situation pushes you into an action, or lack of action, that creates anxiety and a sense of wrongdoing, you should rebel against it. That feeling was the voice of your intuition, and its presence served a purpose.

Of course, preaching to yourself never yielded quite the same results. All too often we were the first to belittle ourselves, to judge too harshly and dismiss too quickly. Without realizing it, the person we were all undoubtedly the worst to was ourselves.

Giving myself a shake, I shuffled into an upright position. A pity party was the last thing I needed. Enough with the repetitive reflection. Hindsight and contemplation were going to get me nowhere. I didn't need a complex plan. Aside from protecting my mom and Kasey, I needed to pick up where Aamon had left off. To finish the work he…I started to wobble. Clasping my hands together, I forced the swell of grief and guilt to one side. It wasn't like I was in danger of forgetting about them.

Aamon would want me to succeed, and using his memory, his teachings, and his power would give me the strength I needed, but not if I fell back into the rabbit hole of tormented sorrow that had held me captive for weeks.

My brain was a multicolored wheel of contradiction. I could spin that fucker and land on a winning idea or wipe out. My ability to think straight had been lost for weeks, but the void of darkness that had occupied my brain just hours earlier was lifting. A thousand lights flooded from all angles, illuminating the space to reveal a plethora of facts, suspicions, and possibilities. It snapped me into a level of sensory overload that had the potential to tip me into meltdown mode.

I had to get my shit together and fast.

Doing so meant facing some hard truths.

I was alone. The thought stung, but I needed to suck

it up and move on. All hopes of common sense prevailing had gone down the toilet. Regardless of what Griffin did, the other three continued to exist in an impenetrable bubble of denial. Their staunch loyalty and inability to see Griffin for who and what he truly was could no longer be my concern. I'd tried, and I'd failed. It was time to move on. Right?

It wasn't going to be a walk in the park, and maybe I wouldn't succeed, but I'd damn well go down swinging. Fighting against a stranger was easy, but the closer to home the enemy was, the harder it became, and when that stranger was no longer a stranger and was instead part of a home, of a family, of a unit of love, well, it was like cutting off a limb of your own. Painful and damaging and sickening and dangerous, but also sometimes unarguably necessary.

Except he wasn't part of my home. My home was long gone. In both life and death, I'd been ripped from any semblance of a family. The thought was strangely freeing. Could I have reached my point of no more fucks to give?

I glanced toward the house. Were Kasey and my mom really my weakness? Against Kerwin last summer, absolutely, but with Griffin...

I cracked my neck, then my shoulders, then my knuckles. For a dead person, my joints were shot to shit. I pulled my focus back from my crappy skeletal system.

In a war, enemies form alliances. I had a direct line of contact to Aamon's allies, and given Griffin's demeanor since his return, I'd guess his name had worked its way onto a number of other hit lists. It could be worth investigating for sure. I swung my legs down from the couch and paced the porch, my mind whirling with a thousand possibilities. Long-lost energy had returned, and with it the ignition of a small passionate flame somewhere deep within my chest.

It wasn't just Sygans Griffin had made enemies of. Some were much closer to home. Amelia and Noah may always be quick to defend Griffin, but Steven was a different matter. Initially he'd shared their mindset, but as time went on, he became a little more reserved. At the beginning, he neither condemned nor defended Griffin, quietly observing, always a step back from any scene. The more Griffin succeeded in manipulating everyone and everything, the more arrogant he became, constantly testing the extent of what he could get away with. With me broken and silenced, and Aamon out of the picture, he became an invincible force.

Over time, the line between what was acceptable and not began to blur, and I stopped being the sole victim in his twisted games. In retrospect it was clear. Of the group, Steven was the one who saw through Griffin's ploy, and if I recognized it, so did Griffin.

I froze mid-pace. I had watched the unraveling of Griffin and Steven's relationship in real time. But my anguish and heartbreak had shrouded me from comprehending what that meant, until now. It started with me, but the sadistic methods he used to exert dominance and garner sick enjoyment filtered through to everyone he came into contact with. Even Amelia wasn't immune.

Holy crap! How could I not have seen this?

I sat down heavily on the porch step as I replayed scenario after scenario in my head. Each recollection fanned the tiny flame, causing it to writhe and coil, eager to fight back.

Griffin would constantly incite arguments, seemingly for no more than his own sordid entertainment. His favorite subjects for such a game were Amelia and I. When I refused to participate, he would use Amelia to goad me, encourage her to throw insults and make hurtful comments about Aamon. She loved and trusted him, and he exploited her loyalty at every opportunity.

The wiser I became to his tactics, the more I refused to be a pawn in his game. I constantly removed myself from conflict with Amelia, stonewalling her before my emotions could escalate. I started to preempt his attempts, often succeeding in defusing situations before they had barely started. Characteristics I was not known for.

What I'd failed to acknowledge was the consequences for Amelia. When her best efforts failed to rile me, Griffin would turn his full attention to her almost like a punishment for her failure. He would often make suggestive comments toward Amelia, grope and fondle her despite her repeated requests for him to stop. Make sexual gestures that she clearly was uncomfortable with, and accuse her of being a tease.

When Steven interjected, tried to distract Griffin, made any attempt to instill peace, or imply that Griffin's actions were inappropriate, he would become public enemy number one. Griffin would use the most effective weapon he knew of against Steven, and that weapon was Noah.

Griffin's punishment of choice was to ostracize and alienate Steven using psychological abuse tactics to manipulate and control Noah. He was the master at distorting facts and consistently placed Steven as the instigator, all the while painting himself as the victim at every given opportunity.

No consideration was given to the consequences of his actions. He was tearing the group apart from the inside out, and each member seemed blind to his actions outside of what was happening directly to them.

Griffin was losing his control as quickly as he was losing his mind, but his massacre had achieved one positive. The extremes of his actions had finally succeeded in ripping me from my burrow and booting me back to reality. I guess even in the direst of circumstances everyone has their limits, even when they're broken.

Meanwhile the voice inside of my head was getting louder and as such was becoming harder to ignore. It was a dangerous combination.

Within the group, there wasn't a single relationship that wasn't suffering because of Griffin. The more he pushed boundaries, the more infallible he thought he was, seeing no harm in his games. He crossed lines and bullied those around him beyond the point of no return, oblivious to the irreparable damage he was inflicting. Or maybe he did know but just didn't care.

Each person had something to conceal. A secret they were afraid to share. Whatever hold Griffin had over Noah seemed impenetrable. Amelia was too afraid to trust anyone, including herself, preferring the devil she knew over one she did not. Steven was the only member of the group I could potentially trust. But to what degree I was still unsure. Steven wouldn't risk confiding in me. One error in judgement could jeopardize his relationship with Noah, which was hanging by a thread at best.

My fingers tapped the step, drilling out a steady

beat. We each had too much to lose, and unfortunately, this benefited Griffin's agenda, giving him the power of puppet master over us all. For now, at least.

Whatever I decided to do, I would have to do alone. More than that, chances were if the rest of the group weren't with me, at some point they would be against me, meaning once again we would be on opposing sides.

If I was going into this alone, then there was no point in putting off the inevitable. No point in continuing this ridiculous façade with Griffin. No point in denying what every fiber of my being implored me to do. I wouldn't hide my intentions anymore, and I would no longer be guilt-tripped into staying away from my child. Griffin found issue with me when I did nothing at all. I might as well gain the satisfaction of doing what I wanted and give him a genuine reason for being an utter bastard.

That evening, I felt something I hadn't felt in a long time. The prospect of stepping outside of the frozen time loop that had held me captive for weeks made me feel alive.

My steps were lighter on the walk back to the loft. The wheel of misfortune still occupied my brain, but one firm decision had been made. And that was progress.

Tomorrow things were going to change.

Tomorrow I was taking my fucking life back. And it would start with a daytime visit to my son.

Chapter 10

"I thought we'd agreed you wouldn't visit here anymore."

I'd known he was there, following me as he often did. My decision to stick to my intended destination regardless of his presence would cause contention. But I was tired of the games. Trying to care enough to keep him happy had become a challenge. One that was not worthy of the effort.

I stood on the edge of the driveway, at the beginning of the small path that led from the garage to the porch, motionless as I willed myself to take just one more step forward to close the distance between myself and their home. An act that had once come so easily before the crippling guilt that infected every interaction with them had wormed its way in.

"You decided, not I, and I'm tired of the games, Griffin." I was careful even in a state of irritation not to raise my voice. My tone remained even and my face impassive. The anger inside burned fiercely, furious that I still allowed him to force control over every one of my emotions.

Emotions I was damn well entitled to.

As I turned to him, my fingers twitched uncontrollably at my sides, but I kept them there. Visible so as not to imply I was hiding anything. Open as not to illustrate defiance. Everything I said and did had to be mentally rehearsed, assessed for ways it could be perceived as aggressive, defensive, argumentative, disrespectful, or prevaricated. The possibilities for wrongdoing were endless.

I couldn't cross my arms or maintain constant eye contact. Couldn't roll my eyes or look away from his general direction. I couldn't change the pitch, volume, or tone of my voice, couldn't step toward or away from him or gesture, shake my head, or furrow my brows or frown or lose control of my facial expression. I couldn't even exhale too deeply.

So, in a gentle yet resolute voice I told him, "You can't tell me not to visit and then take it upon yourself to do exactly that, weaponizing my own family against me. It's cruel."

For a second, I thought I might have reached him. For the briefest of moments, a shadow of doubt crossed his face, a wisp of guilt that caused his features to soften. But in typical Griffin fashion, he manipulated the situation to place himself firmly in the victim seat.

"I thought I was your family," he responded, staring intently, looking for *it*, the thing that he would use to justify his inability to control his temper.

"Since when did it become an either or?" My voice remined low but unwavering.

Griffin's jaw clenched. The line I walked was a dangerous one. A line that was getting precariously thinner with each step.

"I want to see them. I need to see them, and you have no right to try and stop me," I insisted, feeling the cord of control start to slip from my grasp.

Griffin's eyes flashed; little sparks of anger illuminated the copper tone of his irises.

I swallowed hard but stood my ground.

"I watch them to ensure their safety. I watch them in the hopes that Aamon didn't die in vain saving *your* child," he spat, devouring my every reaction.

I flinched. I had expected no less from him, yet I was powerless to shield myself from the sting of his words.

Just for a moment, I'd had it all. The thought was a double-edged dagger to my heart.

"You remember how and why he died don't you?" Griffin goaded.

"Don't," I snapped. He assumed the pain of recall was too much for me to deal with. In truth my ability to retain control of the burning fury born of my hatred for him was the only thing I truly struggled with.

He foolishly continued.

"Protecting *your* child. The child who grew so accustomed to the energy of the dead that he took it upon himself to cross the threshold. That he entered an alternative plane probably looking for the mother who had left him, the mother who couldn't leave well enough alone. Who exposed him and normalized him to an essence no living being should be subjected to." His cruel taunts sliced through the air between us, smarting my flesh like a whip. Yet still his words were no worse than anything I had already thought about myself.

He lacked the power to punish me any harder than I had already punished myself, not that that prevented him from trying. But his words did serve him to a degree. They sliced through barely closed wounds leaving a raw gaping hole that made my nerve endings scream in pain.

I teetered, preparing to surrender, overwhelmed by the thoughts that swarmed my mind. Thoughts that breached its capacity and made me lose sight of my purpose in ever pushing back in the first place.

The click of the latch pulled our attention toward the house. The appearance of Kasey caused everything around me to melt away momentarily, even Griffin and his callous remarks. But it did something else. It reminded me that Griffin couldn't possibly hurt me any more than I'd already hurt myself. The wounds from loss and pain and guilt were deep, the self-inflicted lashings cut far deeper.

I stepped closer to my boy, thankful that Griffin didn't follow suit.

Kasey stepped onto the porch and took a seat on the front stoop to tie the laces on his sneakers. His basketball was pinned between him and the spindles. He was losing his baby features; he looked far taller and leaner than I remembered. His hair, although still blond, had darkened in shade. It was thicker and longer, with a slight wave that he had inherited from me. His locks framed a now-slender face, and he was missing two of his milk teeth. His growth wasn't just physical. His demeanor had changed too. He seemed so calm and focused with an air of maturity beyond his age. A maturity likely brought about by the harrowing experiences he had endured in his short life.

My heart ached just that little bit more.

I edged forward, his pull on me instinctive and beyond my control. But as I moved, so did Griffin. He just couldn't let me have this moment, could he?

I stood just feet away and watched Kasey as he leapt from the steps. I inhaled sharply when he passed by close enough for me to touch, his scent filling every square inch of the narrow channel between us. He rounded the side of the house. I followed, mesmerized by his every movement, watching with pride as he practiced dribbling and shooting, surprised by the ease and skill at which he controlled the ball.

I'd missed so much of his life.

I leaned against the side of the house, an invisible spectator immersed in his practice. Stubbornly, I refused to acknowledge Griffin. I'd missed enough. There was no way I would allow him to take this time away from me too.

I was aware of Griffin as he moved closer. I was prepared for it. What I wasn't prepared for was Kasey's reaction. It passed by as briefly as the breeze that shook the leaves of the tall cedarwoods out back, gone by the time you turned your attention to it. But it was definitely there. Maybe if I hadn't been so fixated on Kasey's every move it would have passed me by unnoticed, but I saw it, and to my shock I think I understood it.

As Griffin stepped onto the driveway feet away from us, Kasey flinched, jolting like he had been poked by something sharp, something painful. The beat of his heart got a little faster and a fraction louder. His eyes widened, and his pupils dilated. It was fast, it was strong, and it was something that was powerful enough to snap his focus away from his practice.

He was afraid.

His gaze remained forward, but his expression changed to stone. His muscles tensed, and his breathing stopped. I started to stand. My maternal instinct took over as I pushed myself from the wall, alarmed at the sudden chill that had wrapped its way around us both. But as quickly as it arrived, it passed. With a furrowed brow, Kasey shot and missed. He retrieved his ball and lined up to shoot again, but he was distracted. His eyes moved quickly from side to side, looking for something but afraid to turn around.

I retreated slowly, coaxing Griffin away. It was inexplicable, yet I felt sure that he was responsible for Kasey's reaction. But more than that, Kasey's reaction had triggered something else. A memory. A small clue that added credence to my suspicions.

The last thing I needed was for Griffin to realize what, if anything, had just happened.

I needed to draw him away from there. And the only thing he would follow without question was me.

In silence, I headed back to the loft with Griffin trailing slightly behind. At some point, I'd be afforded the luxury of the solace of my room. I desperately needed that time to analyze and try to make sense of what had happened. But I also knew that, before that time, there would be some form of punishment to endure.

I had argued back, barely. I had stood my ground. I had challenged him. Participated in an act of defiance regardless of how well I sugarcoated it, and for that there would be consequences.

He took his time. He knew the longer he took, the higher my anxiety levels would be.

However, this time there was no yelling, no hulking out and smashing the furniture, no accusations. No reminders of my guilt in relation to what had happened to Aamon and Kasey.

Instead, Griffin's egotism took the helm.

It was almost laughable in its absurdity. He really had convinced himself that he could be the object of my desires. But of course, I couldn't tell him that he was beyond deluded. I couldn't tell him that the thought of intimacy with him couldn't be further from my mind, that an infinity could pass, and he would still come nowhere near to measuring up to Aamon, in any sense of the word.

At some point during our journey back, he had managed to summon Amelia. I swung open the apartment door to find her lounging on the sofa. Her booted heel rested on the coffee table, and a smug smile painted across her face.

Safe from Griffin's view, I rolled my eyes. I was sure Amelia hated his feigned interest in her almost as much as I hated having to bear witness to it.

With gritted teeth, I walked into the kitchen. I poured myself a glass of water and worked hard to ignore the chatter and exaggerated giggles from the next room. All I wanted to do was to disappear into my room. But that wouldn't do. Griffin needed to exert punishment, and avoiding this would only prolong the process.

They got such pleasure from flaunting their happiness. Their so-called companionship, reminding me of what I didn't have. Or even worse, what I'd had and lost. The irony of the fact that they were just as lonely and alone as I was clearly lost on them. Amelia sauntered into the small kitchen. She pointedly ignored me, opened the fridge, and rummaged through its contents. Casting a long look in my direction, Griffin sashayed over to her, placed his hands on her hips, and pulled her into an upright position. He snaked his arms around her waist and jerked her hard against him. He laughed at her squeals as he nuzzled her neck before he leaned forward and whispered in her ear, his eyes locked firmly on mine the entire time.

I watched him and shifted my weight as I waited patiently for their little performance to end. I tried hard to make it seem like I was in the least bit bothered when in reality he could have fucked her over the damn counter for all I cared.

I played my part, kept my eyes on them, on him throughout, but my vision was elsewhere. The only way I could muster portraying even the smallest degree of emotion was to allow the most minuscule memory of Aamon to surface.

Aamon.

The thought of his eyes fixed on mine, of his scent filling the air around me, and of his strong arms holding me transported my broken mind to a place far away in time and distance from the kitchen and the sick game that Griffin played.

I'm not sure how long Griffin and Amelia's exhibition had lasted, whether he got the reaction he so desperately sought or whether he grew bored and admitted defeat. Either way they had left, retreated elsewhere to enjoy each other's company, much to my relief.

With heavy legs, I pulled myself through the quiet apartment, carrying the memory of the exchange with Aamon close. Kasey's reaction to Griffin's presence that day opened the door to a memory, one that reminded me that it had happened before.

Chapter 11

When Aamon and I were at our worst, back when his time and focus were occupied by Griffin, I sought the comfort I needed in a familiar place.

I didn't have a plan. Confusion remained strong, and trust issues left me with no one to confide in. I had an anxious urgency to do something, and it plagued my every moment. I withdrew to the only person besides Aamon who could placate me.

Kasey.

Each night while Aamon humored Griffin and his whims, I would retreat to the solace of Kasey's bedroom. Silently I would watch him sleep, illuminated by the muted halo cast out from his night light. To all that passed by, who had the opportunity to catch a glimpse or cast a well-trained eye in our direction, I was no more than a shadow in the corner, a simple distortion of the light.

As the days slipped by and my anxiety increased, I could only contain myself for a few hours at a time. I needed something to distract me from the mass of anxious energy that strummed on my nerve endings and made my fingers twitch.

Evening story time was part of a treasured routine that Kasey and I had shared. Reviving the custom provided a much-needed distraction from my chaotic and confusing day-to-day existence. Revisiting memories past allowed me an escape from my own mind. I could almost fool myself into believing I was simply doing what I had always done whilst alive.

I started to retell from memory his favorite tales. When I'd exhausted those, I created new ones with exciting settings and brave characters. I crafted a world where there was only sunshine, happiness, and good kind people. Although Kasey was soundly asleep, I told myself the stories were for him. My voice, barely a murmur, fell just below the decibels of the softest of winds as they danced beyond the windowpanes. They floated almost silently between myself and my sleeping boy. Almost.

The content of the tales changed often, from recounting the precious moments we had shared woven into fiction, the melodies of the lullabies and songs that he had loved, the fairytales recited from memory inspired by the books that filled his book basket and shelves, and of course my own creations.

Slowly, over time my stories became altered versions of his favorite tales. As it became harder to distract myself from the desperation and fear that Griffin brought, the tone and morals of the stories started to transform. Started to align with my more recent encounters.

Trials and tribulations were amended to correlate with the circumstances at that time. Without really realizing it, I often found myself using the stories to rationalize what I was experiencing. Delving into fables and metaphors and the true meaning of familiar fairytales, whispered words deciphering the messages we all eventually comprehend as we transition from childhood.

It wasn't all for Kasey; in fact, it was mainly for me. He was the vessel to which I channeled all of my focus. I suppose a part of me enjoyed the feeling, however convoluted, that I was serving a purpose for Kasey's sake. That my role was to educate him on the dangers that surrounded him, that I was taking steps to try and protect him by providing child-friendly warnings.

I was afraid that Kasey didn't have the luxury of time, slow boating gently from childhood to his teenage years. Even though he couldn't hear me, even though my efforts were fruitless, my ritual at the very least made me feel like I was doing something. They gave me purpose.

That is how it started. The explicit instruction not to trust the ones that seem trustworthy. The story repeated in as many different modes and fable forms as I could think, but each time the meaning was clear. Size and strength were no match for cunning. I implored him to recall how the tiny mouse outwitted the Gruffalo. To remember how Red Riding Hood was tricked by the wolf's disguise. I repeated my point of emphasis over and over, don't judge a book by its cover, think carefully about what is expected, and always question why. Know that the true wolf will have the face of an angel, and the one who resembles the wolf may on occasion be your savior. Above all else, trust your intuition.

I realized early on that the reassurance was more for me than him. The fables and fairy tales offered comfort, and just the smallest sliver of hope that against overwhelming odds, a resolution may still be possible. A fantasy that, if sought out, an answer will eventually be found and wishes at some point would always be granted.

Isn't that all we really hope for in times of

desperation? That when we fall, when the odds are against us, that something impossible arises to catch us, be it the hero of the story or our own strength that transpires. After all, who doesn't want to be saved.

Each evening was the same. Except one.

In the hours of one early morning, weeks into my regular visits, I was getting ready to leave. Dawn was approaching, and Kasey was an early riser. I kissed his soft hair, humming a lullaby as I made my way to the window. I had one leg through the frame when I froze. My hum had stopped, but as quickly as the melody ceased, it started again. Without skipping a beat, the next notes floated softly through the air between us. I turned slowly, terrified at what I may see. But Kasey remained soundly asleep, his hum quietening as he drifted back into a deep slumber.

He had heard me.

At the time, I had not contemplated the possible ramifications of this. Only after, when I was held responsible for his disappearance did I consider that moment as a sign that Kasey was able to perceive things beyond his plane of existence, and even then I saw it as a disability inflicted by me and his constant exposure to my energy.

But his reaction to Griffin was on another level. He was awake, fully cognizant, and able to identify his presence.

What if it wasn't me?

Magda had spoken of the gift that some living people possess.

What if somewhere between sleep and wake something had penetrated the membrane that separated the planes? Something that had allowed Kasey to hear me, that had opened up the possibility of a line of communication between the living and the dead.

Or maybe even the dead and the dead. What if this was a way to reach Aamon?

It was a stretch, but I had to believe it was possible. I became convinced that whatever door had opened for Kasey that night had never fully closed, and it started in his sleep.

But what that meant for him I had no idea.

Chapter 12

The day Aamon died, a void formed deep within me. Some days, the empty hole weighed heavy, making every task arduous and painful. Getting out of bed became a challenge, cohesive thoughts impossible, and normal functioning fell beyond my capability.

Today was not one of those days. The void was still there. The unending river of pain continued to flow fast and strong somewhere just below the surface, but my encapsulation within a vacuum of despair, a soundproof well that held so much at bay, had started to subside.

What I had witnessed with Kasey the day before invoked something. It opened the door to a possibility I had previously not considered. The realization plunged me into the deep end of what I had, up until that point, been blinded to.

My brain had a lot of catching up to do. The last thing I needed was unnecessary distractions from Griffin.

Pulling myself out of bed, I didn't bother to dress. I scraped my hair into a messy bun and shuffled into the kitchen selecting water over my regular coffee.

Griffin watched every move intently. "You stayed in last night?"

It was a pointless question. One he knew the answer to already, but the boy did like his games.

I nodded, careful to keep my vacant eyes downcast.

He followed me from the kitchen to the window seat that filled the space below the large industrial windows. The sky outside was bright blue and blindingly clear.

I swung my legs onto the oversized padded seat, wrapped my arms around my knees, and stared out across the frozen landscape.

He sat inches from me, studying me closely. "Rough night?"

I nodded, careful to keep my expression blank. I made every effort to mimic the zombified version I had been throughout the first weeks following Aamon's death.

He sighed, reached out, and placed his palm on my knee. I didn't flinch. Today was a good day for my act. The day that followed punishments always left behind a mellower version of him.

I lowered my head to my knee, laid my cheek against his hand, and whispered, "I just want to sleep."

With his other hand, he stroked my hair. "Go back to bed, rest. We don't need you to patrol today."

I lifted my head to gaze at him, wide-eyed. "Are you sure?"

With a small smile, he nodded. He radiated euphoria at the opportunity to play the hero. Like I needed his permission to spend the day alone. Like I belonged to him. Whatever. I needed him gone, and if this is what it took, so be it.

I shuffled back to bed with no intention of actually sleeping. One minute I was counting the seconds until Griffin left, the next I was dragged into a world from which there was no escape.

I was dreaming yet lucid. An unnatural and unsettling experience. My conscious and subconscious minds had convened in the same time and space, and in doing so transported me to somewhere I was not supposed to be. Despite comprehending the situation, I was unable to convince myself that the impending sense of danger was not real.

The setting was vaguely familiar. A location that existed in the real world, pulled from the dregs of my childhood memories of the first place I called home. The place my parents had lived before they separated.

Like any dream, the familiar was mixed with the unfamiliar.

Close to their home sat an apartment complex that in reality did not exist. I was drawn to it, and in an instant I knew why.

Aamon.

I could feel him the way I'd always felt him when he was alive. My heart started to race. It was all I'd longed for. The chance to see him, to hear him, and to feel him again. My footsteps quickened. The closer I got, the stronger the sense of him became.

The building was ugly and cold. A gray concrete structure that belonged in some inner-city neighborhood filled with crime and poverty. The thought of him existing in such a place horrified me. What made it worse was how close to home he'd been, yet he'd remained undetected, forgotten.

I raced up dimly lit concrete stairwells, pulled forward by an invisible force. Pangs of guilt poked and prodded at my chest. How could I have left him here? Why the hell had I wasted time with grief when I could have been trying to find him?

On the nineth level, I stopped.

I don't know how I knew he was there; I just did.

I didn't wait to knock. Didn't pause to read the small number at the side of the doorframe.

With my heart racing at dizzying speeds, I rushed into the dark, dank, and sparsely furnished apartment. Everything within it was a muted dull shade, dominated by the color gray. On a threadbare sofa in a dimly lit room sat Aamon.

I couldn't just see him; I could feel him with a force that exceeded the ability of a dream. He was real, and he was there. I was afraid to run toward him in case his image evaporated before me. I tried to speak. I had so much to say, but my words became lodged in my throat, silenced by overwhelming emotion. Filled with confusion, elated to see him, yet heartbroken and panicked that I could awaken at any moment. I was terrified that if consciousness dragged me away I would never manage to find him again.

That possibility was almost worse than death. Knowing he was somewhere but unable to reach him. The thought of him being alone hurt more than the experience of losing him. He stood, and I could see that he was trying to tell me something; I inched closer. My attention focused on his mouth as it moved, but try as I might I was unable to make out his words. I reached for him and our hands clasped together. His energy, heavy with his scent, coiled across the small space between us. It ignited my senses beyond the capability of a simple memory. He was absolutely real and in existence somewhere.

I wrapped my arms around him and pulled him toward me. I craned my neck to try and decipher what he was trying to tell me, but no sooner did the words travel between us than he was ripped away.

"I'm right here."

Unlike the rest of my dream, his words remained, suspended in the air, carried from my subconscious to my conscious world. They surrounded me like static as I jolted upright in bed. The space around me was charged, making me feel like I wasn't alone. My eyes darted to the side. My bed remained empty, and the sheets undisturbed. I glanced nervously around the room, but there was no one there.

I fought to steady my breathing. I had no desire to try and analyze what I'd experienced. All I wanted to do was to return. But try as I might sleep evaded me. The adrenaline persisted long after it should have diminished.

It was early evening when Griffin returned. He passed by my closed door twice, each time he paused to listen. I remained silent and was thankful he left me in peace.

Sleep and I battled straight through the rest of the night until dawn, when frustration and pain eventually gave way to sobs that had to be smothered by blankets. Crying myself into exhaustion acted as the harbinger of sleep and was what finally allowed me to creep back into a world where if I looked hard enough, I might just find Aamon.

The first thing to greet me was darkness. But not the darkness I had become accustomed to. My usual version was vacant and engulfed by nothingness. This one was anything but empty. It was filled with unknown energies. Things that crept closer and filled me with dread.

It took me a moment to adjust to my surroundings. To recognize that the darkness was created by walls, a ceiling, and a floor, of sorts. My bare toes nudged to one side, feeling out the grainy edging of a timber beam. I balanced carefully as I crouched down and reached beyond the beam. My fingers brushed over something soft. A mass of wadded fibers, like cottonwool but prickly.

I pulled my hand back sharply and rose cautiously to reach above my head. Low lying beams sat just above me, confirming where I was.

The attic was vast, dark, and without windows. I didn't immediately recognize it, but I understood that I'd been there before. Maybe a memory from too long ago for my mind to have kept hold of.

As my eyes became accustomed to the dark, I began to pick out shapes. Unmoving mounds, cubes, boxes, and bags that filled the space as far as I could make out, which granted, was not very far.

Carefully I edged myself forward. There was no sign of movement, yet still I felt the presence of something else there, something nocuous just waiting in the shadows. The attic stretched on; I had taken many steps before it occurred to me that I should have checked for some point of entry, a hatch possibly, before I wandered off into the darkness. Too little too late. I turned to see if the point I traveled from was still in view but was greeted with a yawning blackness that refused to share its secrets.

As I moved, so did the thing that shared the dank space with me. It filled me with dread and left my skin coated with a thin layer of sweat. I wanted to double back, to find the hatch that was there somewhere. To jump through it back into a world of normalcy and light. But something in the darkness pulled me forward. An answer to an unknown question that I had to find.

So I persisted, inching deeper into the blackness as the thing that terrified me drew closer. As I moved, the darkness grew, and with it my understanding. Whatever it was that resided in the shadows, I was responsible for. I put it there; I brought it into existence. Some wrongdoing by my own hand that had somehow manifested over time into an entity capable of harming me.

When my fear was at risk of causing me to pass out, I noticed a dull light far off in what looked like another area within the attic. Still a part of the original space but partially separated. Balanced on the rough wood, I stepped from beam to beam over wads of fiberglass, moving toward the light. As I got closer, I realized that the light's source came from an area that branched off from the main body of the attic. There was no door. It was partially obscured by joists and rafters that sat fence-like between it and the darkness. The only way in was to crawl between the thick horizontal timber supports.

Who creates a room with no entrance or exit?

Without hesitation, I clambered between the dusty old wooden beams that crossed before the space and entered a small rectangular chamber, its single high-set window nestled amongst bare bricks on the far side. Through it I could see only sky, dominated by a setting sun that cast an amber glow through the small panes of glass. Tiny specks of dust danced in its sunbeams, and everything within the room was bathed in a sepia glow.

Unlike the rest of the attic, this space had a floor, smooth slats of wood the color of cinnamon. It was warm and safe. A sharp contrast to what lay just beyond.

There were wide shelves on either side of the room, all packed with objects that were instantly recognizable. Objects that stirred a wave of nostalgia so intense that tears sprung from my eyes and streaked my sweat- and dust-covered face.

Everything in there was from my childhood. Hand-knitted baby blankets and crocheted shawls. Stuffed animals, strollers, and toys. My crinoline doll stood proudly, held in place by the metal hand of her stand, the frills of her red and white dress cascading in layers. The first doll pram I'd received as a toddler, a gift one Christmas morning. Its orange base and a dark pink plastic hood as preserved as the image captured by my mom's old Kodak. My red metal tricycle with the pink elephant sticker on its seat, and my Matchbox Play Boot and tree house, with figures and furnishings still inside.

I crept beside the shelves, touching, smelling, and exploring each object.

On the floor to one side was my highchair. Its vinyl seat coverings adorned with orange and brown flowers, its once-white tray now a faded shade of yellow. My baby carriage, a navy-blue carrycot upon a silver chassis with huge white wheels was beneath the high window. A matching chunky blue blanket covered with rows of white pompoms rested within it.

I became as safe as a baby bird returned to its nest. For the first time in what felt like forever, I was at peace. I wanted to stay there, surrounded by nostalgia and love. The thing that frightened me wasn't in that space. Being alone there wasn't sad or lonely. It was peaceful and shrouded me in protection.

It wasn't just that I was okay being alone. It was so much more.

A yearning I'd had for as long as I could remember. A need that I had thought could only be fulfilled by the company of others, a significant individual, or the love and acceptance of someone else in my life, had suddenly been fulfilled by this room. A room in which I was the only person. A room that contained nothing but elements of me, of objects that captured memories from my past and that chartered my transition from birth through childhood.

All I needed was me.

A wave of sadness hit unexpectedly. A sadness for all of these objects, abandoned and forgotten. They deserved so much better. I didn't want to leave anything behind, even though none of it was truly mine to take. Even acknowledging that they were exactly where they were supposed to be, the thought of deserting them filled me with a sadness I could not explain.

I sat down on the floor and gazed up at the sunset, mesmerized by the perpetually changing sky as a summer's eve was ushered in with an array of orange, pink, and red shades, all of them deepening as they spread above me. My only distraction was the dull and distant ticking of a clock.

My eyes shot open as I gasped for breath. My clothing clung to my now damp skin.

There it was again, the swinging pendulum. Incessant and unstoppable, counting down the time to something ominous that was yet to reveal itself. When I closed my eyes, every image recalled from my sleep held the same clockface as it stood solemnly, unanimated yet able to stare through me. Its face ever-present in every scene, whether it was somewhere in the background or off to one side. It was invisible in the moments of darkness, but its steady ticking reminded me that it was always present.

A constant reminder that time was running out.

But for what, or for who? For me? For Steven? For

Griffin?

For Aamon?

The thought functioned as a cattle rod that jolted me from my numbness. The temperature in the room plummeted, sending my skin ice cold while the buzz of static again filled the silence. I was no longer alone. An uninvited guest had entered, except it wasn't the room that had been violated, it was my brain.

Where the hell had that thought come from? Who put it there and why? Why would any part of my psyche be so callous? My heart rate accelerated sharply, and a sharp pain radiated throughout my chest. Icy particles formed intricate patterns that danced before my eyelids every time I closed them, spelling out a horrifying possibility previously concealed.

It was true.

I couldn't explain it. It was beyond reason and contradicted every scrap of evidence, every feasible possibility, yet it rang so true.

What had been an innocuous background ticking suddenly transformed into a doomsday clock. Its beat thumped out a perpetually aggressive rhythm as the arrow-spiked tips of its cold metal hands moved quickly. It challenged me. It berated me. It dragged me outside of my shelter into a storm that rained a million shards of glass-like hail upon my flesh.

Time no longer stood still. It mocked what I had wished for, releasing me from the suspended capsule of the void to show me there was a much worse alternative to my imprisonment. Without compassion, it flung me into a far more terrifying reality.

My misplaced focus was suddenly aligned.

My hope had been to contact Aamon, believing he

was dead. I had never even considered the possibility that he was in fact very much alive.

Alive and running out of time.

Chapter 13

When I awoke, I was not alone. The dream had traveled with me. It clung to me like the seemingly constant sheen of sweat that glazed my skin. The dream permeated my thoughts. It fogged my brain with recollections so powerful I was almost convinced that I was still dreaming.

My breathing was raspy, and my eyes stung. At some point I had cried, a lot.

I felt suffocated by the volume of unanswered questions. The biggest of which reverberated loudly above all others.

Was it even possible?

I had been skeptical of everything Griffin had said or done since his return, so it wasn't like I'd ever taken his version of events with anything more than a grain of salt. The only credence I'd given him was that he had managed to use some half-truths to weave a story that at the very least had fit the timeline.

The bottom line was Kasey was here, Aamon was not.

According to Birsha, there had been evidence of a struggle when Aamon was killed. There was a body that, for all intents and purposes, appeared dead, again a fact from Birsha.

However, the most damning piece of evidence I had undeniably constructed myself. Not one particle of

Aamon's energy could be detected between any of the three planes, of that I was sure. That fact alone was what had booted me roughly over the edge of a cliff.

I shuffled backward in bed until I was upright against the headboard. I pulled my legs into my chest and wrapped my arms around them, balling myself as tightly as I could. Gently I rocked as I dissected the scraps of information I had in an effort to separate the facts from the fillers.

I had no idea where to start, specifically how far back I needed to go. Walking through the sequence of events since Griffin's return would have been the most logical approach, but what if I was right?

Revisiting memories but maintaining control is one of the hardest things I've ever had to do. Like swimming against a mighty rip tide. Just the tiniest lapse in concentration, the slightest delay in dodging the undertow, and you're sucked far away, powerless against it.

As dangerous as it was, I needed to revisit the past. To see the circumstances in the correct order to gain some small semblance of understanding. Even without the presence of a clock, I was acutely aware that, if it was in fact true, if Aamon was alive, his time was running out.

I walked steadily through the timeline of events, circling a maelstrom that threatened to pull me into a vortex at any moment. Casting myself backward was easy.

Pulling myself from it was not. I uncoiled stiff limbs and rolled from the bed. Staggering to the bathroom, I tried to focus on the now. A splash of cold water on my face helped, so did cleaning my teeth. Normal functioning to persuade my body I was back in the present frame of time.

Frustrated, I changed quickly. The painful journey back had taught me nothing new.

I hadn't seen Birsha since that day. Instead, I'd chosen to crawl into a desperate hole from which I ignored every attempt made by others to reach me. Each thought process led me back to the present, yet still I could not identify what it was, if anything, that I could have missed.

Where I had gone wrong? What piece could I possibly have misconstrued? Again, I walked backward, refusing to stop until I had examined every possibility, questioned every scene. There had been a fight, but no evidence of with whom. There had been a body, according to Birsha, but how close he had been I'd never questioned.

I picked at my cuticles and left the bathroom.

I walked to the window. My eyes, transfixed on the dove gray clouds that moved steadily across the white winter sky, blurred. My movements stilled as my mind raced.

Birsha didn't state definitively that he had seen Aamon unquestionably dead. He'd seen him only for the briefest of moments before he'd been forced to flee with Kasey, moments after his rescue from Laeon. Griffin and Aamon, significantly weakened by the effects of Laeon, had exited with Kasey straight into an ambush.

I'd assumed a lot and proven nothing. I'd been so wrapped up in my grief I'd stopped functioning, stopped questioning, stopped challenging.

Stopped caring!

No! It wasn't that I had actually stopped caring. It

was that I'd cared too damn much to even try to comprehend surviving it. I stupidly thought the only one who would suffer the consequences of quitting would be me.

Idiot.

But there was something else. I'd questioned the how's and where's of Kasey's disappearance, and following his return would probably have continued to seek out answers had it not been for losing Aamon. Having both things happen in quick succession, I was left no time and no inclination to revisit the unanswered questions.

I massaged my temples.

How had Kasey just wandered unnoticed from his home and traveled such distance without detection? Likewise, how had he continued his absence for such a substantial period without exposure? And why?

I'd had the theories of others thrown in my face over and over but never thought to actually ask the questions myself.

There was no point in asking Griffin. Not only could I not trust any answer he gave, but I would then be subjected to scrutiny for asking and probably punished for even daring to question him.

The only other person who had been within the vicinity and may have been able to shine a light was Birsha. Luckily, he was one of the few beings I trusted.

Desperate for answers, I wasted no more time. Throwing a thick sweater over my head, I stole from my room. Without looking back, I slipped silently from the building.

Chapter 14

I didn't mean to pound on the door the way I did. The high-speed sprint over to Birsha's home had done nothing to pacify the adrenaline spike brought on hours earlier.

Birsha's initial alarm quickly gave way to amusement as I fervently paced the living room of the large, somewhat ostentatious home that he shared with fellow Sygans.

"I think I know. I think I'm starting to understand. I was wrong, I mean, not entirely I don't think, but there are definitely things that I missed. These dreams have to mean something, don't you think? He came back too soon, and something wasn't right about the ambush. I mean, how would they have known and where did his body go? And why the hell would I be having these insane dreams now?"

Birsha listened patiently to my ramblings. Sitting in a leather high-back chair, he remained silent. His brows were furrowed just a little and his eyes glinted, yet his mouth remained pulled into a tight, straight line.

I took a shaky breath and waited for Birsha's response. He stood, left the room, and returned moments later with a glass of water. Silently, he handed it to me and sat back down. As I gulped from the glass, he calmly announced, "Aamon isn't dead."

My brain screamed in astonishment at both his

words and his nonchalant delivery as water sprayed from my nose and mouth like a high-pressure fountain.

Birsha raised one brow and ducked slightly as I launched the glass with a screech. It whizzed centimeters from his head before it impacted the wall behind him and shattered into a million shards, its path tracked by the small stream of water it left behind.

"Griffin set it up," he explained quickly, "at least that's my theory."

"He's *alive*?" The room tilted, and I had to fight to remain in an upright position, my wrath momentarily forgotten as the enormity of his words took hold.

"Where is he?" I demanded, my voice almost a shriek.

Birsha stood quickly. He approached me like one would approach a feral animal, cautiously, slowly, and with hands and arms open wide. He chose his words carefully and kept his tone even and low.

"I don't know for sure, but a few of us have been looking. We are making progress, but it's slow going."

"And you didn't think to fucking tell me!" I yelled, all attempts to retain control and composure long gone.

"How?" he challenged softly.

I stopped, frozen in my tracks as the realization of how the situation must have looked from his standpoint hit me. I shook my head. "It's complicated."

It was, but either way, I had allowed Griffin to take what everyone must have assumed was control of everything, including me, regardless of the reason.

"I was trying to finish what Aamon had started," I explained weakly.

Birsha nodded. "I wasn't questioning you, Alyssa, just defending my actions. You don't think you were the first person I tried to approach?"

Somehow, I had managed to fail Birsha along the way as well.

"What do you know so far?" I sniffed, my brain still reeling.

"That Griffin wasn't working alone. That he was careful, and that he kept his circle small." Again, Birsha's voice was low, and his words chosen with great care. "You need to know something else."

The hair on the back of my neck stood on end.

"Kasey didn't just wander away. He was taken."

I inhaled sharply as the needles of suspicion morphed quickly into steel blades.

"Please don't tell me Griffin did this," I hissed, as my worst fears began to materialize before me.

"I believe so," Birsha admitted.

That bastard had taken my baby, my innocent child, from his bed and abandoned him to wander Laeon alone. I felt my insides burning like a furnace, ignited by my anger and hatred of Griffin. The small flame that had been barely a flicker for the longest time was now a raging fire. It blazed through my veins and seared my nerve endings as it searched desperately for a way out.

I shook my head. I fucking knew it! I started to pace; my brain had finally returned from its hiatus and was working double time to catch up. Adrenaline made it impossible to stand still.

My questions came in quick succession. Birsha leaned forward in his seat, his body tense as he fired back answers, understanding the urgency and thankfully cutting straight to the chase.

"Who else knows?"

"Zagan, Seraphina, Eli, Steven."

"Steven?" My eyes widened in surprise.

"Yes." Birsha nodded.

I pointed at him mid-stride exclaiming, "We're going to circle back to that one another time. Did you see who took Aamon?"

"No."

"Do you know the extent of his injuries?"

"No."

"Do you know how anyone could conceal his energy from my detection?"

"Yes, possibly. In the furthest point of the outer realm of Daeon, just before you enter its inner core. A combination of the depth and the energy are the only things that could potentially suppress him," Birsha explained.

"And you think Griffin took Kasey, meaning it's reasonable to assume he orchestrated the whole thing. Right?"

Birsha stood solemnly, his gaze met mine, and the look he threw me halted my erratic steps. "To be very clear with you, Alyssa, I don't think, I know."

"How can you be so sure?"

He drew in a deep breath. "Kasey told me."

I balked. Jerking myself to face Birsha, I whispered, "What did you say?"

"He spoke to me, Alyssa. At great length."

For a moment, even the pendulum froze. Moving at warp speed, I snatched a chair from across the room and slammed it in front of Birsha. I sat just inches from him and leaned in with my hands clasped, afraid to hear what he had to say almost as much as I was afraid of missing a word.

"Tell me," I pleaded.

Birsha released a sigh. He rubbed the back of his neck and closed his eyes, transporting himself back to the moment in question.

"Griffin threw Kasey at me, told me to get him to safety, which of course I did. I assumed the poor kid would be too traumatized to speak. I mean, he shouldn't even have been conscious being so close to such potent energy, but it barely seemed to affect him. As soon as we were a safe distance away from Griffin, he started to talk, and he didn't stop until I made it to his home."

If the circumstances had been different, I'd have laughed at his last comment.

"Keep going," I urged.

Birsha opened his eyes but focused on the floor.

"He asked me if I was a dressed-up wolf. I told him I was just a person. He said I looked like a wolf but felt like an angel. Then he asked me if the other man was okay. I assumed he meant Griffin, but he described Aamon."

Birsha glanced up at me before continuing. "Alyssa, he told me that Aamon had saved him, and more than that. He told me Griffin was the one who took him out of his bed. He said that Griffin would watch him from the shadows at night, that he scared him, and that one night he came out of the shadows and carried him away. He told me that Griffin was the bad one."

A wolf?

"Why would he ask you if you were a wolf? He knows what a fucking wolf looks like. Are you sure he was conscious?"

Deep within the recesses of my brain, as if it was some distance away, an alarm started to ring.

"Yes, one hundred percent. I mean, I know it doesn't

make sense, but he's a kid and kids say crazy shit, right? What did you tell him about Griffin?"

"Huh?" I was genuinely baffled. "Birsha, I haven't communicated with him. I visited him often. I thought that might even be the reason he sought out Laeon, trying to follow the energy he got so used to being around. But he couldn't see me."

"He could hear you."

I shook my head. "That's not possible."

Birsha paused for a moment. "Wait, you visited him at night, right?"

"Yes."

"Did you talk to him, you know, as he slept?"

My breath caught in my chest as I recalled exactly how the hours had been spent by Kasey's bedside.

"Yes." My eyes widened as I remembered the tune he had hummed in his sleep.

Oh shit!

"What would you talk to him about?"

"I would tell him stories."

Birsha's brow furrowed. "What kind of stories?"

My voice was barely a whisper. "Fairytales."

Birsha looked hard at me, his brows raised and his eyes wide. "The kind of fairytales with wolves in disguise?"

"Oh God, he could hear me." For the first time, I started to realize the extent of Kasey's exposure to the other side. Slowly the pieces started to fall into place, like a Tetris-constructed flawless wall, the pieces fitting with synchronicity and perfection. Desperately, I racked my brain to remember as much as I could of what I had said to him during my nightly visits. Familiar stories and alternative versions filled my mind. And of course, that damn song. He had hummed the fucking melody of it without skipping a beat. How had the magnitude of that slipped by me? How the hell had I written that off as a coincidence?

Then another more recent memory tore through my brain.

The chair scraped loudly on the wooden floor as I stood. I tried to pace, my body desperate for movement, but again the floor began to tilt. I grabbed the back of the chair to steady myself, my knuckles whitening as each muscle tensed beyond my control.

"The other day he reacted to Griffin," I croaked.

Birsha's eyes narrowed. "While he slept?"

I shook my head, "No, while he was very much awake."

Birsha paused before continuing. "He spoke directly to me, so we know he sees and hears us. It could have just started as sounds to him, and his ability may have developed over time. He told me about the wolf, and how his mom had told him that, when it came, it would look like a normal person. It didn't make sense at the time, I assumed he was confused and talking about things you had said to him when you were alive. He wasn't afraid of me, and he wasn't afraid of Aamon, but he was afraid of the Sygans that had hunted him, and he was afraid of Griffin, or as he put it, the bad wolf."

"I thought he was in Laeon," I gasped, horrified as I swayed on unsteady legs.

"He was, but he knew he he that he didn't belong there. He was trying to find his way out; he was trying to find his way home."

There it was again, right before me, the gleaming wall of colored pieces, seamless and almost complete.

The answer to Aamon's whereabouts the final piece outstanding.

Of course, every Earth-dwelling dead entity would have been alerted by Kasey's presence as he crossed forward and backward between the planes. Such a small child with the ability to see and hear across existences—that kind of energy would be like a beacon, a tempting trophy worthy of a fight. Kasey had been hunted.

"Griffin set Aamon up. Waited for him to enter Laeon to rescue Kasey, knowing how much it would weaken him and knowing the reception that would be waiting for him on the other side."

"The ones who were waiting, they were working for Griffin?" My heart sank a little, how much had I underestimated Griffin?

"Not all of them. Like I said, he kept his circle small. We located all but one of them. The ones we caught knew nothing, believe me."

I paused; the final unanswered question caused a wave of nausea that rolled through me.

"Birsha, why is he keeping Aamon alive? It doesn't make sense."

Birsha sighed. "With Aamon alive, he has leverage. If breaking and gaslighting you into submission didn't work, he still had options. Besides, if Griffin had killed Aamon, you'd have known the second you laid eyes on him. Aamon's residual energy would have remained with Griffin for days. Griffin isn't completely stupid; he knows you'd have killed him in a heartbeat."

Well, he got that part right at least.

He continued, "Not knowing precisely who was to blame made it easy for Griffin to assign blame to whoever he saw fit. An effective control method evidently."

I cringed. "I was just so fucking lost." Tears pooled my eyes.

"And he took complete advantage of that. Everything he's done has been calculating. He waited till you were at your weakest. You blaming yourself is one of the greatest power hands you can give him," Birsha warned.

Anger and shame burned through my veins. "I fell for it."

"Good." Birsha nodded.

I recoiled. "What?" It was hardly the sympathetic response I'd expected.

"That's something we can use." He stepped toward me and added, "Without a doubt, the most powerful enemies are the ones that used to be friends."

"I already know how much power I've allowed him to take," I remarked.

Birsha's smile widened. "Stop looking at this from a victim's perspective. It's time to change seats."

I folded my arms tightly across my chest and tried desperately to regulate my breathing as I shifted my weight. My gaze fell away from Birsha as I focused on the window on the far side of the room. Watching the slow-moving clouds, my voice was barely discernable as I whispered, "If Griffin has a Sygan working for him, guarding Aamon wherever the hell he is, why not just instruct them to…" It was a sentence I couldn't finish. I had reached my limit of allowing the words Aamon and death to be used in the same dialogue.

"And rob himself of the satisfaction of doing it? No, he won't do that," Birsha hissed through clenched teeth.

I hadn't eaten for days, yet a nauseated feeling

continued to plague me. With every new question, every new realization, I was flung back onto a ship caught in a storm. The constant motion left me fighting the urge to dry heave.

My voice cracked as I turned back to Birsha. "We need to find Aamon. I don't think he has much time left."

Birsha's jaw clenched. "It isn't that easy."

"Yes, it is. I'll get Aamon's location out of Griffin. I'll quite happily torture the bastard before I kill him."

"That won't work, Alyssa. You'd be handing Griffin the satisfaction of knowing he won, that he'd succeeded in taking you from Aamon."

"I'm going to kill him," I insisted.

Birsha's eyes pierced mine and with a strained voice he declared, "Then Aamon will die."

My head snapped toward the clock across the room, the sound of its ticking suddenly demanded my attention as its second hand moved faster than it should.

As his gaze followed mine, Birsha sighed heavily.

Images of my dreams flashed quickly before me. I shuddered.

Aamon was running out of time.

"What do I do?" Panic rose like a hot and acrid bile in my throat, but Birsha remained unresponsive, his brow again furrowed. "What do I do?" I rasped, grabbing wildly at him. "Birsha, *what do I do?*"

"Breathe," he commanded.

"Breathe!" I started at the shrillness of my voice. "That's your advice, to fucking breathe."

I was teetering on the edge, a place I'd come to know all too well.

"You need to get a fucking grip, Alyssa, and the reason you need to get a fucking grip is that you *can* fix this, but you get just one shot, that's all, just one."

With anticipation, I stared at him. I tried my best to take a deep breath as I fought down the acid that had caused my throat to spasm. I was barely able to hold back the tears that had seeped into my eyes. Through gritted teeth, I asked again. "What do I do?"

Birsha paced in front of me, his words falling quickly as he summarized.

"Right now, you can't win against him. Right now, and in every feasible scenario, he comes out on top, and we lose everything. At this moment, you cannot win in a fight against him. Do you understand?"

I blinked rapidly and shook my head just slightly.

Birsha pointed toward me as he yelled, "Don't shake your fucking head. You need to accept it; you need to believe it; you *can't* win."

"So, what am I—"

Birsha cut me off. "You let him win." His pacing stopped, and I inhaled sharply.

"I don't..."

He stepped toward me, leaned in close, and enunciated each word as he whispered, "*You let him win.*"

I felt the color as it drained from my face, felt my hands turn to ice as the blood rushed from my limbs to my chest in an effort to sustain the rapid erratic beating of my heart.

"What?" I gasped.

"You give an Oscar-winning performance, Alyssa. You make yourself believe Aamon died already, you convince yourself he is no more, and when it's plausible, you give Griffin exactly what he wants, the one thing he's always wanted, the only reason he implemented this entire fucking plan."

I tried to swallow, but my rigid throat was constricted, catching even my air in its frozen grip.

"You give him you."

Chapter 15

As hard as I tried, my brain could not fathom how I would pull off such an act with any degree of success. I had no choice, there was no question, and I had no doubts that Birsha was right. However, rationalizing what needed to be done would not make the execution of such actions any easier.

Birsha's words silenced my manic mind. They snapped me out of hyperventilation mode and, for just a moment, held me suspended in a state of numbed shock. But only for a moment.

As the realization hit, I plummeted.

"Bathroom?" I gagged.

With wide eyes, Birsha gestured to the entrance hall. I sprinted wildly and swung open the first of two identical doors to the right of the lounge. Luckily for Birsha and his roommates, it was the correct door for the restroom.

I slid on my knees to the toilet and vomited hard. The nauseous waves continued long after my gut had been emptied. Drained and shaking, I lay on the white tiled floor, my clammy cheek pressed against the cold surface. It was the only way the room would stop spinning.

I didn't think throwing up was a thing post death. I'd experienced stress-induced queasiness more than once. The sight of my body at the hospital morgue. Walking step by step back through the final moments of my life. Each and every time I lost what was positive and good in any of my lives, and the near loss of Kasey, twice. Yet each time I had battled against such a human reaction and won.

Not that day.

That day was the final straw.

There had been so many red flags. In hindsight, it was hard to comprehend how I had not seen then what now seemed so obvious.

"If I bring you more water, do you promise not to hurl it at my head?"

The door was open, but Birsha remained firmly outside of the bathroom. I can't say I blamed him. I groaned and pulled myself slowly into a seated position. My eyes and nose streamed, and the ground tilted as I moved.

With my back pushed against the wall for support, I took small sips of the ice water Birsha brought me. He sat opposite me on the bathroom floor. He didn't say anything. He didn't need to. His silent solidarity was enough.

I didn't contemplate leaving until I was sure I wouldn't hurl again. I took the time to get control not just of my guts, but of my mind. The only way I could get through this was to lock away who I really was, not just conceal her as I had done previously, but truly imprison her.

From that moment on, I would wear a disguise not just for Griffin but for everyone, including myself. I knew that the only way to keep my mask from slipping would be to avoid acknowledging the existence of the real me, to keep her hidden from mind and from sight.

To silence her voice and extinguish her thoughts. No more slipping back into the past. No more seeking comfort in what was. From this point onward, I was no longer me.

"Thank you," I murmured to Birsha as I handed him the now-empty glass.

He took the glass and held my gaze. "You can do this. You know that, right?"

I nodded and waited for him to leave before I dragged myself up off the ground. With stiff legs, I hobbled to the small basin, splashed my face with water, and paused, my hands gripping the edges of the sink.

"You're dead," I whispered to my reflection. To the person I was. To the person I hated. Then I turned away and left. I held a slow but steady pace as I journeyed back to the loft, all the while working on my new persona.

The fake me had a different backstory, different experiences, and different hurts. The best part of my new role was that everything related to the real me—the trauma, the anxiety, and the pain—was rendered nonexistent.

At the loft, I stopped at the seventh floor and tentatively tapped on the door. They were all there, Noah, Steven, Amelia, and Griffin. I could feel each one of them from the distinctive energies they omitted.

Griffin opened the door, but he didn't step back to let me in. Instead, he stepped forward and pulled the sliding door shut behind him, leaving us alone in the hallway.

"Are you okay?" He looked me up and down.

I nodded and forced a small smile.

He folded his arms across his chest. "Where have you been?"

I drew a deep breath. "I went to see Birsha."

He raised one brow, the muscles in his jaw clenched just a little.

"I need to know what happened to him. I thought Birsha could help me." I shrugged.

Griffins brows furrowed, and he rocked back on his heels. "You know what happened. I told you already."

I looked at him, my eyes unblinking held his. My face remained passive. "I want to know who was responsible," I whispered.

His frown deepened. "It won't bring him back."

"I was looking for closure, not reincarnation," I hissed.

Griffin's face softened. My shoulders sagged, and I didn't resist against the gentle hug he gave me. He nodded toward the door. "Do you want to come in."

I shook my head. "I'm just going to go up." I started to step away, then stopped and looked back at him. "Hey, Griffin, don't be too long."

He blinked, unable to contain his surprise. With a small smile, I left.

The beginning was frustratingly slow. I couldn't launch into a different persona overnight. Over the ensuing days, I lingered a little longer than I had to around Griffin. I allowed him to intervene with success when Amelia and I argued, and I permitted his self-centered conversations to flow at length without cutting them short.

As the rapport between us grew, I stopped walking on eggshells quite as much around him. I argued back only when the point did not matter to him or when he was right. The more he won, the more confidently relaxed he became. I allowed just a little of the fire out, fully aware of how much he hungered for the warrior I had become with Aamon. How he yearned for the fiery version of me to return without Aamon there to monopolize my time and attention. The woman of ice and fire but fully within his control. Such a paradox.

I fed his ego and his eyes, choosing clothing that was just a little less, a little tight, or a little more threadbare than usual. I would occasionally borrow his sweatshirts and return them still heavy with my scent. I flinched less when he stood close and tried hard not to tense when he touched me.

Reeling him in wasn't the problem. Succeeding without skepticism was the challenge. Just as he started to savor the changes, I would withdraw, just briefly. Just enough to eradicate any suspicions before they had barely formed. Just enough to make him want it even more. Just enough to fuck with his head the way he had become the master at fucking with other people's.

Over time, that reel became shorter. Just a glance could shift the tension between us. It was still that same old story, the less interested I appeared, the more ravenously he longed for my attention, only now he believed he stood a chance. There was just one small hurdle preventing me from giving him what he wanted. From giving him me.

Aamon. It clung lightly to each interaction like a delicate thread that refused to snap. The problem was that Griffin seemed in no great hurry to make efforts to sever it, maybe fearful that such an act would send me spiraling in a direction far away from him. Time was not a friend, and I quickly reached a point where I could wait no longer.

The argument I started with Amelia was petty and

much more her style. I had grown accustomed to her goading me with her constant bitchy comments. I rarely responded; in fact, my brain barely registered them anymore. But not this morning. This morning, I was ready to go hard.

Sitting on the kitchen counter, surrounded by the smell of coffee and Steven's orange and cranberry muffins, I waited for Griffin to pass me by, playfully kicking him as he did.

He stopped and raised one eyebrow, unable to conceal the grin that spread across his face. Leaning back on my hands, I tilted my head to the side and opened my eyes wide and innocent. He stepped close, placed one hand on either side of my thighs, and leaned forward until he was inches from my face. "Did you just kick me?"

Slowly I shook my head with a feigned expression of shock. "Never."

With a laugh, he stepped away. As he did, I raised my right foot and swung it toward the back of his legs, only this time he reached out and caught it. He spun to face me and tugged my leg forward, jerking me across the counter.

I laughed.

From the other side of the kitchen, Amelia watched our exchange, her face darkening with each passing second.

"Careful, Griffin, I would hate to think what you might catch if you get to close," she hissed.

Griffin ignored her. His eyes swept over the low neckline of my top.

I shuffled closer, balancing on the very edge of the counter. "Hey, Amelia, bite me," I snarled.

"I'd like to bite you," Griffin whispered, his voice husky.

I smirked at Amelia.

Her nostrils flared, and her hands coiled into tight fists.

"Truth or dare, Amelia. How often do you fantasize about fucking Griffin?"

"I don't know, Alyssa. Who made you come harder, Griffin or Aamon?"

Griffin gave a low laugh, dropping and shaking his head. "Amelia!"

Without missing a beat, I snatched up the plate of muffins, flicked it sideways to send the food tumbling to the counter, and skimmed it across the kitchen toward Amelia.

With a ferocious yelp, she leapt to one side. The plate missed her by millimeters before it smashed against the wall and shattered.

With a bloodcurdling shriek, she flew across the kitchen. I shoved Griffin sideways and launched myself at her. She swung wildly and caught my jaw as I tried to duck away. I retaliated by raining blows to either side of her head. She grabbed a fistful of my hair and yanked my head to the side and downward before she attempted to knee me in the face.

Steven rushed into the kitchen, but this time he didn't try to separate us. He stayed close to the doorway and observed silently from the sidelines with hooded eyes, aware of what was transpiring even if he wasn't clear on why.

Noah was out of the room and with no one else to intervene Griffin had little choice. When his demand to stop fell on deaf ears, he grabbed me from behind and pulled us apart. He wrapped one huge arm tightly around my waist and lifted me three feet from the floor as his other arm crossed over my chest, immobilizing my arms. Yet I refused to be subdued.

"Get off me," I yelled as I squirmed and struggled against his restraint. He carried me, still clawing to break free, from the room as Noah, alerted by the commotion, appeared from wherever he had been and rushed forward to hold back Amelia.

"Jesus, woman, calm down." Griffin panted as he dropped me to the floor on the far side of the living room. I pressed my back into wall, pushing off from it to propel myself forward. Griffin grabbed me and pinned me back against it. I paused, relaxed my shoulders, and held my hands up in defeat. But as soon as he stepped back, I ducked to the side and sprinted past him back toward the kitchen. With a deep laugh, he chased me, swept me back into his arms, and hauled me back to the wall.

Amelia's voice reverberated throughout the loft as she hollered at Noah to get the fuck out of her way, putting up a similar fight against him.

I stared hard at Griffin. "Let me go. She deserves to get her ass kicked, and you know it." He narrowed his eyes, but his face held a bemused grin. I tried again to break free, but he pinned my arms by my sides and pushed me harder against the flat surface. His gaze drifted downward to where the lace trim of my bra peeked above my top as my chest heaved.

He shook his head and lifted his hot blazing eyes to mine. "We're leaving."

"The hell we are," I screamed, squirming against his grip.

With a chuckle, he pulled me from the wall, spun me

around, and crossed my arms over each other in the style of a straitjacket before he lifted me off the ground and carried me from the loft apartment and up two flights of stairs to our place.

But removing me from Amelia did nothing to dispel my fury. Griffin dropped me roughly onto the sofa only for me to rebound and sprint for the door. He laughed as he gave chase, cutting me off just before I got there, and wrestling me back over to the sofa. Each time his hold on me stretched on a little longer, each time it got a little tighter, and the whisper in my ear to calm down and behave got a little huskier.

The final time I paused, allowing him to believe just briefly that I had indeed calmed down. When he stepped away, with a sense of almost disappointment, I again bolted for the door.

When he blocked my exit, I swung for him. He caught my wrist, spun me around, and pulled me backward toward his chest. He grasped hold of my other arm and crossed them both swiftly across my chest, placing me back in a straitjacket hold. As he held me tightly, he murmured in my ear, his voice unable to conceal his growing amusement and excitement.

I was exactly the way he wanted me.

I fought against every instinct and pushed myself against him. The reminder that my window was closing at an alarming rate spurred me on and encouraged me to fight against the impulse to recoil from him.

His chauvinistic temperament misread my elevated heart rate and the aura of anxiety that billowed from me, despite my best efforts to conceal it. He assumed my reaction was brought about by an attraction to him. So, I let him continue, doing what I could to feed his illusion.

I relaxed my posture and murmured that I was calm. Reluctantly, he loosened his grip, which allowed me to twist free and snake around him, but I remained close.

He assumed I would reach for the door, his muscles tensed, ready to spring the moment my hand grabbed for the handle. But I made no such move. Instead, I stepped closer to him.

Griffin's eyes narrowed, the briefest shadow of surprise and doubt passed over his features. I lowered my eyes to the ground, twisted my head away from him to avoid the snare of his direct gaze, saving it until the last moment as I continued to edge closer. As I continued my act, I could feel the disgust of feminists past turning in their graves, no doubt.

The stereotype I had rebelled so vehemently against in life I now manipulated to my own gain. I wished I'd learned to be more conniving during my living years, accepted the way of the world, and learned new ways to play it, rather than continuing to fight a losing battle to change the staunch inequalities. But as my mother would say, hindsight is a great thing.

I had to fight hard against the flames of anger that threatened to break free. To blanket the voice that dripped with revulsion and echoed scornfully throughout my head. Did Griffin really think that he could be my Aamon? That anyone would think I could replace Aamon at all was infuriating, but least of all with Griffin.

My heart rate was still elevated, and Griffin was too opportunistic to delay his chance any further. He moved toward me; broad strides closed the short distance between us swiftly. A small smile played across his lips, an arrogance brought about by his assumption of victory clearly apparent.

Instinctively I stepped backward, but the door was right behind me and the result provided him with exactly what he wanted. I was cornered.

He pushed his body roughly against mine, his hands assuming a vise grip on my waist as his mouth started on my neck, his stubble grazing painfully against my skin.

The short sharp intake of breath I took in horror was again misread by Griffin, mistaken for enjoyment, for arousal, and he responded by grinding against me.

"Stop," I gasped, as I fought to catch my breath. Gently, I placed an open palm against his chest.

He paused. His eyes, inches from mine, flashed angrily, and his jaw started to clench.

Shit!

I softened my tone. "I can't do this without closure. I can't start a new beginning without an end."

His muscles started to tense, and he began to pull back, his eyes filled with distrust as he studied me.

I slid my hands from his chest to his hips, ran my fingers lightly from the sides of his waistband to the front. Hooking my fingers through the front belt loops I pulled his hips close to mine, a small pant escaped my lips as I felt him, swollen, press against me.

I looked up at him. His forearms rested against the door on either side of me, caging me in as he allowed himself to be pulled forward. He lowered his head, and my lips brushed his. Hungrily he lurched forward, but I turned away, resting my head against the door as I repeated, "I can't do this without closure."

"Then closure you shall have," he promised, his breath warm against my ear before he pulled himself away, leaving the room and me.

He didn't need to question how or why. The only

closure possible would be the swift death of the individual responsible for taking Aamon from me. The age-old concept of revenge. An eye for an eye. I needed it more than the air I breathed, and Griffin, for all of his faults, understood that.

Chapter 16

The fact that Griffin had backed himself into a corner did not slow the arrogant bastard down one bit. The search started the following day. With his eyes on a long-awaited prize. Griffin saw no reason for delay. He carelessly discarded the notion of caution, and with time against me, I did all I could to grease the wheels.

In Griffin's mind, his final hurdle was my closure. The only way to achieve that was to hunt and kill the Sygan responsible for Aamon's supposed death. Attacking a pure one isn't something deniable. Aamon's essence would be easily distinguishable, probably more so if he was indeed alive.

Of course this came with a substantial risk. Griffin had to betray his comrades. Not that being disloyal would concern him, but he would need to silence them before they realized what was happening, before they had time to retaliate and blow his cover. Of course he had me, with a barely containable rage. All he needed to do was lead me to the gas canister and open the door. I would be the naked flame entering the flammable atmosphere. I would be the one cleaning up his mess, all he needed to do was watch and enjoy.

He played a precarious but necessary game. To locate the Sygans responsible meant he would have to guide me dangerously close to the only place capable of concealing Aamon. The son of a bitch would probably take me right to him, fueled by arrogance and secure in what he believed was my ignorance. I was sure his sick mind would get a twisted kick out of leading me within reach of an incapacitated Aamon. In fact, I counted on it.

The mysterious Sygan had to have remained close to Aamon since his abduction in order to avoid detection as Aamon's essence would have clung to him, and by doing so placed a target on his back. He would be clueless as to Griffin's treachery, and when he did realize, it would be too late.

In just a few days, Griffin's persona had shifted to that of a complete stranger. He no longer bothered to mask his true character. Embroiled in a battle between who he was and who he had become, he reveled in doing whatever he could to spite his former self.

There are many aspects of the "bad boy" image that some females find alluring. But the volatile toxicity that Griffin had started to exhibit fell far short of any female fantasy, even by Ameila's warped standards. The speed at which he had spiraled was unprecedented, and as his fragile mind disintegrated at an alarming rate, my already tiny window became precariously smaller.

I had made him a promise, intimated a reward, and now I walked a thin line between running out of one-time constraint and holding the other at bay.

I knew the fabricated search for Aamon's alleged killer would be concluded as quickly as Griffin could manage within the realms of believability. I also knew that Griffin would have no choice but to lead me into the depths of Daeon to maintain the pretense. My plan was simple: whatever direction he took, Birsha and his crew would take the opposite direction covering double ground. Zagan and Steven would track us from a safe distance, their presence concealed by the stifling strength of Daeon's inner core. They would note the identity and location of those questioned for later interrogation, should they survive.

Simple is probably an inappropriate word to use. The concept may have been uncomplicated, but the execution would be on a whole other level.

If the intensity of Daeon's inner core was of such a magnitude that it had concealed Aamon's pure energy so effectively, I could only begin to imagine its impact on us, physically and mentally.

The first time I entered Daeon, it had robbed me of almost every function. Over time, as I worked to understand and accept my power, the peace I found internally became mirrored in my reaction to Daeon. Instead of the walls of two oceans crashing together in opposition, my power and Daeon's power flowed with synchronicity. Born of the same source, finally reacquainted.

But that was only the outer rim.

The first day was undoubtedly the worst. Our descent was slow and painful. Our bodies' ability to adjust to the extreme pressure of the concentrated energy decelerated. Removing the cap of a soda bottle that had been shaken vigorously could only be done so gradually.

Griffin's recovery rate was far quicker than mine, a response he failed to conceal. He had clearly made this journey numerous times before. Although he'd adapted to Daeon's conditions, to endure it was the best he could achieve, which was far different to my experience.

As I acclimated, my internal power synchronized with the external force. Instead of draining me, it fed me. With each visit, with each descent, the layers of weighted numbness were peeled away, revealing something raw and fresh.

The creatures of Daeon didn't know me. To them I was brand new, but my energy was old and recognizable. By some I was revered, by others I was feared. Either way, I was rarely challenged and inexplicably deeply respected. They recognized something Griffin failed to see. The extent of my abilities.

Their reaction was something that Griffin manipulated to his own advantage of course. The more time he spent in Daeon firmly by my side, the less refuted his reputation became.

Day after day we scoured Daeon. The mission and I quickly became the sole focus of Griffin's attention. Whether by my side for the search or guarding me closely in the shadows as I slept, he diligently ensured that my every waking moment was spent with him. As I occupied his time completely, his faithful family were cast aside and long since forgotten. Out of sight and out of mind was where they remained, exactly as we had hoped.

When I visited Kasey, he trailed me closely, unbothered that I was aware of his presence. I didn't question his motives. While he was there, I didn't need to worry about Aamon's safety, and it freed his former friends to work undetected.

As much as Griffin disliked my visits with Kasey, he was not stupid enough to do anything to jeopardize his relationship with me, not when he was so close to getting what he had worked hard for.

Each time we entered Daeon, we traveled a little deeper. The beings we had started to encounter were not surprised by Griffin. He was clearly no stranger to them.

He acted quickly to silence them, wielding me as a weapon and often leaving a trail of bodies in his wake. I understood quickly that this was a clean-up job for him as much as a façade for me.

Deep within Daeon, there were clear divides between the social structure of its inhabitants. Opposing clans were easily identifiable, and they were all like for like except for one. I don't know if they had a collective name. I only knew the name of their leader, Calligan.

Their crew was tighter than most, they reigned quietly, but their methods were brutally effective. Feared by the other groups, they remained unchallenged. Each member bore a brand located to the right of their neck, precisely over their jugular. The rounded scar depicted the severed head of a serpent upon a triangle which made them easily identifiable.

When our path crossed theirs, Griffin's demeanor changed. He didn't charge ahead; instead, he allowed me to take the lead, the coward. They surveyed me with an amused interest but left me to continue on my way, nevertheless. On the last day of our search, we crossed paths with two of Calligan's clan, only this time one of them recoiled in horror at my presence. Griffin had given me strict instructions not to engage, an order I had been relieved to follow, but on that day the uncustomary reaction had garnered my suspicion a little too much.

Without hesitation, I stepped forward. The first of the Sygans had a shaved head and dark goatee. His broad shoulders matched Griffin's, who he surveyed with a look of disgust. The other was as tall but with a slender build. His dark hair was long on his neck, partially obscuring the crude design of black ink that covered most of the skin below his face.

The first held my gaze unwavering. The second's step faltered.

I took another step forward. The smaller of the two stepped backward, his eyes wide. His mate's stance changed. No longer relaxed, he leaned forward, his shoulders hunched, and his cold eyes stared at me unblinking.

I ignored him, continuing to move closer. Griffin pulled me roughly back as he nodded for the two to continue on their way.

"Get your hands off me," I hissed watching them disappear down one of the many winding catacombs into Daeon's darkness.

"That's a useless waste of our time and energy. They are not ones to fuck around with."

"You're afraid of them?" I sneered.

Griffin's face darkened. "If your intent is to come down here for a fight, go for it. I was under the impression our journeys here had purpose," he hissed, watching me intently.

I took a breath. Maintaining my act was becoming harder the farther into Daeon we traveled.

"We should be doing a thorough check of everyone. Isn't that what you told me four days ago?"

"For any potential leads, yes. For stale ones long since exonerated, no."

"Fine," I muttered, crossing my arms and turning my head just slightly. Griffin's shoulders relaxed as he exhaled deeply.

I let it go. At least on the surface. He was lying. Although neither of those particular Sygans were the ones responsible for Aamon's alleged demise, the fear that my appearance had generated was undeniable. One of them at least had something to hide, whether that was knowledge of Aamon's whereabouts or Aamon himself. It had to be about him. There was nothing else that could possibly invoke such a degree of fear. There was nothing else I would kill for, and they knew it.

"We should call it a day. We're both exhausted, and I'm sure you'll want to see Kasey tonight, right?"

I hid my grimace behind a sweet smile as I replied, "Sure."

Griffin relaxed even more. "Should I lead the way?"

I rolled my eyes. "Griff, you know I have no idea where I'm going down here."

His smug smile grew. "God only knows where you'd end up without me." He laughed as he swaggered ahead.

I let him take a couple of steps before I followed. With a flick, I removed a hair tie from my wrist and dropped it silently to the floor. The energy it had absorbed would be a beacon in the darkness to Zagan or Birsha or whoever had been designated the role of tracker that day.

That evening, I visited Kasey, a normal occurrence but with a different intent. That would be the last time for a while. We were close to finding Aamon, and our time was almost up. I was adamant my son would not be used as collateral again.

As always Griffin hung back, secure in the knowledge that I was within his reach. The immeasurable comfort the tiny form huddled beneath the patchwork duvet provided was the only thing that alleviated my anxiety. Being close to Kasey gave me a much-needed time out, the chance to breathe and gather my thoughts. The time to plan and the strength to keep going.

According to Birsha, Kasey had heard the stories I had recited night after night. He wasn't afraid of Birsha or Aamon. But he had been afraid of Griffin. That was understandable, the only piece that didn't fit was his apprehension for Laeon.

Seated in the old nursing rocker that still occupied the corner of Kasey's room, I closed my eyes and recalled one of the conversations I had shared with Magda. She had told me about the living who possessed the ability to see and hear beyond their existence, insinuating that it was entirely probable that some of Earth's missing children could have easily wandered across gateways and found themselves in an alternative plane.

Everything about Daeon repels the living. But Laeon, on the other hand, had the power to conjure the opposite reaction, especially to the gifted.

"When that happens, do they ever return to Earth?" I had asked.

With a small smile and a shake of her head, she had replied "No. Very few, if any, would choose an earthly existence over Laeon. It's a place of immeasurable peace and love, providing everything anyone could want, especially a child."

My eyes fell to Kasey. He had told Birsha he knew he did not belong in Laeon. But how and why?

As I studied his face, his eyelids flickered open. I jumped slightly. Shock coursed through my body and elevated my heartrate as his eyes glistened across the dimly lit room and fixed firmly on me. I froze, afraid to make any movement, any sound, afraid to even draw a breath.

He stared.

I began to believe he was still in a state of slumber, doing one of the many freakish things kids do when they sleep.

"It's okay," I murmured, as much to myself as to him. "Ssshhh, you're just dreaming, baby."

"No, I'm not." His voice cut so sharply through the twilit room that I involuntarily yelped, snatching my feet from the ground and onto the chair instinctively. An animal coiled ready to pounce, or more fitting of that moment, flee. Hunched up, my white knuckles grasped the arms of the chair, and my breath caught in my throat.

He smirked.

Yes, that's right, he fucking smirked at me. I mean, I must have looked ridiculous, but still. Wasn't he the one supposed to be petrified in this scenario, not the other way around?

"Kasey," I croaked.

He propped himself up on one arm. Concern replaced the badly concealed amusement as he asked, "Are you okay?"

The look in his eyes reminded me of the day I died.

"Am I…" I stuttered, incredulous. "Wait, no, I, are *you* okay? I mean, you can see me, and I'm…dead."

He shrugged his small shoulders, replying cooly, "I mean. Sure. You come here all the time. Why would I not be okay?" His eyes darted to the window. "I don't like him, so you should probably be a little quieter, so he doesn't hear you."

To say I was unprepared for such an exchange would be an understatement. I had envisioned over the year and a half since my death what I would do, what I would say if I got just one more chance to communicate with him. Yet here I was, floundering and unable to string together a cohesive sentence. If he wasn't afraid of me before, he bloody well would be after this encounter.

A gentle laugh drifted across the channel between us. "I never thought you'd be afraid of anything, Mom."

"You've always been able to see me?" I sniffed as I swiped quickly at the tears I failed to contain. He shook his head. His little face creased into a frown as he worked hard to remember the beginning.

He wriggled himself to a seated position. "At first I just felt you. Then I could smell you. Then I could hear you." With eyes like saucers, he leaned across the bed and whispered, "When the man with the long hair was out front, I saw you but only for a second. Then *smash*"—he gestured wildly with his hands—"you broke the pot, and Nanny pulled me inside."

His face fell and his shoulders slumped as he continued, "Then I didn't see you for the longest time. And then you came back."

I lowered my feet to the ground, watching his reaction carefully. I slid from the chair to the floor and edged slowly toward him as I asked, "Can you tell me what happened, when the man took you?"

His eyes flicked to the bedspread and held his attention, hyper focused as his fingers plucked at the tiny loose threads. I immediately regretted my question. "It's okay, buddy, we don't need to talk about that."

But with a look of defiance I recognized as my own, he raised his head, held his chin high and exclaimed, "He lied."

I swallowed and scooted across the carpet a few more inches. "We don't need to talk about that, Kase," I reassured him.

"He told me he would take me to you. But that place didn't feel like you. I knew straight away that you weren't there. I thought he might have hurt you, so I was trying to find a way out to rescue you."

My hand flew to my mouth holding tightly to the sob that fought to be released. My seven-year-old little man had tried to rescue me. A thousand emotions flooded my mind and my heart, and amongst them was overwhelming guilt. Griffin's accusations had contained an element of truth. I was at least partially to blame. I had made Kasey vulnerable by remaining in his life.

Eyes wise beyond their years flitted down to meet mine. I was still on the floor but now within reach of the bed. He laid his head on his pillow and reached for my hand. The touch of his skin, so soft, so warm, so familiar against mine, tipped me over the edge and sent me on a freefall beyond control. I softly placed my other hand on top of his, cocooning his palm between mine. I rested my head on his mattress, my eyes inches from our clasped hands, and I cried a river of silent tears that could willingly devour me.

I don't know how long the hysteria lasted or how I pulled myself from its all-consuming current. When I did, Kasey slept soundly. I climbed into bed next to him, wrapped my body around his and murmured in his ear. A special story this time, about an adventure he would embark upon, and the friends he would meet along the way.

As a new day dawned, I pulled myself from the nest of blankets and the small stringy limbs that had swaddled me during the wee hours of the morning. I left my mom's house expecting nothing less than an interrogation, only to be greeted by the complete absence of Griffin.

I had been waiting for this moment and seized it, conscious of how close I had come to missing it entirely. Griffin had loose ends to tie up, a feat not possible with me in tow. It was the only chance I would get to do anything free from his watch.

I traveled with speed in the direction of the loft and ran straight into a breathless Steven at the building's entrance.

He grabbed at me frantically "Where have you been? We have to do this now."

My heart skipped a beat. "Did you find something, was it the place I went to yesterday?" The thunder of feet pounded the stairwell as Birsha and Zagan descended. "Affirmative," Zagan bellowed as he rushed past me without pause.

Steven followed suit, but my fight or flight response failed me. Encased in a concrete vault constructed of fear, I was immobilized. The voice in my brain screamed furiously, and every fiber willed me to move, but try as I might, I remained frozen to the spot. Birsha paused midstride. He sprinted back over to me and placed both hands on my shoulders.

He stared into my eyes, and in a voice far calmer than I deserved, he reassured me.

"You can do this. I promise you, trust in yourself, Alyssa. You are stronger and smarter, and you will absolutely fucking win. Just one step at a time, that's all you need to do."

His words awoke something within me. My limbs may have lost their function, but I refused to let my mind abscond. I closed my eyes and felt for whatever restraint it was that held my darkness down. Feeling Birsha's hands on my shoulders, remembering Kasey's hand cupped in mine, and envisioning Aamon standing before me allowed me to summon the last ounce of strength that I had as I clung desperately to the final strands of my sanity, and with a rough jerk she was released.

With the heat of a hurricane and the force of tsunami she broke free, her iron grip dragged me along at speed. The forward motion forced my limbs into compliance and gave my backside the sharp swift kick it needed.

Pure fear and desperation propelled us onward. As we entered Daeon, we slowed, cautious that Griffin could be somewhere close by. Only when Zagan received confirmation that Griffin had been located in an area far from our intended destination did our speed pick up again.

In silence, we journeyed into the deepest recesses of Daeon. I didn't know what had been confirmed, if Aamon had been found and, if that was the case, what state he was in. The urgency emitted from Zagan, Birsha, and Steven was strong. Questions could wait; Aamon could not. Nor could the slender timeframe we had to work with.

The farther we traveled, the faster the already dim light faded. The tone of the shadows deepened, and the space around us closed in. The air mutated into something thick and alive. Slyly, it stole away my senses as it morphed into its own tangible entity. It blanketed my ears and deafened me to everything, save the repetitive thrum of the low frequency vibrations. It shrouded my sight and confused my nerve endings, combining a thousand pinpricks with numbness until nothing remained but hands that could have belonged to someone else.

I could sense no one. Birsha, Zagan, and Steven

were swallowed by the yawning blackness. I hoped they were still there, somewhere in the shadows, still present and still focused on the mission. I clung to blind faith in the literal sense. For the first time, I was able to understand the appeal of religious belief.

My footsteps slowed when I no longer felt alone. The thick cover that had smothered my senses shifted just slightly, and I was alerted to a familiar presence. But it was not a good one.

One of Calligan's Sygans was ahead. Stationary within the depths of hell for only one feasible reason. As I got closer, my suspicions were confirmed. He reeked of Aamon. His blood and his sweat, his energy and skin cells, overpowering the creature's own essence.

My speed may have decreased, but my forward motion continued. If I stopped, I would probably not start again. The dense energy kept its grip tight as it pulled me backward and made each step a fight. My dry throat rasped, and my lungs burned. Still I pushed on, praying the momentum would carry me to the Sygan with enough strength to incapacitate him.

He sensed my approach and braced himself for the impact. I barreled into him with as much force as I could muster and slammed him into the hard surface of the wall he stood before. He grabbed blindly at my neck, but I lowered my chin, rotated my shoulders inward and sharply pushed my arms up, driving my rigid fingers around his neck. I clamped one palm over the top of my other hand on the back of his skull. With my forearms locked tightly against his collarbone, I leveraged my weight against his head and jerked it in a downward direction, whilst I simultaneously thrust my knee upward and smashed it squarely into his face, caving his skull in.

It was a blow delivered with such ferocity that he was killed instantaneously.

He crumpled at my feet, and I scrambled over him with outstretched hands. My palms skimmed the cold stone wall as I searched desperately for the opening he must have been guarding. When my nails scraped against a thick door, the wood felt warm even against my desensitized hands. My breaths came fast and heavy as I searched despairingly for a way in.

There was nothing. It stood strong and flush to the wall, no sliver of space, no handles or keyhole, no hinge or lock. Solid, thick, and impenetrable.

Drained, desolate, and out of time, robbed of my ability to function physically and mentally, I faltered. With my once-burning flame of rage and fury now reduced to barely an exhausted ember, I started to break, succumbing to the ominous energy as the final remnants of my fight were extinguished.

I sank to the floor, and my mouth opened wide. I felt the raspy scream as it erupted from my chest, but I heard nothing. With my palms pushed against the floor, my heavy head swung gently to the side; the wood grain of the handleless door pressed against my cheek. The thud of my overworked heart added a heavy bass beat to the constant hum that infiltrated every square inch of the air that encased me.

The beat got louder. Its pulse doubled. One thud from inside of my chest mimicked immediately by an external thud. My eyes shot open; I was not alone.

Aamon.

Chapter 17

The sudden realization released a high voltage shock that traveled wildly. It resuscitated my deadened energy and released a swell of adrenaline that engulfed me, electrifying every nerve ending with a jolting force.

Aamon.

There were no thoughts, no clearly devised plan. Like an entity governed by its most primal instincts, my body went into autopilot, while my mind remained locked in a frozen state somewhere far left of Neverland, unable to function beyond a single thought that played on an endless cycle of repeat.

It was real. He was alive, and more than that he was within my fucking reach.

My arm shot forward, and my clenched fist struck the door full force. It shuddered but held fast. I was not deterred. Over and over, I persisted, immersed within a manic trance. A steady beat echoed through the shadows as my blows rained relentlessly against the heavy wood. Even the sickening crunch of broken bones and the steady stream of blood failed to snap me back into reality.

Like a being possessed, I continued. The sane and lucid cords that had tethered me just barely to reality had snapped, and my conscious mind was left tumbling silently through a lightless, soundless vortex. The small circle of light at the end of the tunnel held one image alone. Aamon.

I don't know how long it went on for. When the door finally gave way with a groan, the shock of the sound severed the tenuous relationship that gravity and I had shared. With the last of my balance decimated, I collapsed across the threshold and landed heavily on my knees.

I remained there for a minute, trying to figure out a way to stand without the use of my arms which hung corpse-like, weighted, mangled, and bloody at my sides. The rasp of my ragged breaths was amplified in the dense air. Its loud echoes held any other sounds momentarily at bay and allowed my mind to hang suspended somewhere just beyond reality.

Screams and curses pulled me back to the present. Birsha lunged forward and dragged me back to my feet while twin thuds reverberated on either side of us. As Zagan and Steven's feet hit the ground, I shrieked, just one word, the only word I could say as I hurled my body in the direction of the yawning darkness.

"Aamon!"

I repeated it like a mantra, a hysterical chant over and over. My feet may have been planted firmly on the ground, but my mind was still far away, freefalling into hell.

Zagan and Steven sprinted forward without hesitation. Birsha paused, his eyes wide as I swayed. I was beyond the ability to speak, save for his name, but Birsha heard what he needed to loud and clear. He hooked one arm around my waist and pulled me along with him as he moved.

Aamon was everywhere, the thickness of his energy made the air buzz. I felt him half a second before I saw him, bloody, beaten, and scarcely conscious. His deadweight arms were swung over Steven and Zagan's shoulders. His feet scraped the ground as they yanked him roughly from the black hole of suffocation. His shoulders were stooped; his head too heavy to lift.

"Aamon." My roar was reduced to a croak. But it was enough.

His head lifted, and his eyes met mine. With a force of nuclear proportions, I flew at him, the last threads of my restraint annihilated. As my arms encased him, his scent coursed furiously through every vein, every nerve, every molecule, and my heart exploded. The concrete vines that had compressed my ribcage were blasted to dust, and a powerful rush of Daeon-rich air swept through my chest. The atmospheric density transformed abruptly from a force that restrained into a power that surged. Each lock, gate, and cage that had imprisoned my strength, my thoughts, and my very soul were obliterated.

With a low growl, he pulled his leaden arms free of Zagan and Steven and held me hard against him.

With what sounded like a sob, he rasped, "You can't be here. He'll kill you."

My eyes flashed with anger as I pulled back to stare into his. "The fuck he will." I reached for him again, but he jerked away, his roar echoing as he staggered sideways.

"I don't need you to fight my battles!" He grasped Zagan's shoulder in an effort to regain his balance. "Leave now, all of you!"

An acidic wave of panic rose rapidly in my throat as I screamed at him. "Fuck you, Aamon!"

He blinked in disbelief at my reaction. "You need

to—"

But I didn't let him finish. "No, *you* shut up and listen to me for once. You don't get to do this; you don't get to be a willing participant in the creation of what we had, what we have, to then just quit!"

I pointed a bloody battered hand at him. "I surrendered everything I had, every damn part of me, and you fucking let me. So no, you don't get to tell me to fuck off because you're overcome with a martyr complex. I'm not leaving, so unless you want to fight me as well, I suggest you suck it the fuck up and stop acting like a pussy!"

Ignoring the tears that fell uncontrollably and the sobs that made my chest heave, I pulled my shoulders back and squared up to him. My glare, defiant and unwavering, bored into his coal-black eyes which were alight with hostility. He was the last person across all three planes that I wanted to fight against, but if a battle was what was needed to keep him, then so be it.

"I love you."

His words caught me off guard. Cold fingers snatched my breath away.

"I love you," he repeated as he stared at me intently. "I love you."

The earth beneath me crumbled, the shift of tiny grains reminded me that the notion of a solid foundation was no more than a fallacy. My voice cracked as I tried desperately to make him see reason.

"Then why are you trying to leave me?"

"I'm trying to save you."

"The only way to save me is to save yourself."

Zagan's pained voice sliced through the shadows. "He needs to retreat."

Four bewildered sets of eyes turned toward him.

"It's the only way." Zagan explained, "His injuries are too great. He can't hide from Griffin and there isn't a cat in hell's chance that Griffin will let him escape a second time. As soon as we leave here, he will track him with ease and kill him."

Aamon's face hardened, but he said nothing. The silence hung thickly while tendrils of vines snaked their way through the shadows. They coiled deftly around my torso, and when in place, they squeezed firmly around my ribcage as they morphed to stone.

I tried to speak, but the constriction held everything, including my voice strongly within.

Steven was the first to murmur, "Retreat where?"

I blinked away the membrane that had blurred my vision to focus on Aamon. His expression told me everything I needed to know. The sudden scream startled me, and my brain scrambled to locate its origin, realizing with horror that its source was me.

I lunged toward Aamon and was captured midleap by Birsha. Like a wild animal I fought, all logic lost at the prospect of losing him again. It took Birsha, Steven, and Zagan to hold me at bay.

Aamon stumbled forward and pushed their hands roughly away to hold me one last time. "This isn't forever," he promised. "I will heal, and I will return for you."

I wanted to believe him; I willed it with all my heart. But what was plastered across the faces of Zagan and Birsha were a contradiction to Aamon's words.

"He came back before. Don't look like that," I spat between sobs.

"He needs to go deeper," Zagan muttered, almost

afraid to share his words.

Aamon ignored him. His full attention on me. With a small smile, he pressed his lips softly against mine. "Kill him. But only when he can't see it coming," he whispered.

Birsha turned to Steven. "You need to take her. We need to get the fuck out of here now."

"I'll come too. I can help you to get him there," I begged.

Birsha shook his head. "We can only get him to the doorway. If you come, you'll be like a walking tracker for Griffin. The only chance we have is if time is with us, not against us."

"Then take Steven," I squeaked, desperately trying not to break into a million pieces.

"Griffin keeps his distance from me. I'll stay away from the loft. He won't get anything from me," Steven promised.

Zagan opened his mouth to protest, but Birsha interjected. "Can you run?"

I gulped and nodded. "Wait, how do I explain being here?"

Steven pointed to the remains of the guard.

"You found Aamon's killer and got your revenge. We'll drag him back up to the entrance. By the time Griffin realizes his security measures were thwarted and Aamon is missing, it will be too late. You need to be the fuck outta Dodge by that point, Alyssa, understand?"

I didn't get to bid Aamon goodbye, didn't get a final kiss or embrace. Our collective energy had drawn attention, and Sygans were closing in quickly. If I ran, they would follow me, leaving a clear path of escape for the boys, and so alone, with a broken heart and not a single glance back I fled.

Chapter 18

Breaking free of the darkness offered little relief. At its deepest descent, Daeon may have been a source of affliction, but the suffering that I carried came from the reality of what had happened and yet another loss. The daylight stabbed at my newly restored vision. Instinctively, my reflexes reacted by pulling me backward, back toward a darkness that had become a source of comfort.

My arms hung limply at my sides. The warm flow of blood that dripped steadily from my mangled hands soaked through my pants and splashed to the floor creating a design of crimson polka-dot splatter at my feet. I thought I had reached the epitome of pain in believing that Aamon was dead. But knowing he existed somewhere just beyond my reach had somehow exacerbated the agony and sense of desolation.

Initially, the inner core of Daeon had stifled my ability to breathe. The potency of the dark energy that closed in around me like a weighted blanket had previously served to feed my power, but that day and at that depth it suffocated me.

Earth's air wasn't much better. I was a canary in a coal mine, caged and frail.

I staggered like the walking dead, the irony of which did not go unnoted. I had to keep moving; I could not stop. For the second time that day, I was afraid that if I did stop, I would lose the ability to move at all. If I sank to the ground, it would surely swallow me whole. I was unsure of so many things. A fog of confusion clouded my recollection of what had just happened, but of one thing I was certain.

The familiarity of an essence that had hung faintly in the air surrounding Aamon's confinement. One that had gone unnoticed by the others. Its existence I had chosen not to share. It was a being I knew all too well. A being I had been close to for a long enough time to recognize, even when only the finest wisps of her energy had remained after her departure.

Amelia.

She had been there, circling around him like a vulture would its prey. Recently, and possibly more than once. I had felt her deep where she should not have been, deep within Daeon's core, her imposter energy as strong as solar radiation to me.

At that moment, she became my focus. I watched myself, my level of disassociation unprecedented, as I dragged myself through the backstreets of town. Despite the ability to heal at warp speed, I was still a mess when I reached the industrial estate that housed the loft. But my bleeding had stopped, and the feeling in my hands had returned, not an entirely pleasant experience but still something I was thankful for.

Noah was there with her. They both reacted to my approach. Blackness surrounded me. Its presence served to protect and heal, yet it appeared ominous to those on the outside looking in. I paused as I entered the building. Griffin's energy was absent. I glanced down at my arms, pressed my palms to my pants which were still drenched with blood. I would need to change and quickly. There was no feasible explanation for the state I was in should Griffin make a sudden appearance, an occurrence that could happen at any moment. He would no doubt be trying desperately to track me if he hadn't already.

With a newfound energy born of fear, I sprinted up the stairs, stripping items of clothing as I went. The blood that coated my arms and legs had started to dry like a thin layer of paint. At least I would not leave a path of red droplets in my wake. I darted into the kitchen and grabbed a canister of lighter fluid from beneath the sink. I dashed back through the lounge and bundled my bloody clothing into the fireplace, squeezing the accelerant over the wads of material as I lit the flames, which ignited with a roar.

I was careful to return the metal tin to the kitchen cupboard before I rushed into my bathroom, where I removed the final pieces of clothing from my body. Beneath a steaming shower, I washed away the last traces of blood, dirt, and tears from my broken self as I forced my mind back into character.

Leaving my wet hair to map a path with beads of water, I made my way to the sofa. Only then did I towel dry my hair before I stormed down to the loft. Acutely careful to leave no trace, I needed to make every effort to conceal what I was about to do.

I entered the loft without knocking. It wasn't like the element of surprise was a possibility. Noah froze. His eyes darted quickly between me and Amelia who had just descended the last of the stairs as I strode across the room to confront her.

"What the actual fuck were you thinking?" I hissed, my voice trembling with anger.

"I had no choice," she snapped. "You may want to

consider stepping down from your high horse given your most recent choices," she responded with narrowed eyes.

"This isn't a game," I yelled, louder than I had intended.

She stared at me, her shoulders squared, and her chin raised. "Who's playing?"

"Amelia, I never—"

She cut in. "You never what, Alyssa? *You* never meant for this to happen? This isn't you. This has never been you. It's him, all fucking him." Her voice echoed louder than mine. "Stop trying to carry the weight of the damn world on your shoulders. You understand how tying yourself to a burning stake will end, don't you?"

I opened my mouth to speak, but Amelia stepped forward. She placed one hand on my shoulder, and with her other hand, she touched one finger to my lips, murmuring, "Sshhh, it's okay." My eyes softened seeing the smile that lit up her face. "We did it."

Noah started forward and, for the second time, froze, his mouth slightly agape as the hamster wheel in his head spun rapidly in a desperate effort to catch up. I couldn't blame him for being confused. The conversation between Amelia and I was panicked and fast, responses fired before sentences were finished.

I placed my hand over hers which still rested on my shoulder. I grasped it firmly and tried to make her understand the gravity of the situation. "Griffin is going to sense your energy there. Or he'll sense Daeon on you and probably figure out pretty damn quick that you were the one to inform Zagan, or even worse, he could think you told me. What do you think he'll do then?"

"Was there time to do anything else?" she asked softly. Her eyes locked on mine as I choked on my response. "Did he have time?" she pressed. "Would he still be alive if I'd waited to confirm? If he'd been left there for another twenty-four hours, maybe more?"

Unable to hold back my tears any longer, I shook my head. Amelia wrapped her arms around my neck and pulled me into a tight embrace.

"*You* found Aamon?" Noah croaked, his eyes wide on Amelia as he finally understood our exchange.

I ignored him, there wasn't time for explanations. "Amelia, you have to go, *now*. Before he gets here." I pulled away from her and pleaded, "I can make him believe that Aamon's energy came from me attacking one of his guards. He already trusts that I believe Aamon is dead. He set up this whole ruse to cover his ass. The only thing he didn't account for was my impulsiveness." I started to pace. "I'm sure he'll believe me when I say I sought out and killed Aamon's murderer. He has no reason not to. But that won't be the case if he catches wind of you being there. Or if your paths cross anytime soon. You have to run, and it has to be now." Begging, I turned toward her.

Defiantly, she shook her head. "I will leave the loft, but I will not run. I will do what I intended to do in the first place. I'll take them somewhere safe, I promise."

Noah charged between us, his eyes wide and frantic as he hollered, "Just stop. Both of you just stop, just for a second. You played him, I get it, award-winning performance, bravo!" He waved his hands above his head. "So you don't detest each other; it was an act. I get that too, and I understand why. But I need to know what's happening right now. I need to know where you're going." He grabbed Amelia's arm and pulled her toward him, so she was inches from his face as he lowered his head. "Let me help, I'm begging you. Alyssa's right. Griffin is dangerous. He isn't the person we once knew, and I'm afraid of what he might do."

"I'm taking Kasey away. Her mom too. I'm telling no one where," Amelia responded calmly.

"What?" Noah croaked. "Why?"

Amelia glanced toward me. "Because I told her to," I rasped, "and everyone includes me."

"Do you think he'll hurt them?" Noah stammered.

"Do you not?" Amelia and I answered in unison.

Noah fell silent. His face crumpled as he whispered to me, "Why don't you want to know where she's taking them?'

I couldn't answer. Hearing someone else say the words out loud made them so much more real, and the thought of being blind to the whereabouts of another person I loved stabbed at my heart like a hot poker.

"Plausible deniability," he surmised, his face pale.

I turned my attention back to Amelia. I opened my mouth to speak, but she held up her hand, stepped forward, and gave me a brief but tight hug. "I'm gone already," she whispered before she turned on her heels and scurried to the door, leaving without further hesitation.

Noah flapped like a fish out of water, hyperventilating as he paced back and forth across the living room.

"You need to chill out," I hissed. "As far as you're concerned, I followed up on Griffin's leads and tracked down the Sygan responsible for Aamon's death. I slaughtered him and got my closure. If anything, it's a day of fucking celebration. Oh, and if asked you have no idea where Amelia went, okay?"

He nodded. I waved my arm in his direction as I headed to the door. "You should find something to do. You have too much anxious energy whirling around you right now."

"Alyssa."

With one hand still outstretched toward the door, I stopped dead as the tone of Noah's voice sliced chillingly through the air, causing the hairs on the back of my neck to stand up straight.

"He's here."

Chapter 19

My feet barely touched the floor as I swept up the stairwells and into the apartment I begrudgingly shared with Griffin.

I could have showered in bleach and boiling water; it still wouldn't have eradicated the final wisps of Aamon's essence from me. I prayed my lies were good enough to hide the truth, that Griffin would believe I had remained ignorant to Aamon's imprisonment and that he'd assume any lingering remnants had merely hitched a ride from the confined space outside of Aamon's cell.

Griffin would be pissed that I had ventured into the depths of Daeon alone. He would claim his fury was born of fear for my safety, rather than his fear of being incriminated. But he couldn't possibly stay mad for long, not if he truly believed he had achieved his goal.

The pressure was on to deliver an Oscar-winning performance, the final necessary step to conclude my sought-after closure and the successful completion of Griffin's master plan.

The tears I needed came easily. Their purpose was to deceive him, but their source was authentic, procured from a biting pain that refused to fade. When I reached the couch, I positioned myself cautiously so the damp towel I had discarded earlier lay close to my head. My eyes darted toward the still roaring fire, no scraps of clothing remained, the last pieces reduced to ash way before my return.

My sigh of relief caught mid-exhale.

I sniffed.

"Shit!"

The clothing may have been incinerated but the scent of lighter fluid still hovered lightly in the air close to the fireplace. Griffin's paranoid mind was on hyper alert at the best of times. I couldn't give him any reason to be more suspicious than he already would be.

I darted into the bedroom, careful to avoid disturbing the water ring marks on the floor. I skidded into my closet and frantically ripped aside an array of T-shirts until I found what I was looking for. With my breath held, I dashed back to the fireplace and tossed the item into the flames. But the flames had burned too low and the dark gray material I had flung upon them only acted to smother them. A feeling I knew well.

The clock didn't need to tick to tell me I was almost out of time. Griffin's heavy footsteps struck each step loudly, even they sounded furious. He rounded the last corner and stomped briskly down the hallway.

With a panic that threatened to tip me into hysteria, I sprinted into the kitchen and snatched up the lighter fluid. Like trying to run underwater, I just couldn't get my legs to move fast enough as I ran back into the living area, a petrified sob jammed painfully in my throat.

Ten feet from the couch.

Griffin's footsteps paused as he reached the door. The distance between where I was and where I needed to be yawned ahead, resembling the length of a football field.

Eight feet from the couch.

Griffin's hand grabbed wildly at the handle, sending

my heart rate into a frenzy. He cussed loudly when he realized it was locked and fumbled for his key.

Six feet from the couch.

Without hesitation and using every last molecule of energy I could muster, I propelled myself forward, flicking open the small canister as I reached the four-foot line. Still moving I aimed the nozzle toward the dying flames and squeezed the tin. A stream of liquid surged forward. Its first droplets struck the waning flame and caused the fire to roar upward angrily in response.

Two feet from the couch.

I flew across the final stretch simultaneously as the end of the thin line of liquid traveled through the air, its trajectory directed at the revived blaze, my body flung in the direction of the couch. The soft thud of my impact was concealed by the loud bang of the door as Griffin flung it open. The fire writhed and spat, its mood a perfect match for Griffin's as he crashed through the door.

For a second, I remained still, maintaining the position I had landed in. To anyone who hadn't seen me take flight over the coffee table, I appeared to be lying in a semi-fetal position, my head resting on a cushion close to a damp discarded towel.

I glanced down, the drips on the floor may have dried, but their ring marks were still evident for anyone inclined enough to cast a careful eye in their direction. There appeared to be no clues as to my erratic movements just moments before.

Griffin's steps slowed. Edging forward, clearly suspicious of everyone and everything as he surveyed the scene before him. I couldn't fault him for that.

I decided to strike first in the hope of deflecting, my

feigned aggravation an excellent channel for my overwhelming anxiety.

"Where were you?" I demanded, holding tight to my defensive mode, accusations fired quickly before he had a chance to fire first. An action that created a tiny coil of satisfaction derived from using one of his own methods against him.

His voice may have emanated concern, but his eyes remained stone cold as he pointedly ignored my question and instead asked me where I'd been. His fists clenched when I answered him with a single word, "Daeon."

I stared at him, my red-rimmed eyes still pooled with tears as I added, "Alone, thanks to you and your disappearing act." I turned my head from his in anger and gazed into the dancing flames of the fireplace.

He followed my gaze and paused as his eyes fell on the burning scraps of Aamon's favorite shirt. An item I had clung to like a safety blanket during my first weeks there.

His attempts to conceal a smug smile failed. The tension in his shoulders decreased just a little, and he sat gingerly on the same couch as I, but at the farthest point from me.

His anger remained, flowing just below the surface with a life of its own. He struggled to conceal it as, between fake apologies, he directed a barrage of questions my way.

"Why would you go without me? Did you go alone? Who gave you information? Where exactly did you go? What did you find?"

I responded to each with a short to the point answer, moving through them quickly without time for elaboration. Except when he asked the final one. That was the point at which my head turned, and my eyes met his. My voice cracked just a little, and my arms wrapped tightly around my knees as I hugged them close to my torso.

"I found him," I whispered, my voice barely audible. "The one who was responsible, the piece of shit who murdered Aamon and tried to kill you."

That was good, feeding into his fantasy and implying that I'd give a shit if someone had actually tried to kill him—like I wouldn't have backed the assassin.

There was a fleeting shadow of relief at my words. Griffin still believed that I considered Aamon dead. No sooner was it there than it was gone, replaced with feigned pain for my loss and worry for my state of mind, falsified guilt and remorse at his unintentional abandonment in my hour of need, all the while artfully dodging the questions I asked him.

He scooted along the couch and pulled me into a hug as he murmured into my hair, "How did you know it was him?"

"I could sense that Aamon had been there. His energy clung to the Sygan. It was so strong, almost like he was still there, somewhere in the darkness."

Griffin's diaphragm froze. His hug squeezed just a little too tightly as every muscle involuntarily tensed.

I waited, relishing every moment of pleasure I garnered from toying with him. With wide-eyed innocence, I asked Griffin, "Was that because of Daeon's energy? Or because they made him suffer before they—"

"Don't." Griffin pulled back; his hands clamped against my shoulders as he held me far enough away to study my expression. "Don't think like that. It isn't going to bring him back, and you've experienced enough pain for him."

Again, the stream of tears tracked down my cheeks. Again, Griffin pulled me close; his arms held me against his chest, obscuring my face and the smile that I could no longer contain.

He wouldn't wait for long, but I'd hoped to at the least be granted that day. For the remainder of the morning, he didn't leave the apartment. Playing the dutiful partner role to a tee. Usually, I would have hated to have him so close for so long, suffocating my every thought and action, especially at a time when I desperately needed alone time to plan and assess my next move. But that day I was grateful to hold his full attention. It allowed the whereabouts of others to remain unchallenged.

I used every subtle technique I could think of to maintain his engagement. For a solid four hours, it worked. But by lunchtime, his patience had started to wane. It wasn't that he was becoming bored of me. It was that his desire for more was increasing. As far as he was concerned, he had delivered his end of the bargain. Now it was my turn.

I'll admit, my focus had wholeheartedly been on locating Aamon followed by securing his safety, Kasey's safety, and basically the safety of everyone who could be implicated in my scheme. I hadn't thought beyond that. I hadn't planned for what was happening at that moment.

I wanted Griffin dead. I wanted him to suffer first, but I had no idea if Amelia had succeeded in getting Kasey to safety, nor did I know with certainty that Zagan had managed to get a seriously injured Aamon to the sanctity of the inner realm.

I had no choice but to maintain the act. Griffin needed to trust me; it was the only way to entice and keep him firmly on the road to ruin. When he handed me a glass of wine before joining me on the couch, I accepted it and drank it far faster than I should have, especially given the early hour. When I leaned across him to place the now-empty glass on the side table, he seized his moment.

He wound one arm around my waist and hooked his other hand behind my knee, pulling me on top of him in one sharp movement. He held me there while his eyes drifted from my face to my breasts. A small, smug smile danced across his lips as he jerked my groin closer to his. The kiss wasn't his, not as I remembered it. It was savage, self-serving, and cruel, correlating perfectly with who he now was.

I closed my eyes and willed my mind to take me anywhere but there. But I quickly realized that I would not be extended the luxury of fading out of this experience. Not when I had to exert every effort on controlling my inner self, who furiously beat against her reinstated restraints, demanding she be released from her shackles and extended the opportunity to defend the girl who was on her way to discovering a whole new level of hell.

Griffin used eroticism as an excuse to assault me. He squeezed my throat, forced me down with unnecessary brutality, and savored every moment. The rougher he was, the harder it became to smother the fire within me.

As he started to rip at my clothes, my body tensed, an involuntary reaction to what was about to happen. He paused. I forced my eyes to his, questioningly. He reached for me, ground against me, and again paused.

I was losing him.

I wriggled my arms free from beneath him, pulled him toward me, pushed my lips against his. And for the briefest of moments, I thought it had worked.

It had not.

Gently, he pried his lips from me, lowered his head so that his cheek rested lightly against mine, and whispered, "You do remember I fucked you when you wanted it, don't you?"

Silence filled the space between and around us. It made the air thick and charged, not dissimilar to Daeon. He ran one finger down my face and carefully traced the contour of my cheek bone as he continued, "Don't you think I remember exactly what you feel like, what you sound like, and what you smell like when you're turned on, you stupid whore. It's etched in my memory, carved into stone, and weighing me down."

I froze as my muscles turned to lead.

With a snarl, he leapt from the couch. Slowly I rose, my eyes locked onto his, my body tensed, ready to pounce at him or away from him, my choice dependent upon his next move.

He paced before me, making no effort to close the space between us. I calmed, just a little. Maybe he had decided to give rational a go. With a fluid stride and in a steady monotone, he started to speak.

"We're taught to be good." He shook his finger admonishingly in my direction as he continued, "That being a source of light and peace, a being that emanates kindness and love, and making the right choices will ultimately equal happiness and contentment. Any deviation from this will ensure hatred, karmic consequences, darkness, and misery. It's an age-old concept reinforced in literature, and TV shows, in songs and movies, in the preachings of religion, and society in general."

He paused and gave a half smile as he added, "And I fell for it all. I believed it wholeheartedly. I fucking strived for it and tried desperately to drag you into it."

My heart rate notched up slightly.

"Acceptance and understanding, but only when what is to be accepted and understood fits snugly within what our society deems tolerable, right?" His head cocked slightly to one side as he searched my face for a response. When I remained silent, he continued to pace, only this time his steps became a little faster as his speech descended into a rant.

"It's bullshit. To set impossibly unrealistic standards and deny the most basic of human emotions and impulses. It's a fucked-up belief that neglects to consider who and what we are as a species. It does nothing but dictate self-control."

He stepped closer.

"You were right. The path you chose was right. And the power you got from leaning into the darkness far supersedes any power you had by denying it. I see that now."

I opened my mouth to respond, but his rant continued, his voice getting louder with each word.

"I had longing, I had desire, I had love, I had regrets, I had sorrows, and I blindly believed they were all good. If I couldn't have you, I would just have to get over you. They were my only options. You see, I never thought I would feel liberated by not missing you anymore. I told myself I would rather take pain over the nothingness left by you." He struck his chest hard as he growled, "I was afraid to feel empty."

Another step closer. I fought hard against the urge to jerk away, instead I repositioned my stance so that I was sideways to the couch, prepared should I need to step back.

With narrowed eyes and a smile that chilled, he snarled, "Now I have nothing. And that is the most beautiful and liberating thing in all of the worlds."

As my mind raced to digest Griffin's words, of one thing I was sure. I may not have been certain of what to expect, but this reaction was the furthest from any of my expectations and placed me in a situation far more dire than I had originally anticipated.

With forced nonchalance, I retorted, "So you're saying you're happy now. Okay. What do you want, congratulations?"

Griffin leaned closer. "I'm saying I'm free now. And fuck, yes, that makes me happy."

I shrugged my shoulders, genuinely unsure of what response he had envisaged. Despite my cool demeanor, icy fingers of fear had clawed their way through my body. With cunning, they concealed their source but made their presence known, nevertheless.

With a frosty glare, I attempted to retaliate. "Here we go again, your efforts to make me responsible for your breakdown. You took no culpability for your own actions. As long as you weren't the one to blame, as long as you were faultless, you had nothing to fix. The gospel according to Griffin. But you didn't really believe I had that power, did you?" I scoffed. "Blaming me was just one of your many tools of manipulation. But guess what? It backfired. I believed you, and by doing so, I opened a door no one knew existed, me included. I may not have possessed the power to break you before, but I damn well do now. Now I get to do what you wrongly accused me of over and over again."

He chuckled. "No you don't. Not as long as those bonds exist like millstones around your neck. They will always weaken you."

There it was, the jugular exposed. My mom and Kasey, the only things that every enemy believed they could manipulate as a method of control. Would they never learn?

I rolled my eyes. "Really, Griffin, that's your end game? To threaten my mom and Kasey? It feels kinda old."

He held his hands up in mock surrender. "I would never do such a thing. I am not a threat to them. You are, and as long as you remain tied to them, little Kasey in particular, nothing will ever change."

Furious, I realized that in the most twisted, convoluted way he was right, but I kept my expression passive. "I disagree. Did it never occur to you that life tethers you for a reason? Look at Icarus. But that's the difference between you and me, Griffin. I don't need to be swallowed by the darkness to harness its power. What you neglected to consider is that, when you submit completely, you retain no control."

"You only need control for them," he countered as he walked backward toward the door. "And I only needed it for you. You were the only thing that confined me to sanity and reason. You think you've witnessed the dark side of me, Alyssa—you have no fucking idea. I will come back when there's nothing left, and I will fuck you whether you want it or not, and I won't give a shit if you want it or if you hurt. I'll fucking relish every microscopic drop of pain that I inflict on you."

Griffin reached for the door, throwing me a final scowl as he swung it roughly open. "You'd better believe this is all your doing."

Chapter 20

I wish I could have just snapped on command. Transitioned to dark mode with about as much effort as it would take to flick a switch instead of having to endure a full-on breakdown each time.

When Griffin left, the room shook, and the wooden doorframe splintered. He slammed the door with so much force it bounced back open and impacted the wall, its handle creating a dent in the brickwork.

Fear-induced adrenaline raced through my veins. The thud of my heart was so loud it became a struggle to hear anything else. It was inevitable that Griffin would figure out the truth, that the complicated network of lies I had constructed would eventually fail to conceal my deceit. I knew this with certainty, but I had hoped for more time.

In hindsight, I probably should have run through at least a few potential scenarios to better equip myself for what was coming. However, the possibility of Aamon's return from the dead and the revelation that Kasey could see and hear me had taken front and center stage, and in doing so had left little time for anything else.

I tried to talk myself down from the precipice of hysteria I was steadily moving toward. I accept that talking to oneself may not scream sane and rational, but then neither is having an internal argument with oneself, something that had become a regular occurrence between my somewhat condescending inner critic and I.

"When you think of climbing Everest, your sole attention is on reaching the summit, not the descent," I murmured to myself, a vain attempt to feel make myself feel better about my monumental fuck-up. With a disapproving tut, the voice in my head retorted, "That is probably why the damn thing is littered with bodies."

Of course, *that* element of my psyche was still alive and well, beating me down with self-loathing and disapproval. I couldn't have lost her along the bloody way, could I?

But she wasn't wrong. Careless and foolish. That's what I had been, and that was what had landed me exactly where I was, up shit creek without a paddle.

I paced the floor, forced deep breaths, and tried to shake away the pins and needles from my hands.

Think.

Griffin had considered my reaction a form of rejection, and that alone had nearly made his head fly off his shoulders. I shuddered to think about how incensed he would be when the full extent of my deception became apparent.

I shook my head free of the possible outcomes. That was a bridge I would have to cross when I came to it. For now, I barely had the capacity to focus on the present.

My immediate concern was Aamon. Was what had just happened severe enough for Griffin to punish him?

For a reasonable person, absolutely not. For Griffin, possibly. No scrap that, probably. If that was the case, I had just run out of time. My hands started to shake, and small beads of sweat dampened my forehead and neck. I had to fight hard against the urge to bolt.

If Griffin was on his way to beat out his anger on

Aamon, we were all royally screwed.

I guided my shaky legs in the opposite direction to the doorway, not trusting myself not to succumb to my impulses. I moved quickly into the bathroom and clutched the sink as I stared hard at my reflection, the same reflection I had vehemently avoided for months.

"Get it together," I hissed. "Everyone is safe. Everyone is hidden. The only person he can come for is you, and you are stronger than him."

My reflection stared back. Pale and trembling, she was not selling it.

Somewhere along the way I had lost a part of myself. No, that wasn't true, I didn't lose her. I destroyed her. I had spent so many months smothering her in order to reel Griffin in and sustain my act that I had given no consideration as to how or even if I could ever retrieve her when the time came.

What a great time for such a revelation, when the unstoppable series of events had already been set in motion. I had lifted the brakes on a freight train without any thought as to how I would stop it before it annihilated everything in its path.

Shit! Shit, shit, shit.

The back of my throat burned as I fought against the urge to vomit. Today was not going well.

I wasn't sure what I needed to do but knew I needed to do something. My freak out in the bathroom most certainly was not serving any purpose, and my reflection only proceeded to remind me of my failings.

I gave myself a mental slap and strode as confidently as I could toward the door. I tried desperately to ignore the voice of my inner critic, which resounded throughout my head as she sneered, "What the fuck is that? Fake it till you make it? What a great way to get yourself killed, dickhead."

I jolted. I felt it. The smallest of reactions.

The self-ridicule and contempt had finally struck a nerve and ignited the tiniest spark, so inconsequential it was there one minute and gone the next. A minuscule flicker of anger. Too fleeting to grasp, but still there, nonetheless.

The realization warmed me. It thawed the edges from the icy fear-ridden aura that hung heavily in the air that surrounded me.

I still had it; she was still there, somewhere. I just had to figure out a way to access her.

And I knew exactly who the most effective catalyst was.

No one made my blood boil the way Griffin did. So instead of caving to every instinct that willed me to flee, I made a decision. The wait was over. Before my inner voice could make another snide or critical remark, I stormed from the apartment to find him.

Noah was alerted to my speedy descent, either due to the thundering of my steps as I leapt between the flights of stairs or the contradictory cocktail of anger and anxiety that emanated from me in a thick fog. He shot from the loft as I passed by and held his pace a few beats behind me.

I slowed as I crossed the scrubland that separated the disused industrial estate from the quiet winding roads that led into town. My quota on worry was filled. I did not need him to give me another person to have to think about.

After he ignored my first few requests that he return home, I stopped and with irritation turned to him.

"I know I said you needed to find a vent for your energy, but I did not mean trailing me. Please go back."

He fixed his gaze on something in the distance. His jaw set in a stubborn line, and he clenched and unclenched his fists, which caused a rippling motion up and down his muscular arms. My eyes flashed with the anger I had tried to keep out of my tone. I had neither the time nor the patience for an argument with him. He remained unresponsive.

"Noah," I snapped.

He turned slowly to face me. I expected defiance. I expected him to yell and insist on being my backup. I expected a confrontation. What I didn't expect was for his face to crumple, for his shoulders to slump, and for his heart to break, right there in no-man's-land on the outskirts of town.

"I can't," he stammered, his voice quivering. "I can't just do nothing, but I don't know what to do." He glanced around, like a child afraid of their surroundings. "I don't know where to go. Steven is AWOL. Our relationship is in tatters. Amelia is on a secret mission, and no one knows where, and now you're leaving too…" His voice cracked, and his words dissolved into soft sobs.

My heart sank. I leapt forward and wrapped my arms around him, around this huge man who had saved me more than once, but I said nothing. There were no words that would make this whole shitshow any easier. So I did the only thing I could. I hugged him long and hard, so that he knew he was not alone, so he understood that I wasn't abandoning him. Because really, that's all anyone needs, be it in a time of crisis or not.

I stayed locked in that embrace for Noah's sake. The

truth was that it served me just as much as him. It reminded me that I was also not alone. It gave me a much-needed moment to catch my breath, and it gave me the strength to see a clearer path to success.

I didn't want to worry about Noah. I didn't want to put him in a potentially dangerous situation, but like it or not we were all in danger and leaving him behind wouldn't change that. I wouldn't argue with him, I would let him make his own decisions, and I would respect and support him, just the way Aamon had with me.

When I left the building, I was fragile and afraid. By the time my feet hit the concrete sidewalks of town, my resolve had returned, just a little, just enough to keep me moving in a forward motion.

In hindsight, Noah's breakdown added to that. No matter how weak you feel, when someone leans on you for support you are forced to be strong, often finding a strength you may never have known existed.

With each step, I became more determined. With each step, I forced myself to recall the humiliation I had endured, the pain and the suffering at the hands of a narcissistic, gas-lighting control freak. I compelled myself to recollect the many months of abuse, the frustration and anguish of being stripped of my power, of my rights, and my voice. Of being emotionally bound and shamed. Of being guilt-tripped and ridiculed, all under the sickening guise of protection.

Each memory quickened my step and warmed my blood until I had transformed from a blubbering wreck to a wild animal chewing at the bit and hungry for a fight. The revenge that I craved came from many sources, not simply mine alone. Griffin's victim pool had been wide and varied. He showed no prejudice when it came to being an utter bastard with strangers and acquaintances alike.

As much as it shouldn't have, the drive to right the wrongs done to others superseded my desire to find retribution for myself. I found putting myself before others an almost impossible feat, or maybe I simply struggled to accept myself as the victim I truly was.

Focused on reaching my destination, I remained silent, but mentally I had twenty tabs open and at least four narratives in full flow.

It wasn't until my feet crossed the line that separated Earth from Daeon that I was able to comprehend the relationship between my mindset and the impact of the dark plane's power on me. When driven by fear and apprehension, Daeon's energy restricted me in every way. It drained my energy, fogged my mind, and slowed my reflexes.

When I crossed over with intent, its energy invigorated me, exactly the way it had when Aamon's prison door had lost its life. It narcotized me to the negative effects of its potency and altered my perceptions. Without effort, my body absorbed from its surroundings, its charge intensifying my strength, my clarity, and my speed.

Noah on the other hand experienced a reaction not dissimilar to what I had the first few times I had crossed. Suffocation in its cruelest form, every sensation numbed yet agonizing at the same time.

I half carried, half dragged him deeper and deeper into Daeon until he begged me to stop. We were only a short distance from the last place I had seen Aamon, so with strict instructions not to move, I left him propped up against a large boulder and darted down one lightless winding labyrinth after another until I reached the point I recognized as the opening to Aamon's prison.

Down here, the air had become so heavy that even with Daeon's power surging through my blood, my chest still tightened.

If memory hadn't served me well, I'd have located it from smell alone. The partially rotting corpse of the Sygan remained in the same spot he had met his end. I could detect no sign or sense of another being visiting that place since I'd left. Griffin had not been there. My assumption had been wrong. My heart skipped a beat, if he wasn't there and hadn't been there, that meant he was still oblivious to Aamon's rescue.

I let out a long exhale and ran my hands through my hair, muttering thanks to a nonexistent entity. Disaster avoided, right?

Griffin's continued ignorance of Aamon's release was obviously a good thing, but the realization spawned a gnawing sensation that filled me with unease. The image of Griffin as he thundered from the apartment flashed like screenshots across my brain. The sound of his venomous promises as he fired them like weapons, the flash of his eyes as they raged incandescently. He did not leave in an effort to cool off. He left to exact revenge, to dole out a punishment fitting of his fury. A punishment specifically for me.

Despite the thick dense air and the smoldering heat of Daeon, a shiver rippled through me.

If he wasn't in Daeon, and Aamon wasn't his intended target, who the fuck had he gone after?

Chapter 21

I made it back to Noah in seconds, driven by a combustible combination of Daeon's power and pure panic, the latter a byproduct of fast-growing uncertainty and nervous anticipation. My error of judgement had extended Griffin the opportunity to strike somewhere else like a serpent unimpeded.

I couldn't decide who I was angrier with. Him or me.

And that damn mental clock was ticking yet again.

Noah's feet skimmed the floor as I hauled him from Daeon without breaking a sweat. When the sun's harsh rays blinded us, I let him go, fully expecting him to find his feet. Instead, he collapsed in a heap to the floor, wheezing and spluttering. It reminded me of my first encounter with Aamon.

"What the hell was that?' he gasped as he struggled into a seated position.

"Daeon," I retorted. Had I underestimated the extent of oxygen deprivation his brain had experienced?

"Not that." He nodded toward the opening.

Gesturing in my direction, he croaked, "*That*. I've never seen anyone travel that fast. I have motion sickness."

"I guess I'm getting more attuned to it in there." I shrugged as I paced impatiently. Maybe I should have left Noah back at the loft. He was being more of a hindrance than a help. I massaged the back of my neck in a futile attempt to relieve the mounting tension. My temples had begun to throb.

"Care to share?' he asked as he attempted to heave himself from the ground. He was momentarily held in a genuflection as a bout of rapid, forceful coughs caused him to double over.

I stepped forward, but he raised one hand and waved me away. "I'm fine, I'm fine, it's starting to pass." He pulled himself upright and took a deep breath before he continued. "Are you ever going to tell me what happened back there?"

"Well, it was a little hard to explain anything to you when you were circling the drain," I snapped, my tone way harsher than he deserved. I immediately regretted it.

He had extended me far more grace each of the many times I'd struggled to wrap my head around things that had happened, and besides, none of it was his fault.

"I'm sorry." I blurted before he had time to respond, relieved to see him break into a small reassuring smile.

"Griffin hasn't been here, not recently at least," I explained.

Noah's smile was quickly replaced with a frown.

"Aamon would have been my first guess too. Maybe he wasn't as angry as he sounded," he offered.

My cheeks flushed; Noah must have heard the entire exchange.

"No," I insisted, "he was seething. There's no way he isn't retaliating."

"Kasey?" Noah's voice was barely above a whisper.

Our eyes met and widened simultaneously. I shook my head sharply as I fought down the panic that had doubled in size since we crossed over from Daeon.

"No. He doesn't think I know about Aamon. He'd assume Kasey would be the first one I'd run to. And besides, the only place he'd have known to check is my mom's house, and neither of them is there."

The moment the self-assured words fell from my lips I wanted to snatch them back. One lesson I'd learned very quickly was that assumptions, much more than pride, came before a fall.

"Are we sure?" Noah's words, spoken softly, carried eerily between us.

"What do you mean?" I clipped, as a feeling of dread washed over me.

"Alyssa, how do you know your mom and Kasey were home when Amelia got there. Say they weren't, and she had to wait..." His voice trailed off.

The silence hung thick between us as we both calculated the very narrow timeline that Amelia had been left with.

Fuck!

My stomach lurched as the ground transformed from a level surface to a steep peak with an incline to rival the wildest coaster. I felt myself slipping.

This couldn't be.

"What day is it?" I barked.

"Tues...no, wait, Thursday, it's definitely Thursday," Noah responded, his body rigid, ready to launch.

"Time?" I screamed as the panic refused to be placated any further and rose like a wave of acid through my chest.

"Oh God," Noah croaked, his feet moving as the words tumbled from his mouth. With a resounding clang, the tick of the clock that had taken up permanent residence in the corner of my mind stopped.

We ran.

A million thoughts swarmed my brain as we traveled. How could I have been so careless? I was so out of touch with real life and Kasey's daily schedule. Of course he would be at school, and my mom probably at work. Each in the opposite direction of the other. Again, my head tried to do the mental math, but I hadn't thought to take note of the time that Amelia had left. Nor had I tracked it since then, everything had happened so quickly.

At the time I was running underwater, each movement was painfully slow. But speed is irrelevant. Everything takes too long when you know you're out of time.

Griffin's energy was everywhere. I felt it as we charged through neighbor's yards, scaling walls and fences, driven by dread and far too panic-stricken to stick to sidewalks and roads. Fear stabbed at my chest over and over, wounding me indefinitely. When our feet hit the front path of my mom's house Noah tried to hold me back, but I pushed free of his desperate grasp, and his pleas to approach with care fell on deaf ears.

No time.

I stopped in the hallway. My pause was only to strain my eyes and ears as I searched for any sight or sound of my family. The silence that reverberated was louder than a thousand-watt bass speaker and the force that hung in the air more sinister than anything I had ever experienced in Daeon. I closed my eyes and scanned the energy. I followed each intricate thread that weaved around me, Amelia, Kasey, and my mom. All intertwined and all strong.

And one more, one differing from the others, an unwelcome imposter.

Griffin.

They'd all shared the same space and time, and their encounter had been emotionally fraught. The strands left behind mapped out my worst-case scenario right there before me, sequencing the sorry tale like a live performance.

Noah's normally heavy steps were almost soundless as he moved through the house with stealth. He crept toward the dining room as I tiptoed through the kitchen. The scene that met me was not pretty. Lunch box, backpack, handbag, and car keys lay strewn across the floor. One barstool from the counter was on its side, and the fruit bowl was smashed in two on the ground, its orange and green contents dotted across the white floor tiles.

The back door had been kicked in with an unnecessary level of ferocity. The perpetrator had made no attempt to cover their tracks. The wood and glass frame teetered at an angle, two of its three hinges ripped clean away. Large, jagged cracks crossed over the glass panels that remained within the structure, and shards of the rest were scattered across the threshold.

I backed out gingerly and with a renewed sense of urgency moved through the downstairs level. I swept the closet, mudroom, and lounge, and made it up the first four stairs before Noah came into view. He moved hastily as he rounded the second-floor landing and sprinted down the stairwell. His eyes remained downcast and without breaking his pace he barreled straight at me, lifting me from my feet as he descended the last few steps. He tried to carry me outside, tried so hard to remove me from that situation. To protect me from being exposed to something that could never be taken back, something that could never be unseen.

I knew.

I knew, but I refused to believe.

I was rigid. With the precision of a marksman, my intuition had hurled spears of fear that had electrocuted me from head to toe. The scream that escaped was guttural and animalistic. The connection between my brain and throat severed. I was beyond the ability to form thoughts or words. I thrashed wildly against Noah's strong arms and for the second time thwarted his efforts as I quickly broke free.

I don't remember the movement that carried me up the stairs. I don't remember pausing at any other rooms before I arrived at my destination, my course mapped by something unseen, something that harnessed my deepest instincts and pulled in only one direction.

I have no recollection of pushing the slightly ajar door open. In my memory, I see it creaking open independently, insidious and alive, like the room itself had been awaiting my arrival, waiting to share its horrifying secrets with me.

Her image filled my field of vision, and I heard nothing but the thundering rush of blood that echoed from within, filling my eardrums with its deafening roar.

She hadn't died peacefully.

Her last moments had been brutal and violent, the evidence of which was painted crudely across her face. It contorted her features into a frozen mask of terror. Her unnaturally wide stare held an empty gaze at the ceiling. A thin sheen of fluid stretched across eyes that bulged beyond their sockets. Her mouth was held in a perfectly preserved silent scream.

The broken bones beneath her chin protruded convex against the pale skin of her neck, jutting sharply at all the wrong angles. Her beautiful hands had been reduced to rigor mortised claws, and a single tear glistened on her left cheek, defying gravity, too dead to move.

Momma.

I floated forward, carried by an invisible breeze. The smell of violets from the vase on her dresser danced lightly on the back of the zephyr, the dark purple petals the same hue as her overstretched lips. The scent was fleeting, only discernible for a moment before it was overpowered by the stench of urine.

There was no rest here. Dark clouds sat motionless, filling every dead space in the room. Her soul had left without a trace, ripped from its body with a savagery I had never seen before.

I fell to my knees. With unblinking eyes and short raspy breaths, I dragged myself over the thick carpet and reached across the crisp, powder pink bedspread.

Momma.

My fingers brushed lightly across her cold, blanched flesh. I moved gently across the bed to deliver a last ever kiss. A kiss of love that I place softly on her head, an excruciating final goodbye filled with love and sorrow, promises and apologies.

A kiss that came too late for a mom long dead.

Chapter 22

Noah's arms were warm, but his body heat failed to cross the membrane of ice that shrouded me. I caved, a collapsing star pulled in on itself, powerless to fight against the draw of a bitter end. I wanted to fade away, but he pulled me back, murmuring a single word over and over. The only word capable of dragging me back and grounding me.

Kasey.

My eyes flickered. Earth seemed so far away. From the deep dark hole of despair, I gazed upward. Its cavernous depths numbed everything—sight, sound, and pain. For that, I was thankful.

Noah's voice was filled with anguish. "He isn't here, Kasey isn't here."

I flinched, and he carefully placed me down, reaching two huge arms out to grip me as I swayed. We were outside. I almost laughed, the sky was a cloudless canvas of cyan blue, and the sun shone brightly. A twisted and cruel contrast to that moment and the minutes that preceded it.

"Stay with me," Noah's voice boomed, and my head snapped back as he shook me hard.

I blinked my eyes back into focus and, in a voice I did not recognize, whispered hoarsely, "I will."

Noah exhaled deeply, releasing a breath he had held onto for too long. His eyes locked on mine. "We need to find Amelia and Kasey."

I was impressed with how composed he was. The warmth from his hands, which were still clamped firmly on my shoulders, and the calmness of his voice weaved intricately together to create a cloak that melted away my icy shroud. But even without it, the numbness remained.

To most, disassociation is seen as a crutch, a disability that harms. For me, in that moment, it was a buoyancy aid in rough seas. It carried a soul that would have sunk quickly beneath the churning water without it.

In the absence of fear and grief, I was able to assess with laser focus. It was no longer a game. It was a war that only one side would survive. It was a dance I had done before. Only last time, I had evaded any real loss.

I steadied my body and my mind, and from my position on the sidewalk, I forced myself to face the house. I studied it, plucked and absorbed every negative energy that I could from it, of which there was an abundance. The ringing in my ears reached a painfully shrill pitch, but still I held the door wide, as every last particle was ushered in.

As it traveled through me, it brought pain to everything it touched. Giant hands of steel squeezed each bone, the intensity of which made my knees buckle. It sought out and suffused every fiber of my being. It darkened and hardened whatever it came into contact with. My body strained and cried out against it until I could take no more. The air around me knew. I was now a part of it; each accepted the other. Slowly the pain started to subside, and the fear was finally silenced.

The actions Griffin had undertaken to destroy me had become my sustenance. They fed my power, armored it, and transformed all of the pain and suffering into a weapon to use against him. It renewed my strength, a strength from which he would have no escape.

As the seconds ticked by, the air pressure shifted. My hyper-attentive eyes were able to pick out each atmospheric molecule that pulsated around us, transforming from an opalescent shimmer to a shade of gray. The gradient deepened, and the molecules hardened the closer to the house they were. Noah's small gasp let me know I wasn't the only one witnessing the phenomenon.

"We need to go," I murmured in a gravelly voice, completely unidentifiable as my own. It wasn't just the pressure surrounding us that had shifted. Whatever it was that I had invited in was strong. It had clung to each cell and had started to amalgamate into something new, something that compelled me to move.

We didn't run; we walked, yet the time taken to cover the distance to our intended destination was equivalent to if we had sprinted. Whatever had affected me had seemingly affected Noah as well. All we ever had to do was invite it in instead of fleeing from it.

I had never managed to do so before, but now the instinct to survive, like the rest of me, was dead.

Each movement was controlled and calm. There was no conversation as to where we would go. We just knew, each of us guided like a person possessed, and neither of us surprised when we arrived at Aamon's building.

Being there, in the place I considered home, comforted more than hurt. The memories of Aamon hung lightly in the air. His smell, the scent of cedarwood and musk, wrapped around me like a blanket, warm and safe, tugging me gently back from a state of complete disassociation. I turned to Noah.

"I need to reach Zagan. Do you still have contact with Steven?"

He nodded, reached for his back pocket, and pulled out a cell phone. With his eyes on the screen, he mumbled, "So that's where he is."

I stopped; it hadn't occurred to me that Noah was still unaware of Steven's alliance with the Sygan group.

"You didn't know," I responded with a voice devoid of emotion.

He waved my words away. "It's not a surprise. Griffin treated him like shit, and I stood by and let him."

"Why was that?" I ventured. I too had enabled Griffin, convincing myself it was for good reason, so there was no judgment from me.

Noah shrugged as his face fell. "That's the worst part. I don't even know. It was just little things at first. Sometimes I thought Steven was at fault, sometimes Griffin. I felt like Griffin deserved a little slack for some things, given everything that had happened, but Steven refused to give him an inch."

He pulled out one of the wooden chairs from the large dining table and sat down heavily, raking his fingers through his hair. "When I look back now, it's easy to see how Griffin played me, but at the time I was so preoccupied with trying to keep the peace, all I did was belittle Steven's concerns and brush aside Griffin's behavior. I didn't know what to do, so I did nothing." Noah shrugged and with a sigh admitted, "I wasn't trying to take a side, but without meaning to, I guess I did."

"Hindsight's a great thing," I murmured.

They were my mother's words; they slipped carelessly from my lips. Hearing them said out loud transported me swiftly back to the image of her contorted broken body. I pushed it away and with gritted teeth forced myself to shove the door to that memory firmly shut. I couldn't think about her, not right now. I muttered a silent prayer that my mind wouldn't always associate the image of her in death with my memory of her, that at some point in the future I would be able to remember her in life instead of her brutal end.

I wandered through the condo as Noah dialed Steven's number, giving him the privacy and space he needed.

Everything was how I'd left it on that very last day. Every room was immaculate. Cleaning had been an outlet for the nervous energy that had built to a fever pitch in the days that followed Kasey's disappearance.

With trepidation, I entered our bedroom. A room I had avoided in my last few weeks there. It was the place of our last exchange, and the place that held the strongest memories of Aamon.

Our conversation from the last time I had seen him alive and well drifted back. It was not pleasant; I'd been so angry at his refusal to open up to me. We'd made so much progress over the prior few days, yet he seemed to have slipped back into secrecy mode, holding his cards close to chest from everyone, including me.

He hadn't even tried to deny that he'd uncovered something, potentially something that related to Kasey's disappearance. His insistence that being kept in the dark was for my own good only served to infuriate me further.

His final words were a promise to return and explain everything, but only if I promised to stay home and wait for him to complete whatever stupid bloody task he'd insisted on undertaking alone.

Out of other options, I had dolefully agreed. We

made a promise to each other that day, a promise that I had honored. And one that he had not.

I'd remained in the condo for the first few weeks that followed Aamon's death, but in that time I'd been unable to bring myself to lie in our bed. I rarely slept, and when I did, it was for a few snatched hours on the sofa.

I walked over to the dark-framed king size and perched on the edge. I kicked off my boots and swung my feet up. Slowly, I lowered my head to the pillow before I rolled over to face Aamon's side. I ran my hand over his pillow, my fingertips skirting lightly over the soft cotton as I made another promise I would without a doubt keep. "I will get you back."

I felt their approach long before they arrived. I pulled myself up from the mattress into a seated position and pushed my feet back into my boots. I remained sitting on the side of the bed, my eyes staring dead ahead through the wide window, but I didn't see beyond it. All I saw were images of Griffin and a hundred different ways that I could kill him.

Noah gently pushed the door fully open fully open and leaned against the frame as he waited patiently. His energy was a beacon of safety that cajoled me back to the present. Somehow over time, we had both lost our way. His support of Griffin had driven a wedge between him and everyone else, me included.

I had come to the realization that such measures were synonymous with Griffin's coercion tactics. His go-to mode of control was to divide and conquer, a practice he excelled at. He had successfully alienated each of his former friends, manipulating them like pawns to get what he wanted with no regard to the devastation left in his wake.

For a range of different reasons, we had all been complicit participants in his sick little game. His strategy was similar to the one Kerwin had employed, a lesson from which we'd learned nothing apparently.

But then the same could be said for Griffin, who either didn't remember how it ended for Kerwin or was too much of a narcissist to consider the potential ramifications of his actions.

I rose from the bed and turned to Noah. "Are you ready?"

It was an ambiguous question. In the months prior, Noah's relationships with the Sygans had become strained, not dissimilar to his relationship with anyone outside of Griffin. The distrust between the two parties had been reciprocated, yet there I was asking both sides to work in collaboration. And as if that wasn't enough, he had just discovered the love of his life had switched sides weeks earlier, a move he had been oblivious to.

"Yes," he answered.

I raised one eyebrow, to which he added, "For all of it."

I believed him.

The entrance to the condo had been left wide open, granting permission for all to enter. Steven greeted me warmly, but his response to Noah was lukewarm at best. The rift between them was worse than I had initially assumed. With solemn faces, each person took a seat around the large dining table. I read their thoughts as clearly as if they'd spoken the words aloud. There was an air of unease, they expected me to lose it, to go into meltdown mode, and make irrational decisions to the detriment of us all. Yet surprisingly, no one amongst them was prepared to go against me.

I smiled. "I'm okay."

Silence.

"I'm serious. None of you need to worry. I'm not planning on doing anything rash."

Birsha cocked his head to one side, an amused expression flitted across his face. "So, you're a mind reader now?"

I shook my head. "I'm not reading minds, just energies. My point is the only person to have lost their mind is Griffin." I added with a shrug, "For now at least."

All eyes flashed toward Noah. He shifted uncomfortably. "Despite what you may think, Griffin lost my allegiance a long time ago." He looked directly at Steven as he concluded, "I'm with you, if you'll have me."

Steven's face softened, but he said nothing.

Zagan cleared his throat. "Aamon is safe. I know part of your family..." His voice trailed off.

My eyes fixed firmly on his as I finished his sentence. "Was murdered." With a small smile I added, "Don't be developing a sense of humanity on me now, Zagan."

"What about the rest of them?" he ventured.

"Kasey and Amelia are missing. The problem I have is that I had no knowledge of where Amelia was planning to take Kasey and..." I paused, unable to force the word from my mouth.

With his head cupped in his hands, Steven leaned on the table as he concluded, "So you have no idea if they made it to wherever they were going."

I shook my head.

Zagan sat back, he lifted one leg to place his ankle

on his opposite thigh, and with his elbows resting on the arms of the chair, he pressed his fingertips together. "Trying to locate them is going to take time and resources that we don't have. If Amelia was successful, it would not only be a waste of time but could potentially endanger her and the child." He studied my reaction closely.

I recognized immediately what he was doing. He was testing me.

"So we just hope Amelia and Kasey are okay," Noah hissed, "and move on regardless?"

I stared back at Zagan, his gaze held in my iron grip as I responded, "No, he's right."

Steven frowned. "Alyssa—"

I stood, pressed my palms onto the smooth polished wood surface, and leaned forward. "Every feeling and every sentiment need to be left behind. When we exit this room, we leave without our emotional baggage, and if that's something you can't manage, I need to know now."

I looked slowly around the table, meeting each set of eyes with a challenging stare.

"If they are safe, they don't need us. If they are not, their best chance of survival is Griffin's death.

"Griffin was right about one thing. What you love will kill you. It's time to learn from the mistakes of the past." I pushed myself upright from the table and gestured with wide arms. "Look where traditional tactics have gotten us so far."

"Griffin is without remorse, without conscience. He is ruthless and unrelenting, and whatever slim boundaries he may have had are now gone," Birsha agreed.

"The only way to beat him is to become him. He immersed himself in Daeon's power, surrendered wholeheartedly to his darkness, and lost control. I intend to do the same."

That is where the silence ended. The table erupted with fury, shock, and disbelief at my words.

I held up my hands to silence them as I insisted, "I've used it before, let it out, and then reined it back it. I can do it again."

"That's different," Zagan growled, incensed. "You didn't relinquish control, and even with control, you struggled to maintain it. If you let it out, you may never restrain it again. Look at where we are because of Griffin's fucking arrogance, and now you're going to stand here and tell us your plan is to do the same. You've lost your fucking mind!"

"She can do it," Noah insisted.

"What do you think this is?" Birsha snapped at him. "A fucking superhero movie? I know you're not that naïve. It's a suicide mission."

Steven's chair scraped loudly as he stood. "Except it's not, is it? It's not a suicide mission because she won't be dead. She'll be the female version of Griffin, and we'll be powerless to stop her."

Her!

"Hey!" I snapped. "Do you need to speak about me like I'm not right here in front of you?"

"Let's call it practice for the future, shall we?" Birsha snarled.

My eyes seared his as I growled, "You have no idea what I can do."

Birsha lowered his voice as he pleaded, "That is the problem, Alyssa. None of us do, including you. Please, just think about it."

I sat down and placed both hands gently on the table. Grounded and calm, I glanced around at them. "You have a choice. The door is right there. If you want to leave, please do. No judgment, I swear."

Zagan laughed, and Birsha leaned back in his chair, craning his neck to stare at the ceiling, his fingers laced together behind his head.

Steven shook his head. "No, we can't."

I sighed. I should have expected this.

"Assurances made to Aamon are irrelevant. He isn't here," I reminded them. "I'm giving you leave to go."

Zagan stood. "And respectfully we decline. So, we make finding Griffin our priority?"

"I don't want you to stay over some misplaced sense of duty," I insisted.

"Shut the fuck up." Birsha laughed. "You're not the only one desperate to tear Griffin into pieces. No one's jumping ship. We got you, but I think you know that already."

I nodded. "We make finding Griffin our priority," I reiterated, adding, "The narcissistic twat will love that."

Zagan walked around the table; he glanced toward the yawning windows that sat adjacent. Evening was fast approaching. "Can we reconvene tomorrow? I need to brief my team."

I nodded. "Here?"

Zagan shook his head. "No, the last place we know Griffin was. I'll bring a tracker."

"The loft," I answered.

Zagan and Birsha left, Steven and Noah remained.

They wanted to be alone, and that worked perfectly for me. Deeply immersed in conversation, they barely noticed as I stole silently into the bedroom, back to the comfort of my memories just one last time.

Chapter 23

The dream caught me unaware. I had tried to lead my mind with intent down one path, but somehow I had lost my way, misled by some unrecognizable entity that pulled me in a completely different direction.

I sought out Aamon and found Kasey.

Stuck somewhere between reality and my unconscious mind, I found a place of beauty. An open plain with long grass that moved like the waves in a bay, all within a dome of indigo blue. A million tiny lights clung to the stratosphere, providing the perfect illusion of stars, and on the furthest edges, I could see a ring of silhouetted trees, their twisted limbs reaching high.

Just before me, on the stump of a tree, sat Kasey. He was cross-legged and wide-eyed as his little neck craned upward toward the illuminated sky.

He welcomed me with a smile as I approached. I leaned close. He swung his arms tight around my neck and squeezed enthusiastically.

I sat cross-legged on a bare patch of earth within the grassy plain, eyeing the ground suspiciously for ants. It would be just my luck to have biting bugs infiltrate my dreamland. Kasey giggled. The sound made me smile widely and pulled my attention from the paranoid search for creepy-crawlies. Our heads were at a similar height thanks to his tree stump seat.

"Did it hurt when you died?" he asked, his sapphire

eyes filled with concern.

I shook my head with a reassuring smile. "It didn't hurt."

He looked surprised.

"Does it never hurt for anyone?" he wondered out loud.

As breathtaking as the surroundings were, I couldn't tear my eyes from his. I pondered his question. "Maybe not. Maybe things can only hurt when you're alive."

My conscience tutted at my blatant lie. The line between the truth and my attempts to prevent fear blurred when I was with him.

"Who makes your dinner?" he gasped with eyes so wide.

I tried to hide a smile; it was a legitimate concern, given my inability to cook even the simplest of meals.

"You don't need to eat when you're dead."

Wrong answer. His little face crumpled; he was mortified. "No food?" he squealed.

I poked him gently. "I didn't say you couldn't eat. I just said you don't need to."

His shoulders slumped as he gave a dramatic sigh of relief. My stomach churned as the conversation reminded me of a harsh truth. There was no one left on Earth to cook for Kasey. He had no one left. The thought sent icy shockwaves through my body and squeezed my heart.

Kasey's warm hand brushed my cheek. "She's okay, Mom."

With a small shudder, I changed the subject. That was a bridge I would have to cross at some point. But facing the reality of what he had lost was not for today.

A small frown flitted across his face.

Concerned, I reached for him. "What's up, buddy? Are you okay?"

He scrunched his nose. "It's kinda weird. You look the same. You sound the same…" He unwrapped his skinny little legs and scurried into my lap, his ear pressed to my chest. "And I can hear your heart still bumping." He pulled back and eyed me suspiciously. "Are you sure you're really dead?"

I laughed and tweaked his nose. "It's not what you think, being dead. It's not what anyone thinks. You don't stop existing. I guess in a way you really don't stop living. You just go somewhere else."

"But you didn't go somewhere else. You stayed," he astutely pointed out.

He wasn't making it easy. I tried a different approach.

"It's kind of hard to explain. When you're alive, you're in a bubble that you can't see through, so you don't know what's on the other side. Some people think there must be nothing beyond the bubble, because they can't see or hear outside of it."

"Like the bubble I was in when I was in your tummy?" he asked, laying his head back against my chest. His fingers traced outlines up and down my arm.

"Sort of." I followed his gaze up toward the stars which had started to drift, their movements slow and mesmerizing against the dark blue backdrop. "When you were in my tummy, you didn't know that there was anything else. Imagine how scary that must have been on the day you were born, not knowing if it was a beginning or an end."

"So dead isn't a thing?" he concluded.

My heart started to ache. "I think at some point there

is an end. But not before you pass through lots of new beginnings."

The stars began to fall, just a few. They didn't pick up speed as they fell, they traveled at a steady pace as they drew closer, and they seemed to get smaller the nearer they got.

Kasey giggled loudly as a fallen star landed softly on his arm. A small stream of them followed, landing quietly in the tall grass around us. Only then did I realize the falling stars were fireflies.

I held a finger close to a thick green blade, extending an invitation for the small creature that inched along it. Tentatively, it crawled onto the tip of my finger and sat patiently as I studied it closely.

It didn't look like a firefly. Its body was a single segment made up of lavender fuzz, its wings were iridescent, and its large eyes had pale blue irises. Its glow wasn't reserved to its hind end. Instead, a soft muted light radiated from its entire form.

Kasey squirmed in my lap, twisting till his knees hit the ground and he faced me. He thrust his cupped hands an inch from my face and exclaimed, "Mommy, look, this one doesn't have his light." Carefully, he opened up his palms to reveal a small lightless bug with striking silver-blue eyes.

"He's okay," I said reassuringly. "Maybe his light is on the inside."

Kasey shook his head, a stern expression etched across his face. "No. It means he shouldn't be here. We need to get him back inside," he whispered emphatically.

I opened my mouth to ask what he meant, but he had already started to move swiftly through the sea of greenery. I pulled myself up and hurried after him. He moved with speed toward the tree line, glancing back every few seconds to check I was still in tow, a look of determination engraved into his beautiful features.

The house appeared suddenly, just within the wooded area that surrounded the rolling pasture. It was a small and weathered wooden structure, but despite its apparent age, it was untarnished. A single step led to a redwood front porch encased by matching wooden spindles and rails. A large solid three-panel wooden door with a black wrought-iron pull sat adjacent to the porch opening, flanked on either side by small windows, each consisting of four square glass panes.

The dusk hung over us, and the small clearing became shaded, cloaked within the circle of trees. Despite the darkened surroundings, a bright light from an unseen moon bathed the small house in a silvery white light. The windows emitted a soft orange glow. Intrigued, I tried to peek inside, but the glass panes were frosted and obscured my view.

"Try the door," Kasey whispered, his hands still cupped protectively around the bug with no light.

I reached for the handle but paused, opting to knock on the heavy wood instead. I could feel a disapproving glare from Kasey. With a shrug, I mouthed, "What?" in his direction. He responded with an eye roll and a small shake of his head.

When did he become the expert here?

"The door, Mom," he insisted when my knock garnered no response. I gripped the black iron door pull and pushed hard, but the door refused to budge, despite my best efforts to force it open.

I turned back to Kasey, surprised to see him so crestfallen. I moved quickly to his side and wrapped my arms around him. "It's okay, buddy. I'm sure the bug will be okay, even without a light."

His shoulders slumped, and a deep sigh escaped his chest. "I forgot," he murmured.

"Forgot what?"

I followed his stare to the unyielding door.

"I forgot that, when you let it close, you can't open it again."

His words were innocuous enough, but they sent a chill down my spine. I opened my mouth to again request an explanation, but with a small frown he opened his hands. The bug was gone.

"See?" I tried to smile, but it refused to reach my mouth. "He's okay. He probably flew back to his friends."

Kasey slowly shook his head and extended his arm to point at the door. The bug was just above the handle and had stopped mid-crawl across one of the dark-grained panels. Its white glow shone bright.

Its glow came when it accepted the door was closed.

I shook my head; it didn't make sense and suddenly I didn't want it to.

"It was hard to see you when I was in there." Kasey gestured toward the door. My chest felt tight. "But you could always see in, right?"

"I can't see in, Kasey. The windows are frosted," I corrected him.

"Sure you can. Look, I can too." He dashed to the window, grasped the sill, and on his tip toes, peeked through the glass.

Each step closer was painfully slow as my legs refused to comply. When I reached his side, I gasped. The glass had cleared, and I was greeted with the sight of my mother's living room. With a rising panic, I moved to the next window, the room on the other side was my childhood home. I closed my eyes; it was just a dream. It wasn't real, yet I was having a hard time convincing my nervous system.

As hard as I tried, I could not pacify the sense of alarm that continued to increase in size and strength, initiating my flight response. I didn't realize my steps had started to take me backward until I stumbled down the single wooden porch step.

Kasey didn't notice, he was still peering through the window, entranced by whatever was on the inside.

I couldn't comprehend why; I just knew I had to get Kasey back inside of that house. The thought of him being on the outside looking in distressed me.

"Kasey," I gasped, my chest had become so constricted it made talking hard. He turned to me, wide-eyed and innocent. "Kasey, try the door, push it hard," I wheezed. "Please, Kasey, you have to get back in."

With a puzzled look on his face, he shook his head. He glanced between me and the door as he muttered, "I told you already. It's too late."

"Please, please try," I begged.

He shrugged and reached for the door which held tight against the push of his small frame. "I told you," he mumbled as he returned to his spot at the window.

I wanted to move toward him, but as I shifted my weight to step forward the mud beneath my boots started to crumble away.

Horrified, I spun around, the ground had disappeared behind me, the once grassy forest floor now replaced by a gaping black hole. Something had been taken, and what was left in its place was a void filled with nothingness. For the life of me, I couldn't remember what had stood in the space now occupied by the ever-growing hole.

I shuffled backward, my eyes transfixed on the ground as it disintegrated to dust beneath my feet. I tried to move quicker, but my legs were suddenly made of lead. I rocked back on my heels as the soil fell away from beneath my toes and the balls of my feet, and then the ground wasn't there at all anymore, and I was freefalling into the hole, my arms desperately flailing as they made an unsuccessful effort to grab at the sides.

It was my own screams that woke me. I had crawled across the bed in my sleep and had ended up on Aamon's side, clawing at the sheets to save myself from the hole.

My skin was damp with sweat and my throat hoarse. On shaky legs, I wobbled through the darkness into the bathroom. I turned on the light and winced at its brightness. My reflection was a mess, my skin mottled and streaked with tears, my eyes bloodshot. I splashed cold water on my face and crept from the bedroom. Noah and Steven slept soundly in the living room. If there was a God, only he would know how my sound effects hadn't roused them.

I returned to the damp bed sheets and assumed a fetal position facing the window. Light was cast from the moon above and the LED street lights below. I searched for the stars, reminiscent of the dream bugs but found none. With any hope of restful sleep long gone, I dissected the dream in search of any clue as to where Kasey could be.

As the early morning sun pushed away the last of the inky night sky, I pulled myself stiff and sore from the bed. I showered slowly and waited impatiently for time to pass, doing the best I could to ignore the ticking of the clock that refused to be silenced.

I didn't discuss my dream with Noah and Steven, but they buzzed around me as persistent and irritating as flies anyway, sensing the pain and confusion that had been left in the wake of the dream.

We had agreed to meet everyone at noon, yet as the time drew closer I became more reluctant to leave the condo. A contradictory response to my desire to find Kasey. I was sure I had finally started to lose my mind.

When it was time to leave, I stalled and told the boys to go ahead of me.

With no desire to be a third wheel, I informed them that I had items to collect from the condo and would meet them there within the hour.

The door closed softly as Noah and Steven left. I was finally alone, just me and my thoughts, quite the potentially precarious situation, some might say. I let out a breath and walked slowly from room to room, collecting weapons and small pieces of memorabilia. Unsure if I would ever return, unsure if I would survive the next hours to be able to.

I closed my eyes and tiptoed quietly through my memories, keeping any recollection of the dream far from my immediate thoughts. Focused on memories beyond the previous evening, I prodded at the ones that invoked the strongest emotional response, tested the reaction, increased and decreased the accelerant to identify its flash point. Each time, I allowed my anger to burn a little stronger before I tugged it back in line. Each time, I took a step deeper into my darkness, until eventually I arrived at my furthest point, the carefully constructed holding cell hidden away, beyond the reach of my conscious mind.

My darkness was waiting. Not full of fury the way I had expected. It was only then that I remembered the love she had extended me. She needed no apologies. She understood with a patience and virtue beyond human comprehension. My hand rested on the cold metal of the bars of her cage. I glanced around in an effort to locate the key, but her laugh pulled my attention back. I didn't need a key. Remaining incarcerated was her choice. No lock and key could ever truly imprison her, not metaphorically or otherwise.

"Thank you," I whispered to her, in awe of her tolerance and grace. She extended me the support and fortitude I could never extend myself, a sad affliction of humanity. With renewed conviction, I left the condo. My success or failure had become irrelevant. The only thing that mattered was stopping Griffin and hopefully saving my child and best friend in the process.

I hurried across town, relishing the last few moments of solitude. I picked my way across the derelict industrial estate, but as I approached the old mill, something hit me hard. The residue of something familiar but starkly out of place hung heavy in the air. The energy of one who should not have been there. I froze, horrified as I recognized it immediately.

How could it not resonate with me when it was so similar to my own?

Kasey.

Chapter 24

The adrenaline that shot through my body elevated my heart rate and caused my blood pressure to surge, the sound of which amplified like thunder in my ears. I vaulted up each flight of stairs, a runaway train on a red-hot track. Had Griffin crossed my path in that moment, he would have been powerless to stop me.

The energy that remained was residual, a clear message that the beings associated with it were either long gone or dead. I prayed the latter did not relate to Kasey.

There had been death, of that I was sure. It hung like a dank acrid mist in the air within the building. Unmoving and lifeless. The acidity in my blood increased. It burned my veins and made me feel more than I wanted to.

My mind was fixated on my target, my final destination the apartment I had shared with Griffin. I got five paces past the entrance to the loft before my peripheral vision registered the image that had flashed by. The realization stopped me dead in my tracks.

With a sense of dread, I retraced my steps, back to the wide-open doorway. Before I could step across the threshold, Noah's broad shoulders filled the space, his frame intentionally obscuring my view. He stepped forward, a movement that forced me backward.

"Don't," he whispered.

He was joined by Steven, his face ashen and eyes red. They both stepped clear of the loft, Steven reached back and gently pulled the rolling metal door closed. An eerie silence filled the cold corridor.

I wanted to ask, but somewhere between my throat and mouth my words were lost. My eyes begged them, as they stood firm, side by side blocking my entrance.

"It's not Kasey," Noah promised, his face set in stone. I exhaled so hard I felt sure I would crumple to the ground like a deflated balloon. I slumped forward and pushed my palms into my thighs in an effort to maintain some degree of balance. But my relief was short-lived.

Rocking back on my heels, I glanced between a somber Noah and Steven. Again, my voice failed me.

It was Steven who eventually drew a shaky breath as his eyes found mine. Noah grasped his hand and squeezed it hard.

"We were too late," he croaked. He cleared his throat. The sound echoed louder than it should have in the deathly quiet building. In a hushed tone, he continued, "I don't think she died here. I think he put her here after…"

Amelia.

I flinched and drew in a sharp breath, again the sound was too loud as it sliced through the tomb-like silence. I shook my head. My darkness raged, not with her typical anger but with a pain so deep, and so raw I feared it may have broken her.

My feet stepped back involuntarily, only stopping when my back hit the wall opposite, and when it did the crushing weight of the situation broke the last strand of my resolve. With a guttural scream, I slid down the wall to the floor. I buried my head between my arms and rested my forehead on my knees as the ground lurched and shook.

He killed her.

The words on an endless repeat ricocheted inside of my skull.

He killed her, and I let him.

"No, you fucking didn't!"

Noah's snarl shocked me. I was sure I hadn't uttered my thoughts out loud. My head jerked up startled and bewildered. Steven glanced nervously between us, confusion etched on his tear-stained face.

Noah's face contorted in rage as he insisted, "I hear you, and you're wrong."

"You heard what was in my head?" I whispered incredulously.

Steven's eyes widened as his head whipped between us. In one fluid movement, I was on my feet. Noah's breaths came in pants, and his muscles twitched, willing him to move, his eyes darting in panic as he desperately struggled to maintain control. His animal instincts had started to overpower him as his restraint slipped swiftly away.

I edged forward until I was able to place one hand on his chest. But instead of calming him, it only served to intensify his fury. His eyes flashed and narrowed as he hissed, "I will make him pay for this."

I pulled my hand sharply away; I had no desire to make the impossible even harder for him. He was embroiled in a battle I was all too familiar with.

With each life he took, Griffin had molded a new and dangerous enemy whose sole mission became revenge. His toxicity poisoned every person within his reach. The persistent tick-tock from my mental clock nudged me. I was almost out of time to stop him before the damage he inflicted became irreparable.

He had picked off my family one by one with seeming ease. Now only one remained.

"I need a minute," Noah growled through gritted teeth as he stormed down the corridor, his fists clenched into bowling balls at his side.

Steven started to move in his direction, but I pulled him back with a shake of my head.

"Not a good idea."

"I've never seen him like that," Steven stammered in a hushed tone.

I glanced at the closed loft door. Steven followed my gaze and placed one hand on my shoulder. "You don't want to do that."

"I believe you." I placed my hand over his and trained my eyes firmly on the metal door. I needed to hear his words but couldn't face the pained look in his eyes.

"What happened?" I asked.

Steven's haunted voice was barely above a whisper.

"It looks like she fought back. And she paid for it. He slaughtered her, left her to bleed out, then brought her body home." His voice trembled but he continued, "She was on the sofa covered with a blanket like she was asleep. He even removed her fucking boots and put them on the floor next to her."

I might as well have been there to witness her death. Each detail shared by Steven caused the flash of an image to slice through my brain, giving me a play-by-play account in snapshot form.

I understood Griffin's motives. He was stripping us all of every facet of safety. Noah and Steven had lost their sister and their home in one fell swoop. He wanted them as vulnerable as possible. He was succeeding.

Bastard.

We stood speechless, lost and without words. There was no peace in the quiet and the stillness. The silence was heavy and suffocating. It filled my brain with a thick fog that made even the smallest of thoughts impossible and the slightest movement laborious.

Even the ticking of the clock had ceased. Without it, time slipped by almost unnoticed.

Heavy footsteps announced Noah's return. Although somewhat calmer, his anger had not dissipated. His once-golden eyes flickered coal black, and his jaw remained clenched. He was flanked by Birsha and Zagan.

They had not come alone. There were more of them outside, some I recognized, others I did not. I appreciated the support but knew their efforts were redundant. This would come down to the battle of just a few. Griffin would make sure of it.

Zagan surveyed the scene before him. He drew in a breath as if to speak but hesitated.

"Is Kasey dead?" My words chilled the air. The sensation reminded me of my dream.

Birsha and Zagan exchanged a questioning glance before Zagan responded.

"There's no evidence of that. It's more likely he's being held to bait you."

How much more could this poor kid take? I had to be the worst fucking mother.

"Held where?" I stammered.

"I'm relatively certain he isn't on Earth. If Griffin has him, he likely took him to Daeon," Zagan retorted.

Steven interrupted. "I disagree, if Griffin had captured him already, we'd all know about it. He must be tucked away in Laeon somewhere. Given his present state, I doubt Griffin has the capacity to function well enough there to find anything."

We could only hope.

"Our goal remains unchanged—we find Griffin," Zagan clipped.

With the compassion that Zagan lacked, Steven stepped forward. "Firstly we don't know that he's being held. Amelia could have secured him somewhere, then fled to draw Griffin away from him." Concern filled Steven's face as he turned to me and implored, "Please, don't go down that rabbit hole."

Noah agreed. "And when this is done, we will go get him. He'll be in Laeon. It makes perfect sense."

"Then it's the only thing that does." I sighed.

A movement behind Zagan pulled my attention. I'm not sure what exactly I had expected Zagan's tracker to look like, but I certainly had not expected a teenager. The boy that stepped forward looked no older than sixteen at best. Lanky and awkward with sandy brown hair and bronzed chestnut eyes, he surveyed us tentatively. I frowned and opened my mouth, but Zagan held one hand up to silence me.

He opened his palm in the boy's direction presenting him as he announced with an air of pride, "My tracker."

"Didn't know we were in the habit of owning people, Zagan," I responded dryly. My eyes narrowed as I added scornfully, "You brought a child?"

An impish grin spread across the boy's baby features. His warm eyes met mine. "I look younger than I am," he murmured with a bow of his head.

"Well, that's good because you look about fucking twelve," I snapped. Was I the only one who appreciated the time constraints of the situation?

The boy glanced up at me, with a smirk that made me want to slap him as he retorted with a sneer, "I'm actually one of the oldest ones here."

"Then you should possess the intelligence to know not to piss me off," I remarked with a frosty glare. I had neither the time nor the patience for this level of bullshit, least of all from a fucking kid.

He started to laugh, the arrogant little shit, but no sooner had his snigger begun than it was cut short. All eyes turned to him, but he was oblivious. In a trance-like state, his wide eyes stared straight ahead, his body jolted, and his fingers twitched. He took a sudden step back as his eyes shifted upward.

Zagan sidled close to him. "You feel him," he confirmed smugly, a child demonstrating their shiny new toy. "Now track him."

The boy blinked, turned his head toward Zagan, and muttered, "I don't need to. He's here."

Chapter 25

It took everything I had not to bolt from the corridor to find him. A sentiment shared by Noah, who lunged forward with a roar. It took the full efforts of Steven, Zagan, and Birsha to restrain him.

The boy child had vanished into thin air. I can't say I blamed him.

"You know it's not going to be as easy as that, Noah," I chastised through gritted teeth, reminding him sharply, "He could have my son."

With a face like thunder, Noah held his hands up in surrender. He pointed one finger at me and hissed, "You are not going up there alone."

I studied him closely. The muscles in his arms bulged beneath the thin material of his shirt. His jaw was clenched hard, his huge hands were squeezed tightly into fists, and his eyes burned fiercely. He was a ferine beast tensed to attack, but as much as he was compelled by every instinctive drive he possessed to break free, he fought hard against his urges and seemed to be winning the battle. Still, I needed to be sure.

"Can you control yourself?"

He nodded, his glowering eyes fixed resolutely on mine.

"You don't enter unless I tell you, agreed?"

He nodded.

I sighed. Conflicted beyond reason, my preference

was to face Griffin alone. The more people in attendance, the more collateral we handed him. I held Noah's gaze. He knew precisely what I was thinking, and for the briefest of moments, a softness flicked across his eyes. He was still him, still the hero just a little bit damaged, but still one of the very few I could trust.

If I was being honest with myself, having him by my side was probably exactly what I needed. We were synced like never before, and there was a chance that we could hold each other's broken parts together, for a little while at least.

I relented with a small nod.

Side by side, we climbed the two flights of stairs to the ninth floor. The door to the apartment sat open, and a soft orange glow spilled into the dimly lit corridor. True to his word Noah paused a footstep away from the opening.

I stepped warily into the light. Amber flames danced manically in the fireplace, eager to escape their confinement. They threw out a plethora of shadows that flickered across the walls and ceiling, their coiled forms in a constant motion as they twisted and pulled against an invisible shackle that tethered them down.

Griffin sat casually on the long sofa that flanked the hearth, motionless against the ever-moving backdrop. He was composed, appeared utterly relaxed, and paid no attention to my entrance, seemingly too preoccupied with the dark red liquid that he swilled from side to side in the wine glass he held. He took a long slow sip and flashed a smile in my direction.

"You took your time."

I stepped forward softly, careful to keep my back to the door, and the armchair and coffee table between us.

My eyes flickered to the table. It held a bourbon bottle, its contents fully drained and a cabernet bottle which was two thirds empty. A second glass half filled with the crimson liquid stood between the two bottles. Its rich aroma wafted through the warm air.

He nodded toward it. "Not like you to refuse a drink, my love."

I continued to watch him silently, my face expressionless. After all, the only voice he was truly interested in was his own. He rose fluidly from the sofa, and for the briefest of moments, my confidence faltered.

"I've got to give it to you both—you certainly played me. I mean, I really should have expected it from you." He gestured toward me. "But *Amelia*. I really didn't think she had it in her." He chuckled as he shook his head with not a hint of anger in his tone.

He kept his movements slow and steady as he navigated across the room, each step graceful and choreographed. I fought against the urge to retreat. In a hushed tone, he promised, "But to win the battle is not to win the war, and rest assured, I will find him."

My face remained passive, but inside, hidden from his prying eyes, I was in turmoil, unsure if his words referred to Kasey or to Aamon.

He inched closer. I held his gaze, refusing to succumb to the power of his wrath that had started to bubble slowly to the surface.

"She took her secrets with her," he sang. His brow furrowed briefly as he admitted, "I underestimated her. She wouldn't give him up, even with her final excruciating breath, but she did have a request for you."

Griffin paused for dramatic effect, examining me closely for even the slightest hint of a reaction.

"It was like she thought you were there in the room with us, damn near scared me to death she did. *Alyssa, forgive me, I'm so sorry*," he mimicked as he rocked joyfully back on his heels. "Maybe it was the blood loss," he mused, "or possibly the blows to her head that sent her cuckoo, or maybe she was always bat-shit crazy. Who knows, and who cares, right?"

I blinked but held my ground, my mask cemented firmly in place.

Griffin crept another inch closer. "Such a shame that it was all in vain. You see, I will find him; there's only so many places she could have hidden him, after all, and when I do, I won't just kill him, I'll orb his fucking soul and sell it to the highest bidder."

He raised his hand and studied his now-empty glass with disappointment as he mumbled, "Can you imagine the prospective buyers for the soul of a pure one's offspring?"

I shifted just slightly. The movement drew his attention from the glass back to me.

His eyes lit up with excitement, he kept his gaze fixed firmly on me, thirsty for every minuscule reaction as he added, "I'm really hoping you survive long enough to see it."

His mercurial temperament was disturbing. A hurricane force wind that constantly shifted direction and gave no indication of its intended landfall. The instability of his thoughts was a stark reminder of how volatile his mental state was.

Somewhere in the deepest, darkest recesses of my mind, an iron door creaked as it swung open. *Please not yet*, I begged silently.

There was another louder creak, but this time it

came from the corridor. Griffin's words had started to draw more than just my darkness forward.

I had what I needed. Wherever Kasey was, it was safely away from Griffin. He had nothing, no hand left to play.

I smiled; he flinched. The tables slowly turned.

It was I who pushed forward to close the final few inches between us, leaning as close to him as I could stomach. I had waited for what felt like an eternity for that moment. It was time to strike the match I'd held on to for so long. It was time to burn him to the ground.

With his eyes affixed on mine, he called out to Noah. "Take one more step, brother. I dare you."

I froze, so did Noah.

Unhinged or not, his senses were unparalleled, leaving him acutely aware of everything around him.

He started to raise his glass to his lips before he remembered it was empty. Just one more disappointment to add to his irritation.

Moving quickly to refill his glass, he taunted both Noah and me.

"Now I know neither one of you really thought I'd be stupid enough to corner myself."

My eyes narrowed. "Really?" I scoffed. "You have that few options left that you're down to bluffing?" I laughed, an ugly deep-throated cackle. Griffin strode quickly back across the room, and stopped abruptly, a mere inch or so away for me. With a hostile glare, he lowered his head to mine, but his attempt at intimidation only served to fuel me. I leaned even closer, the distance between us now down to millimeters as I hissed, "You're pathetic."

With a small shake of his head, he took a final long,

drawn-out sip from his glass. As he lowered his head, he murmured, "God, I loved you; I may not remember much, but I do remember that." He sidled up beside me, his breath warm against my cheek. His position, the closest he could get without actually touching me, electrified the sliver of space between us. I faltered.

"I would have given anything to have you love me."

I jerked away, just slightly, and he dissolved into laughter.

"Did that cheesy shit really work once upon a time? Fuck, that's embarrassing," he exclaimed loudly. Again, he leaned forward, his mouth uncomfortably close to my ear and his breath hot against my skin. The hairs on the back of my neck stood on end as his teeth gently grazed my earlobe before he murmured, "Now all I want is to see your insides."

A dark flash of anger snapped me back.

"Then you're in for a world of disappointment," I snarled.

"Hmmm, maybe not." He pondered, turning sharply on his heels to stride back to the coffee table. He discarded his empty glass and reached for the wine bottle. As he did, Noah shifted just slightly in the doorway.

Griffin spun toward him and waved his arms wildly as he screamed, "One more fucking step and I will blow you into the next fucking realm!" His overreactive outburst was brief, scarily so. One moment his reddened face was contorted in rage and his body poised to attack, the next he was cool, calm, and collected, tilting his head with an amused expression as he wagged his finger at me with a chuckle and declared, "To be clear, that was not a euphemism, dear. My inclinations were always more toward bitches than dogs."

Wow. He really had entered a whole new level of psychosis.

But he wasn't bluffing. One truth amongst a million lies was easy to identify. And besides, I didn't need to believe him. I could hear it myself.

I had unknowingly heard it all along. The clock that resided unwelcome in my brain had managed to normalize the sound of incessant ticking. I had become so desensitized to its sound that my brain refused to acknowledge it, or anything remotely similar to it, even when the echo originated elsewhere. I glanced around the room, desperate to locate it.

Griffin waved one hand dismissively in the air between us. He raised the bottle clutched in his other hand and navigated it close to his lips, pausing as he confessed, "It's not here. Save yourself the trouble. It's downstairs, pretty damn close to your congregation, as luck would have it."

He finished the contents of the bottle and dropped it to the ground where it hit the thick rug but did not smash. He rubbed his hands together and announced, "Time to go."

"You're not going anywhere," Noah growled from the doorway, his knuckles whitened from his grip on the wooden frame. His body leaned inward; a wild animal ready to pounce.

"I am," Griffin stated calmly, and he pointed at me. "You're coming with me."

"Like hell."

Griffin sighed and shook his head. "Oh dear, sweet, stupid, fucking Alyssa," he spat. "Must we do this dance? You know you can't help but be the fucking hero.

We both know you're not going to risk the lives of the precious few you have left to live for. I mean someone's got to survive long enough to retrieve little Kasey from wherever the fuck your bitch stashed him."

"Don't." Noah's voice bellowed across the room to me, but he remained in the doorway.

Griffin looked him up and down, exclaiming "When precisely did he decide to grow a pair?" He dissolved into manic laughter as he muttered, "Today is just full of surprises."

I turned to Noah and yelled urgently, "Get out now!"

With a loud cuss, he pushed himself from the doorway and darted out of sight.

Griffin crept up behind me, he slid his hand around my waist and held me tight against him. Swaying a slow dance, his acid breath burned against my skin as he droned, "I for one thought he would never leave."

I stood stick straight as Griffin moved from side to side, pulling me unwilling with him, my sole focus on the movement outside of the apartment as bodies scattered wild with panic, out from the building and to a safe distance away.

"You know I'm not leaving here," I told him, softening my tensed shoulders and relaxing into Griffin's dance, my rhythm synchronized to his soundless movements.

"You know I don't want you to," he chuckled, twirling me slowly.

So that was it. He'd allowed the survival of the others to ensure he got mine. A fair trade.

He had no intention of either of us leaving that day. He had no intention of either of us surviving that day.

The thought of him winning curdled my blood.

"You didn't get Kasey," I taunted, "and you didn't get Aamon."

There was a small hiss and a sharp intake of breath. He froze, and every muscle in his body tensed.

I continued to mock him. "You were so distracted by me you didn't even notice when he slipped away."

"Impossible," he snarled.

I laced my fingers through his and held his hand to my waist, knowing how much it would burn. "Hmmm, you have no idea how good it feels to know I fucked you over, you silly little man," I whispered between heavy breaths as I pushed up against him.

He snatched back his hand and pushed me roughly away.

"You're full of shit," he snarled.

My head tilted slightly to one side as his confidence slithered slowly away. My eyes twinkled as I disdainfully remarked, "And yet you're still doubting yourself."

Griffin paced before the fireplace. A full minute ticked by while a thousand emotions fast forwarded across his features. Bizarrely, the final one which stuck was some contorted version of pleasure. He stopped and with a wide grin exclaimed, "So fucking what? I don't care. It's better that he escaped. Now he gets to suffer an eternity knowing he wasn't able to save you."

"Are you trying to convince me, or you?" I mused.

He gave me a wry smile. "This isn't one you're going to win, Alyssa. Whatever your aim for antagonizing me is, whatever reaction you hoped for, you're not going to get it."

I stared deadpan into the still dancing flames. He was right. His mind was too unstable for my original tactic to work. The incessant ticking had slowed, a clock nearing its end.

Assuming my lack of response was some indication of defeat, Griffin rolled his eyes and on unsteady legs turned toward the coffee table. He bent forward to reach for the second glass, still half full of wine.

The alcohol may have impaired Griffin's reaction time by mere milliseconds at best, but that was all that I needed. As he leaned down, one arm outstretched, I delivered a swift hard kick to his back with enough force to pitch him forward. He faceplanted onto the table, and before he had the chance to clamber to his feet, I snatched the wine bottle from the rug and smashed it against the back of his head. He flopped hard against the wooden surface with a thud. I didn't see it happen. I only heard it. I had made it halfway through the window before the shattered glass of the wine bottle cascaded like hail and Griffin, for that moment at least, lost consciousness.

I swung, firefighter style, down the first two floors on the outer edge of the metal fire escape. My feet barely brushed the floor as I leapt from level to level, driven by pure adrenaline. I hit the ground hard and didn't look back as I sprinted from the building and across the scrubland. I was partway down the abandoned gravel access road when the explosion rumbled behind me. The top level of tiny stones shuddered and shifted beneath my feet, and the heat scorched the dry air with its fiery breath.

I skidded to a halt and turned to see the top half of the building obscured by thick black smoke that billowed from every fractured opening. Dark red flames roared angrily, stretching up and outward as they snatched at handfuls of air.

I stood and stared, but only for a moment. I felt the others approach; in silence they formed a loose semicircle around me. A familiar hand rested reassuringly on my shoulder, reminding me I was not alone. But nothing could lessen the pain that caused a warm wet trail of tears.

Tears for a fallen hero, a sister, and a friend.

Chapter 26

"Shit!"

I paced the length of the open plan condo's living area and shook my hands as I tried to rid myself of the pins and needles which had invaded my fingertips. To say that things were not going well was possibly the understatement of the century. My plan to locate Kasey by backtracking Amelia's movements had quite literally blown up in my face.

The only saving grace was that I now knew Griffin hadn't managed to get his claws into Kasey. He was as much missing to Griffin as he was to the rest of us, the secret of his location taken with Amelia to her grave, for now at least.

Once the initial shock of the explosion had worn off, I had cussed and stomped my way back to the condo. On arrival, I had given Zagan, Birsha, Steven and Noah a ranting rundown of the events prior to the detonation, seethed my way through a steam shower, and accumulated enough steps to last two lifetimes with my manic pacing, yet still my anger refused to subside.

I needed to find Kasey, but then I also had no idea if Griffin had in fact perished in the explosion. As pleasant as the thought was, it was highly unlikely. If I had managed to escape, there was no reason to think he had not. It didn't matter how much I hoped, killing him would never be that easy. Going round in circles was costing me the last shreds of my sanity. Each time I tried to make peace with the order of our intended plan of action, my gut told me I was making the wrong decision.

"It is entirely feasible that Griffin didn't escape. You did say he was unconscious when you left, correct?" Zagan offered.

I shook my head. "You don't believe that any more than I do. He's a such a fucking cockroach."

Zagan didn't disagree. He didn't honestly think that Griffin had died in the explosion; his words were merely an attempt to placate me. The mood in the room was somber. The sense of unease was as much about Griffin and his next course of action as it was about me. I was eyed with nervous anticipation, each person watching and waiting for me to snap.

I turned to the group. "So Noah and Steven go to Laeon, start the search for Kasey, while the rest of us corner Griffin."

From his seat at the table, Steven interjected, "What happens if Kasey is found before Griffin is eliminated? I have faith in Amelia. She wouldn't have put him anywhere unsafe. I say we leave him where he is until we know it's secure to retrieve him."

"It is a risk that may be unnecessary," Birsha agreed.

Not one damn person knew where the hell Kasey was for sure. All we had were theories. Again, a monumental fuck-up on my behalf, and most definitely the elephant in the room that day. I didn't need my feelings to be preserved. The collective avoidance of my error wasn't helping anyone, least of all Kasey.

"Am I the only one able to see what the screamingly obvious bigger issue is? How the fuck do we even have the option to retrieve him when no one has any idea where he is nor any way of finding him?" My voice echoed shrilly around the room. The borderline hysteria of my tone sent a ripple of nervousness through the group.

Birsha leaned forward on the table, his eyes fixed firmly on mine as he murmured gently, "Try to focus on one problem at a time."

I stopped pacing and absentmindedly started to pick at my cuticles instead. Right. One problem at a time.

Griffin's main objective would be to prove me wrong. Our confrontation had given me a front row seat to his mental undoing. I had hit a nerve, threatened to obliterate his well-laid plans with my claims that Aamon had escaped. His ego was too big to accept that he had been outwitted by anyone, and the fury brought by such an implication would drive him crazier than he already was, if that was even possible at all.

I knew him well enough to know that this final tip would send him crashing into a place from which he could not be retrieved. My intent may have been to save Aamon and Kasey, but I'd be lying if I claimed that vengeance played no part in my actions. I wanted him to suffer. It was what he deserved. It was a necessary step in breaking him. It also made him more treacherous than ever before, meaning any hope of retrieving Kasey would have to wait until Griffin was dead.

I had interpreted my most recent dream as a warning that wherever Kasey was, he was on limited time, but I had no idea how relative that was.

Time may have been of the essence, but the implication was less dire than the possibility of subjecting him to a psychotic maniac. The safest option, and lesser of two evils, undoubtedly was for Kasey to remain hidden until I had taken care of Griffin as swiftly as I could.

All eyes turned to me, but no one spoke. They didn't need to.

I cleared my throat. "I need to go to Daeon."

Of course, there was about as much doubt in regard to Griffin's whereabouts as there was about his continued survival. He didn't need to be found. We all knew exactly where he would be, and I would happily wager that once he discovered Aamon's cell empty, his fury would exceed anything we had experienced before.

"Absolutely not!" Zagan roared with far more emotion than I thought possible. He leapt from his seat and slammed both palms down hard on the wooden surface.

I blinked in surprise, not just at his reaction but at what such a response meant. "You're afraid of him," I ventured.

With his mouth set in a thin line, Zagan conceded, "We should all be afraid of him."

The thought of drilling holes through my toenails appealed to me more than the notion of confronting an infuriated homicidal maniac deep within Daeon's subterranean core, but I hadn't realized exactly how formidable Griffin had become to the rest of the group.

"He isn't going to win," I said softly, as I looked slowly from face to face. "But logic and reasoning aren't going to get us very far against him. We're all in agreement that he has reached a whole new depth of crazy; I think it's time we meet him at his level."

Noah gave a small laugh. "She's right." He leaned back and rested his elbows on the arms of the chair. "I've never felt more powerful than I did when I had nothing but pure anger and hatred driving me."

Birsha and Zagan glanced at each other. Birsha cleared his throat. "I'm sure I don't need to tell you that coming back from that isn't always as easy as it sounds."

Steven's eyes flickered to Noah. "But it can be done, especially if we work as a team."

Zagan massaged his temples as he hissed, "Jesus Christ, we'll be singing 'Kum Ba Yah' next." He leaned forward and gestured toward Noah and Steven. "If you think you can access your inner Sygan, please be my guest. Let loose and have at it." His chair scraped loudly across the ground as he stood and added, "When we're done, maybe we can all go hug trees or something, but for now, can we please just get this over with."

In an effort to lighten the mood and prove once and for all that I had my shit firmly together, I forced a thin smile on my face and quipped, "Well, if nothing else it should be entertaining."

My penchant for humor at the darkest moments really did leave me questioning my own sanity at times, but my comment did bring a few small smiles at the very least.

The conversation was minimal as we traveled the short distance from Aamon's condo to the closest gateway. I had opted to take a skeleton crew, leaving Zagan's team of Sygans scattered between the condo and Daeon's gateway. I wasn't sure how, but numbers would be irrelevant. It would ultimately come down to just me and Griffin. I secretly prayed that my anticipated scenario would transpire without further loss of life.

The air in Daeon lay thick and heavy. Once upon a time, I would have considered it suffocating, but on that day I found it strangely comforting. It didn't fill the hole that had started to form in my chest, but it did blanket it.

With each step farther, the weight of my chest increased. My body knew something my fractured mind was unable to comprehend.

I felt sorrow for the obvious reasons, but the heaviness went beyond any loss I had experienced. I was entering an end without the excitement of a new beginning, quite possibly my own. Just another screeching alarm that I failed to acknowledge.

I felt Griffin long before I reached him, a sense that was reciprocated. Griffin's excitement became elevated the closer I got. When he was but a few feet ahead, hidden within the folds of darkness, I ordered everyone to stop. From my stance up front, I turned to face them and in a steady voice announced, "This is as far as you go."

A narrow opening sat between two coal-black walls just before me. A sliding frame of iron bars peeked out from one of them, its metal track embedded across the gray stone floor of the lightless aperture.

"Don't be stupid," Zagan barked angrily as I edged carefully backward. Griffin's energy wafted sharply through the air as he emerged from the shadows right behind me. With my back to the opening, I was unable to see him, but I didn't need to, the reaction from the rest of the group told me all I needed to know.

With one final step back, I crossed the worn metal track and yanked the gate closed. Its loud clang reverberated throughout the confined space in a deafening tone, trapping within the confines of the cave me and the beast I once called a friend.

Chapter 27

"Alyssa, don't!" Noah's frantic eyes were wide. He lunged forward, but Birsha pulled him sharply back as the automatic locking mechanism snapped shut.

There was only one way this would end. It was always going to come down to me and him, as if by some higher order design. The paths chosen were irrelevant. The ending would always be the same.

As they fought with the impenetrable barrier, I turned and silently followed Griffin deep into the darkness. We stopped in a familiar spot. The once heavily reinforced wooden door that had held Aamon prisoner had long since been reduced to splinters and strewn crudely across the floor.

Any doubts Griffin may have had regarding my hand in the carnage would have been short-lived. I was everywhere. Remnants of my energy clung to the thick air, and there was an inordinate amount of my blood still evident upon many of the wooden shards.

Surveying my work, I couldn't stop the smug smile as it crawled across my face, which only served to further enrage an already volatile Griffin.

He forced out a laugh between gritted teeth.

"You're a tiny bug sitting in the palm of my hand, with no idea of the danger you're in or of the power I have." He leaned against one of the gigantic boulders that encircled the small cave-like space before Aamon's holding cell.

His words reminded me of my Kasey dream and unwanted images threatened to pull my focus from the here and now.

"I can and I will crush you. But after all you've put me through, I deserve to enjoy myself a little first," he sneered.

My smile faltered, but my stubbornness refused to allow the fear I felt to sneak across my features. Instead, I rolled my eyes.

"Yes, Griffin, it was all me. I am of course the bastard route of all evil," I agreed sardonically.

"Don't you fucking patronize me," he roared as he lunged toward me. "Your sarcastic little remarks won't help you this time."

Did they ever?

"No," I agreed, "but they do entertain me, which is more that I can say for you."

The echoing sound of my group trying to break through the iron bars had faded, now only a stifling silence remained between the words of our hostile exchange.

With narrowed eyes, Griffin asked, "Do you think Zagan gives a shit about you? That Noah and Steven are on your side? You're deluded. And Amelia was no ally of yours either. You have no friends, no family, no man, nothing."

"And yet I wasn't the one Amelia betrayed," I mused.

"You think Amelia was your friend? I'd been fucking her for months." His laugh was strained.

Liar!

"Ahh, then congratulations are in order. You

succeeded in leaving two of us unsatisfied."

"Fuck you," he bellowed.

"You did, hence my lack of satisfaction." I shrugged.

His eyes blazed. "You have no one," he spat.

"If that was the truth, I'd be a lot more okay with it than you are." I smiled. "I don't need anyone else. It was my choice to lock them out, remember?"

He started to turn away, but at the last moment spun toward me and struck the side of my face with a blow I did not anticipate. Unprepared, I crashed to the floor tasting blood.

For a moment I just lay there, like I was on the sidelines watching the drama unfold. A small part of me still could not believe this was the same person I had once known. It was only then that it truly hit me. By denying a huge part of himself, Griffin had enabled two very different personas to form. Neither one was able to find peace or acceptance with the other, so they were forced into separation.

I had already let go of everything that had previously held me back. The perception of control, the fear of becoming lost within the darkness, the apprehension of the unknown. But still I'd compartmentalized a whole part of me, my fear placing me on potentially the same path as Griffin.

My darkness could no longer be treated as a separate entity. She never had been, at least no more than I had made her. I had inflicted the role of imposter upon her, and from a place of love, she hadn't fought against it. She had accepted it and all of the bonds that came with it.

All to my own detriment. I had hurt and hindered

only myself. Fearful of who and what I truly was, afraid not only of the perceptions of others, but of my own jaded convictions too. I was automatically ashamed of even the possibility of being different. I'd never given myself the chance to know the real me, let alone love her.

Never again.

And so, as I should have done on that final fall evening of my first life, I completed my first act of letting go. It was the most simple and obvious of solutions yet one that had evaded me for far too long.

To become who you are supposed to be means letting go of who you were. It isn't without sadness. It isn't without longing. It is a necessary yet painful part of a bigger journey. As someone once said, the fear of falling should never prevent you from flying. I'd come so close; I had opened the door so many times, yet without realizing, I had refused to allow what resided beyond it to pass through without restraint.

What lay beyond it was me. All of me.

Griffin surveyed me, his eyes almost as black as the slick coal walls. His shoulders were hunched forward, and his movements became slow but remained fluid, a beast hunting its prey. He had become something recognizable, a slave to his darkness. He lacked any respect for the power he yielded, a respect I finally appreciated was necessary to understanding it. It was clear now that his heart was filled with hatred for everyone, including himself.

I rose slowly but without effort. With my arms hanging limply by my sides, I made no attempt to wipe away the trickle of blood that weaved a ruby red trail down my chin.

There's a degree of relief in giving up a fight. In the

acceptance of the label that others cast upon you. If Griffin wanted me to be the villain, I could see no viable reason to continue to rebel against it. Fuck it, if he was the good guy in this twisted scenario, then I wanted nothing more than to be the bastard. How much wasted energy had been misdirected in my quest to rid myself of the irrelevant opinions of others?

"You will never leave this hole." He gestured around the confined space with a satisfied smile.

What I didn't realize at that time was that he was finally right about something. That those would be the last few moments of me. The foreboding of an end that had burdened me had not been without purpose, because who I was did cease to exist that day, never to return, and if gone forever isn't the definition of death I don't know what is.

I exhaled slowly.

"Hush, don't speak." Griffin placed his finger on my lips. "I want to relish every second of this, and that involves you shutting the fuck up, please."

I raised one eyebrow, yet indulged his fantasy, knowing he had one last hand to play.

"Interesting fact," he continued. "My extensive research has proved that there are no living souls in Laeon."

He gently pulled his hand from my mouth and cupped his chin between his thumb and index finger. "Hmmm, if we do the math here, what does that tell us?"

My conscious and subconscious states were out of sync. I was still minutes away from understanding the weight of his words, and when I did, that would become the point of realization for my conscious mind, but deep inside me my darkness stirred. Sharper and quicker than me in every sense, she had understood immediately.

That was the time it actually happened. As Griffin stood in a feigned position of pondering, that was the very moment she slipped from my grasp.

Or not. There wasn't any grasping involved. I simply let her go. I let the real me go.

It required no effort at all. I stood back and watched passively as she stepped free. As the old me died, and the new me rose.

Griffin's words echoed on repeat, thrusting me into a dark, soundless corridor of grief.

Kasey wasn't in Laeon.

It had taken me all of a matter of seconds to ascertain that he wasn't in Daeon. No living soul was.

And he wasn't on Earth. Of that we were all sure.

Griffin studied me carefully, my face remained deadpan, my body frozen rigid.

"Please, go right ahead and take your time. It's not like we're on a clock or anything." He leaned closer, intrigued as he caught a glimmer of something, a hardening behind my eyes, the fluctuation in the temperature of the air around me. With exaggerated pity, he mocked me. A drawn-out slow clap with a wide scornful leer. "Oh, we have movement, ladies and gentlemen. The hamster wheel is indeed starting to turn again. There may be a semi-functioning brain beneath that thick skull after all."

I may, for the longest time, have been unaware that deep in the darkest recesses of my twisted, warped mind, the cell door had sat open for a while. The part of me I had ostracized and cast out had heeded my commands and waited with a level of patience my weaker side had been in awe of. But even the most tolerant of beings have their limits. Griffin had in that moment broached mine. A fact I remained oblivious to until I felt new breath fill my lungs, felt the fiery burn of a fresh source of anger course through my veins, and was pulled into an inescapable pool of warmth and power.

I was whole for the first time. I would never let me go again.

This time there was no leash. I would have been powerless to stop it even if I had been so inclined, which I was not.

"Of course he is here somewhere. Just not in living form," Griffin jibed.

I stumbled backward, an unavoidable reaction to the tsunami of thoughts that had flooded my already-overwhelmed mind.

Finally, the pieces slid perfectly into place. And the picture they created was anything but beautiful.

Amelia's apologies, her pleas for forgiveness, the inability for even the most proficient of trackers to locate Kasey's whereabouts, and of course my dreams. The little boy who peered from the outside in, and that fucking clock. That clock wasn't telling me Kasey was running out of time, it was telling me his time was up. The void into which I fell created by the loss of his life.

Instantaneously, I knew where he was, and I understood why.

My head snapped up, the familiar scent and residual energy that I had attributed to my own blood spilled in vast quantities within the small space wasn't only my essence. It was Kasey's too. He had been there, in Daeon's deepest core, moments before he passed through to its inner realm.

"She took him to Aamon." The realization hit me

like a freight train. "Amelia knew, she knew that was the only place you couldn't reach him."

It was an act that saved his soul but cost him his life.

The scream that erupted from my chest cracked against the confines of the cave like a whip. The emotional freight train didn't hit me. I consumed it and guided it straight toward Griffin, lifting him from his feet as I sent him flying across the small space. His airborne body impacted the wall with a bone-shattering crack and bounced back before hitting the floor with a resounding thud.

Dazed by the impact, he struggled to stand. As he pushed his palms into the ground, I swung my leg forward and struck him hard. With flawless precision, my foot slammed into his face, the point of impact perfectly centered with such speed and velocity that the blood which sprayed from his nose and mouth flew sideways like a high-pressure pump.

With a cry, he dragged himself up, one hand again the wall as he staggered and swayed. He launched himself from the wall swinging wildly. Each punch and kick were blocked and returned with ferocity. Griffin hit the wall, and I rushed at him, ready to deliver my final blow. With one fist raised inches from him, I froze.

There was an inexplicable flash of light, white teeth contrasting sharply against his blackened bloodied face, and something else.

Again, I hadn't extended him the credit he deserved.

Even in his broken mind, Griffin had at some point in time been capable of lucid moments and rational thoughts. He must have experienced such an episode when selecting his weapon of choice. I had felt the presence of a dagger but had been unconcerned. What I failed to realize was exactly which dagger he had in his possession.

The only object able to truly impede my power was the dagger I had once used in an attempt to end my own life. The last time I had seen it had been last summer on the rooftop of the convenience store at the foot of the Adirondacks. I had neither contemplated its location nor had I considered the implications of my actions on that day, and the potent force subsequently encapsulated by it.

I didn't see or feel it until it was too late. Seconds from executing a deathblow, I was restrained and incapacitated. Stripped of my power, I became a lamb at the slaughterhouse. For a moment, I remained oblivious, still swinging fury-driven blows until with the shriek of a banshee, I was engulfed by a river of white-hot molten lava which imprisoned my every movement. The pain, so excruciating, rendered my brain's ability to process thoughts beyond my capability.

With the blade embedded in my chest, Griffin catapulted from the wall and hurtled toward me at full force. We crashed to the ground. Landing on top of me, he maneuvered quickly, my dagger-drained attempts sluggish in comparison to his lightning moves.

His knees pinned my upper arms to the ground. He leaned forward and yanked my head upward, his face a contorted mask of rage, his skin a flushed blend of deep red and violet. With my head between his huge hands, he let out a roar as he smashed the back of my skull into the rock-hard floor again and again.

Unable to defend myself, let alone retaliate, I drifted in and out of a forced oblivion.

With dissociation in full force each time the

blindfold of unconsciousness lifted, I listened with numbed shock to the sickening sound of my skull as it was crushed against the floor, only to be replaced with a gurgling sound. Somewhere between a comatose and compos mentis state, I saw Giffin's arms, stick straight and rigid, holding his hands steady in an iron grip around my throat.

A river of red seeped across my eyes, the shallow pool replacing the blackness, but only for a moment. Its shade darkened swiftly until it mutated from ruby to garnet to black, and I started a long and lonely free fall into darkness. Yet again to be consumed by death.

Chapter 28

The flashes came like strobes of light, painfully bright and in short bursts. My consciousness flickered between light and dark. Noise and silence rolled in waves, and my brain fluctuated between activity and stillness. Each bout of darkness stretched on a little bit more every time. Each moment of light became a little shorter and further away.

So tired but I couldn't even sleep. The nothingness did not allow it. Its silence echoed loudly, making no sense to my exhausted, confused brain.

There was something in the midst of a fleeting flash that snatched me from my stupefied state. It tugged at my heart, which reacted by beating furiously, the shock of the blood rush forced my eyes to snap open.

I was on the ground and immediately regretted my return to reality. The semi-conscious state had dulled everything: my vision, my hearing, my brain function, but most importantly of all, my pain.

I tried to inhale, but my lungs would only fill halfway, leaving me gasping for air. I writhed on the floor, my nerve endings electrified to such a state that stillness was not a possibility. I was desperate to escape the red-hot pressure that pinned my chest down, but I was snared; with each moment that passed, the pain grew in intensity. It made me want to smash my head against a rock just to get it to stop.

I blinked; the voice inside my head screamed to be returned to the pain-free, light-free void. It took me forever to convince my arms to work, to strenuously move them from where they were glued to the ground and guide their dead weight to my chest in search of the object responsible for inflicting such agony.

At that point I wasn't trying to escape, I was trying to die.

The dagger burned to the touch, but I grasped it regardless. In full hyperventilation mode, I tried to rip it free in the hopes I would bleed out quickly, but my arms had about as much strength as wet noodles.

Only then did I realize that there was someone else there. Their rapid movements were caught in my peripheral field of vision. Their roar was one of pure rage that made the tiny grains of earth tremble and vibrate as their wrath cast shock waves within the compacted space. I tried to call for help, but the most I could muster was a low hoarse whisper that was barely a sound, let alone an actual word.

I tried again to grip the dagger, but someone had stolen my bones and left me with jelly hands. My eyes rolled back in my head as my useless fingers started to slip from the hot metal. I anticipated the thud of my arms as they hit the ground, but the thud never came. My shocked brain tried to fathom out what had happened. Had I lost my hands? Did someone slice them clean away as they were mid-descent? My eyes flickered, jolted by panic as I tried to regain a focus beyond my blurry field of vision.

I twitched my fingers. They were still there, attached to my unhelpful hands, suspended in midair and supported by hands much smaller than mine. Despite their slight size, they were strong. They cupped and held with strength my flailing fingers. Little yet mighty, they squeezed their fingers tightly to my own, offering the support my gelatinized bones were incapable of.

Carefully, they guided my hands back to the dagger where they held fast and worked with me to tug the searing metal from its position, entrenched deep within my chest. Exerting everything I possibly could, I pulled, and finally with a sickening sound, the blade tore upward, back through my sternum, ribs, and flesh.

I was free.

Without the embedded blade, my lungs finally filled and pushed away the fog of confusion. The burning pain however remained relentless.

I still couldn't move. My broken bones and crushed windpipe required longer to heal. I didn't care though; I had been lifted far from that dank and lightless cave by the vision that had taken center stage and made me forget about my desire to die and the chaos that occurred feet away.

Kasey.

His soft fingers brushed against my face, wiping away tears and blood. He lowered his head close to mine, his huge blue eyes held my gaze transfixed, his voice was calm but concerned as he begged for assurances. I was enthralled by his presence, so stunned at being gifted with what I had ached for yet thought impossible. He was with me again. I could hold him, breathe him in, protect him the way I was meant to. I was so captivated that I managed to temporarily overlook the blatantly obvious danger being with me had placed him in.

The smell of blood and the sound of broken bones dragged me sharply back to reality.

I grabbed at him in panic, I wanted to shield him but even with an adrenaline rush in full flow, the best I could manage was to half prop myself up on one side, and even that made me scream in agony.

That was when I saw him. Embroiled in a vicious and deadly battle against Griffin.

Aamon.

They attacked each other with visceral brutality, their aggression comparable to that of unrestrained rabid dogs. I wasn't witnessing a fight. I was witnessing a homicidal rampage of incomprehensible savagery.

Clutching Kasey behind me, I forced myself up one more inch, making every effort to ignore the screaming pain that such an action generated. I ripped my gaze from Aamon and mustered everything I had, gathered together every thought, emotion, scrap of anger and pain, and dropped it all into the open arms of my beautiful darkness. Then I slumped back.

It appeared no more than a haze to my blurred sight, a dark cloud of anger-fueled vapor that traveled at the speed of light and struck Griffin from the side, immobilizing him mid-swing.

Aamon stumbled, momentarily perplexed at Griffin's sudden statue-like stance. His onyx eyes glinted even in the dimly lit space. He released a deep guttural roar and lunged forward; his huge fist impacted Griffin's temple with skull-shattering force. Aamon's growl rumbled deep and low, making the thick air shudder as Griffin's features froze into a grotesque mask, his pupils hardened to a dead stare, and he crumpled to the ground.

I raised my foot and kicked the dagger toward Aamon but yelled at him to stop before he had the time to thrust it into Griffin's stone heart. He glanced toward me, confusion painted across his face.

"Wait," I begged, as I strained my broken body to retrieve the small glass vessel capable of holding Griffin's soul. The orb.

I lacked the strength to throw it, my feeble arm barely able to sustain the weight of the oval glass and silver container as I extended it toward him.

The ground tremored as Aamon's huge form stepped forward. Blood and sweat glistened on his olive skin, and anger remained carved deeply across his dark as thunder face. As he bent forward to reach for the orb, his fingers skimmed lightly over mine, their touch igniting a magnetic pull. He fell to his knees and placed one hand against my face as his lips brushed gently against mine, the brief embrace was enough to pull me back to life, to refire my eroded synapses and knit together some of the frayed parts of me.

Somewhere behind him, Griffin flinched, Aamon gave me a small nod as he stood. I rolled over to face Kasey, pulled him close, and whispered, "Close your eyes, baby."

With a faint whoosh, the dagger glided through the air and punctured Griffin's skull with a crack. A short high-pitched hiss followed as his soul was snatched from its passing and encapsulated within the orb.

"You don't get the gift of free will, you fucker," I murmured as yet again the floor tilted and the pain dragged me grudgingly back into the darkness.

Aamon's huge arms cradled me and carried me from Daeon, just as they had done the very first time our paths crossed. Earth's air was not so quick to revive me this time, and when it did, I felt like I'd been hit by a freight train.

I turned my back to the light and sank deep into the darkness in search of deliverance amid the relentless grip of the excruciating injuries from which my body refused to heal.

The voices were what brought me back. Their words as sharp as smelling salts, once my sluggish brain was able to comprehend the conversation.

My name, Kasey's name, Laeon, and hunted swirled around trying to find their place within a meaningful sentence. I got the gist. Even with Griffin gone, Kasey wasn't safe, and in my present state neither was I. Aamon's role in Daeon had always been to maintain a degree of order. Without him, chaos had ensued, a situation only worsened by Griffin.

I hadn't healed the way I should. The lingering effects of the dagger seemed to be the prime suspect for my fragile physical state, the prognosis of which remained a mystery. The only safe place for me was Daeon, but not the outer realm. The center was where I needed to be, the place of no return, allegedly. And Kasey, well, his only true place of safety was where he was meant to be already, Laeon.

I was not bloody well okay with that. I suppose really it was my anger that dragged me back more than the voices.

I forced my eyes open. The energy and concentration such a facile action took was ridiculous, a notion that increased my growing rage from a simmer to a boil. I blinked rapidly, willing my full sight to be restored. I was on Aamon's bed, my bed, in the place I considered home. A fact that failed to placate me the way it usually would.

Each breath was labored. I sounded like a cow being slaughtered as I heaved myself onto my side and dropped my lead-weight legs to the ground.

With clawed hands gripping the edge of the mattress, I heaved myself upward and was met with immediate regret. The room spun like I'd drunk my way through a bottle of white on an empty stomach, and my legs reacted like a hundred-pound weight had been dropped on them.

I hit the deck with as much grace as a hippo falling from a balance beam.

"Fuck."

From a crumpled heap on the ground, I rubbed my throbbing temples and tried unsuccessfully to convince my lower extremities to comply. After cussing my legs out, I reached up to the side of the bed and hauled myself halfway up, dragging my infuriatingly useless lower limbs behind me.

Aamon cleared his throat.

His stature filled the doorway. He kept his arms crossed as he leaned casually against the frame, dressed in jeans and a dark shirt with his sleeves rolled midway up his muscular tattooed arms. His dark eyes glinted, and he attempted to conceal a smile. Of course, he looked drop-dead gorgeous, which was fitting given that I resembled something that had dropped dead, been buried for some time, then dug back up.

I scowled in his direction, then winced as I hitched myself up another inch. Aamon's smile faded quickly, and he rushed to my side, lifting me carefully to the bed like I was weightless.

"I'm almost scared to ask"—his deep husky voice only served to make him more damn seductive—"but what the fuck are you trying to do?"

I attempted to sit up and groaned as a fresh wave of pain engulfed me.

Aamon's eyes widened incredulously. "Stop moving! What the hell?"

"I need to sit up," I croaked.

His eyes narrowed. "If I help you sit up, will you stay put on the bed?"

"Opposed to what? Collapsing in a heap again? My options are clearly limited," I growled.

His face softened. "Baby, let me help you."

My stomach did a somersault, and my heart sped up as he hitched me gently into a seated position and rearranged the pillows around me. I exhaled like it was I who had done something strenuous. Just existing drained me. Aamon leaned forward and ran a finger along my cheekbone. His eyes, inches from mine, caused my breath to get stuck somewhere in my chest. His lips brushed against my mouth, and for that moment at least, he succeeded in placing a lid firmly on my little pot of rage.

"Will you leave me again?" I burst, surprising myself.

"I didn't leave you in the first place," he replied softly.

My eyes filled with tears and my breaths rasped painfully. "I dreamt of you."

Aamon perched gingerly on the edge of the mattress. He lifted my hand into his with the care one would extend to bone china or fine crystal. He held my gaze for a moment before admitting, "I know. I was there."

I blinked and my jaw dropped in astonishment. "What...?"

Silence sat heavy between us as my anesthetized brain tried desperately to make sense of his response.

He brushed a wisp of hair off my face as he explained, "It isn't a very reliable method of communication, but it's all I had."

A sudden panic bubbled in my chest. My brain still felt foggy. Was there a possibility that none of it was real?

"How are you here?" I stared at him hard. If it hadn't been for the excruciating pain, I'd have been convinced I was still dreaming.

His dark eyes held mine with a burning intensity. "I had a little helper who guided us both back."

Kasey.

His sapphire-blue eyes flashed before me, and along with his image was Aamon's voice on replay reminding me of the last conversation I'd heard before I slipped into unconsciousness. My heart skipped a beat.

"I heard you," I murmured. "Did you take Kasey to Laeon without me?"

Aamon's smoky eyes searched my face, and his brows furrowed. "You think I'd dare?"

I expected a smirk, but his features remained serious. I fought hard against the tears that pooled. "Where is he?"

"He's sleeping on the sofa, his head in Noah's lap. He likes him a lot."

"But you're going to take him to Laeon?" I croaked.

Aamon sighed heavily. He gently caressed my hands, his gaze never left mine. "We are going to take him. It's where he's meant to be, but I don't think I need to explain that to you."

"I just want the chance to…" My voice trailed off. I

couldn't even bring myself to say the damn words.

I switched my attention firmly away from thoughts of contemplating the inevitable. I reached for Aamon and asked, "Are you okay?"

He looked surprised. "What do you mean? Why wouldn't I be okay?"

"I mean, you had a pretty fucking horrific fight and killing someone you've known, well, across literal lifetimes. It can't have been the easiest thing you've ever done."

Aamon chuckled as he walked around the bed. From the opposite side, he crawled carefully across the king size and settled gently next to me. I shifted my weight to face him. Behind me, the sun was starting to set. Its warm golden-orange glow bathed the room in a comforting, muted light.

"And there was I concerned for how it would affect you." He pushed a strand of hair from my forehead and planted a soft kiss in its place.

I tilted my head questioningly. Talking was starting to hurt too.

He shrugged his shoulders and glanced down. I couldn't take how beautiful he was, his dark eyes beneath thick lashes, the way his shirt clung to his broad and defined shoulders, the top buttons teasingly offering just a taste of his muscular chest covered in ink.

His closeness made my breathing heavy and that hurt too, but it was pain I was willing to put up with. And if it killed me, at least I'd die happy.

"At one time you were close with him, the two of you had a relationship," he mumbled.

It was a bizarre thing to witness. This godlike creature who had mercilessly ruled the bloody underworld with beastlike ferocity, lounged out on the bedspread, afraid to look at me, afraid of what my response might be.

I'd have laughed if I hadn't been so afraid of the suffering such an act would cause.

"You had a relationship with him too, and for much longer," I reasoned.

Aamon's eyes flashed, and he glanced at me, his brows raised. "Not like the relationship you had." He emphasized.

"Oh my good God!" I exclaimed, mortified as I grimaced in both pain and embarrassment. "If you ever make reference to *that* again, I will slap the shit out of you."

His gruff laugh soothed away my embarrassment but unfortunately did little to quell the burning throb of hurt.

I inhaled a shaky breath. "Why won't this pain stop?"

"The dagger did a lot of damage. We need to get you to Daeon."

"I'm not going anywhere until I know that Kasey is safe," I insisted, turning toward the footsteps that cautiously approached.

Zagan knocked on the open doorway. He looked me over before exclaiming, "She's alive." He raised his open palms to frame his face and shook them, mimicking jazz hands.

A small laugh erupted before I had time to stop it. It was gas on a lit flame, and I gasped as a fresh wave of agony swept over me. Aamon shot Zagan a murderous glare, and he dropped his hands quickly in response.

Desperate for a distraction, I gripped the bed sheets

with white knuckles and whispered, "When do we leave?"

"You were unable to convince her, I see?" Zagan responded, his face sour.

"I didn't even try," Aamon answered dryly.

"Well, the crew are here. Everyone's ready. We need to get moving before we lose the last of the daylight." He nodded toward the window and added, "Should we wake the boy?"

"He has a name," Aamon growled.

Zagan became flustered. His eyes flitted to me as he murmured, "Apologies."

I offered him a small smile, as much as I could muster and just slightly, I shook my head.

"Let him sleep," Aamon confirmed. He rolled away gently and walked around to my side of the bed. "Are you ready?" he asked, warning me, "This is going to hurt."

Lying still, I had convinced myself the pain simply could not get any worse. I was wrong. Branding irons seared from the inside as a thousand hot-poker needles pierced from the outside. I had to clench my teeth to stop a scream from escaping as Aamon gingerly scooped me from the bed.

I fought to stay conscious, but as the minutes ticked by, my slips between altered states grew in frequency and length of time. I heard more than I saw, and more than I could respond to. Aamon's voice called out to me, but he sounded so far away my eyes wouldn't open to help find him, and my mouth refused to comply when I tried to speak.

I heard Kasey's voice, and I felt his delicate touch. I wanted so desperately to see him; to hold him and to kiss him but I was encased in a thick stone tomb, silenced and frozen. I felt Kasey leave, felt him move farther away as he passed across planes and left me far behind. My heart cracked and splintered, but still the cold hard confines of my enclosure remained indestructible, giving no clues as to my awareness and my heartbreak.

The walls remained near, yet the darkness became deeper. A low frequency thrum resonated too close. It made my head pound and my chest ache. The dense air of Daeon mingled with Earth's atmosphere and snatched away each breath, while I gasped with what little oxygen I had left in my raw bleeding lungs. The darkness closed in, taking its final last steps. It was not a pain-free passing, as I prayed for the only end I knew.

Chapter 29

I opened my eyes; the pulsating darkness began to dissipate slowly. The color above me altered as particles of light merged and blended with the inky blackness. I propped myself up onto my elbows and turned my head slowly to take in the surroundings from the middle of the meadow in which I lay.

Panic jolted through me. I had no recollection of where I was or how I had gotten there. Cautiously, I dragged myself to my feet. The movement made each muscle tense painfully tight.

A halo of muted white encircled the perimeter of the open space, disappearing into the tree line of a forest, the dark rich greens and browns of which made up two-thirds of the outer edge.

The stiffness in my legs relaxed involuntarily, and I was able to move freely. I picked my way across the grass, which despite being shorter and motionless, shared a striking similarity to the meadow in my dream. Beyond the grass was a landscape of rolling hills, fringed by trees with a backdrop of mountains that were covered by a veil of mist and violet haze.

Nothing was still, the colors constantly mutated, and the tone of the terrain deepened and lightened.

I felt him close behind me. I was afraid to turn around in case he disappeared again. Every fiber pulled me in his direction. I could not be without him.

I stared ahead, mesmerized by the ever-shifting landscape, willing his closeness to remain.

"Where are we?" I whispered.

"Home," Aamon murmured.

"We can't stay here," I pleaded with him.

"What's the rush? Time is for the living, not the dead." His hushed tone crept across the small channel between us, making my skin prickle and testing my dwindling control.

I shook my head, grasped at my focus, and dredged through the quicksand of memories, trying to order them sequentially.

"But I lost him," I gasped. The words made what had happened suddenly a harsh reality, and in the process, it stole away my oxygen.

He rested his hands on my shoulders and lowered his cheek next to mine.

"He was never yours to keep. The ones we are gifted with are just that, a gift to enjoy but only for a little while. The only forever is with the one you find alone, the one you choose when you're without the encumbrances of another life."

Free will.

I winced in pain. He waited.

"You were only ever supposed to have him until the end of your time in that existence. You exceeded that. Now let him have the freedom every living soul deserves."

"But he's so little," I insisted as tears pooled in my eyes. Even in the midst of my sorrow, I understood the selfishness of my need.

"You've seen the other side, you know that age becomes irrelevant. There's no danger, no dependence, no needs that he can't fulfill himself."

"Will he not wonder where I am?"

There they were again, my ego and desires propelled forward beyond truth and reason. He tugged me round to face him. The look in his eyes reaching out to surround my fears, and my pain, lifting me clear of them.

"It isn't your choice for a reason. You'd never choose to open the cage door and let him fly away. No one ever would. It contradicts what life conditioned you to do, what nature embedded within your every instinct. You'll miss missing him, but once you truly let him go, you won't miss him anymore."

"That makes me even sadder," I admitted.

He laughed.

"There's no place for fear or longing here, you'll see," he promised, planting a tender kiss on the top of my head. "He doesn't need you anymore. That's what stings the most, but it is how it's supposed to be. You were the tree that held his nest. You sheltered him and protected him all in preparation for that special moment."

"The moment he flew away," I concluded.

Aamon took two steps back and held out his hand. "Walk with me."

I studied him closely. His once-dark eyes and brooding features had melted almost completely away, making him look younger. The smile that once was such a rarity was now never far from his features. Annoyingly, his happiness was contagious.

I slipped my hand into his, and he pulled me close. His lips ignited a part of me I'd forgotten existed. For a fleeting moment, the embrace stole away my breath and my hurt, and I was reminded that he was the forgiveness I could never give myself.

We walked from the meadow toward the dense tree line. The air was warm and the scent intoxicating, reminiscent of late summer or early fall, dry without the dust, crisp without the chill. The perfect concoction.

The circle of trees familiar from my dream wrapped around the sprawling grassland. I assumed we were destined for the forest, but instead, we stopped at its outer edge. Aamon gestured toward the tree that stood directly before us.

"Look carefully."

Puzzled, I stepped closer, crossing from a field of grass to a floor of soft dry moss. I studied the first tree closely. The surface of its trunk was rough, a blend of dark cherry and chestnut shades that formed bumps and grooves. I followed the path of one of the grooves by running my fingers lightly over its surface. The closer to the center my fingers traveled, the smoother the surface area became. I squinted and leaned closer. There in the middle, faded almost beyond recognition, was the outline of a grandfather clock, not dissimilar to the one that had plagued me relentlessly. Its sepia face gently contrasted against the wood grain, its faint numerals almost completely obscured by moss and foliage, its hands motionless.

I moved to the next tree. This one was clearer to make out. Its trunk was thinner and smoother, even on the edges. Its branches were gangly in contrast, its hands stuck frozen on a different time.

I spun bewildered toward Aamon. A rush of air swept through me, warm and comforting. My mouth fell open. Each tree was the same, constructed from a clock, and aged from the moment its time stopped.

Aamon surveyed me closely, his hands stuffed into

his pockets. "Do you understand?"

With a frown, I shook my head.

"Endings are from what this place was created."

His words crept softly, and like a thief in the night it took something from me, just like my dream. Only this time what was taken wasn't replaced with a colorless void of pain, it was replaced with an inexplicable peaceful relief.

I peered deep into the thick forest as I asked, "It was created by death?"

"From an ending and a beginning."

"An ending and a beginning?" I repeated slowly.

"Each time that ceases adds to the beauty of this place, or another place. Every end just means a new beginning."

We started to walk just within the tree line of the forest and toward the horizon. Moments passed as I mulled over Aamon's words.

The end of my life meant the end of everything tied to it. I winced in pain and pushed the heel of my hand to my chest.

"When you left that life, you also left the roles from that life. You're not a daughter or a mother here. You're simply you."

"It feels so wrong." I frowned.

"That's because you spent one whole life and half of the next tying yourself to the people you loved. You needed them to depend on you more than they actually needed to."

"So if I leave this life, I also have to let go of you?"

The panic that bubbled just below the surface threatened to erupt. Aamon squeezed my hand reassuringly.

"This is the ever after. Everyone has one. Some pass through the outer realms swiftly to arrive here. Others live and die many lives before they are ready to pass in to here. For most, it is a point of no return, but for you and I, we can still transition through planes, and maybe we will one day, but not for a while."

I stopped, alarmed at what his words meant.

"Can Griffin?"

"Griffin has a lot more living to do before he'll be even close to being ready. Until then, he can't pass into here, and it will be a long while before he can cross between even Daeon and Earth. He didn't get to choose, remember? He was delivered to Daeon against his will, and there he will remain."

A small sigh escaped me. "If it's the way it's supposed to be, why do I feel so guilty?" I challenged.

"Guilty?"

I nodded. "Yes, I believe everything you say, I think I will be okay, and I think I can let go." I turned to face Aamon. "And that makes me feel guilty. I must be the worst fucking parent in the world."

He laughed, an irresistible melody that danced on the breeze before it floated lightly away.

"Imagine if each plant and tree kept what they bore, the fruit they grew, the pollen from the blossoms they created, and imprisoned them indefinitely. Eventually, everything would wither. Nothing would grow. Nothing would flourish. We'd be left with a real darkness."

I stood silently as I allowed the full weight of his words to sink in. With infinite patience, he stood beside me until I was ready, and we continued our trail.

As we walked, I glanced up at him. "Was this a choice? Did I choose you over them?"

His mouth remained unmoving, but his eyes smiled brightly. He shook his head. "You didn't choose Daeon. Daeon chose you, but even if it hadn't and you had all gone to Laeon, it would have made no difference. You are now and will always be a form of you. Elements of who you were then are responsible for shaping who you are now."

We had walked clear of the forest; the soft floor of moss and pine needles fell away to a breathtaking view. Before us was a rocky hillside, and beneath it stretched an ocean. I rested against a rock, its surface warmed by an unseen sun. The waves beneath us lapped gently against the soft white sandy cove.

I inhaled slowly. The tranquility wound like tendrils. Their touch permeated through my skin and entered my bloodstream, making me feel a little high.

"It's not quite the burning fires of hell I expected," I murmured.

"Suns and stars burn and are considered beautiful, but when you burn from a source of darkness, it's deemed ugly and evil," Aamon responded mockingly.

I raised one brow as I glanced at him. "Are you likening yourself to a star, Aamon?"

His laugh was gruff and rare. The sound made my heart skip a beat.

"I was illustrating the misjudged hypocrisy. The truth is that the darkness holds the key and the power to all planes. Daeon's size supersedes Earth and Laeon combined."

He leaned against the rock. With one arm wrapped loosely around my waist, his lips skimmed the top of my head. "How did you feel the first time you entered Daeon?"

The memory made my breath catch. The memory of him overpowered the memory of Daeon, but it was not completely forgotten.

"Like I was entering Hell. The energy, the heat, the lack of light—it was intense."

He smiled just a little. "That's because you'd been conditioned to associate that specific combination as an abomination. You automatically assumed that type of energy indicated something deplorable and nefarious." The memory of my first Daeon encounter drifted away. When he was that close, it became hard to think of anything but him.

Aamon tugged me from my resting place and led me down a winding pathway etched between the boulders and patches of beach grass. Upon the sandy shoreline sat large driftwood logs, smooth and bleached almost to a shade of white.

Crystal-clear water rolled over the branches that reached longing arms toward the azure horizon line as the roots that once anchored the tree to the ground sat proudly on the sand, soaking up the light and air they were once denied.

Aamon guided me to the largest of the fallen trees. With ease and agility, he climbed up onto it and extended his hand, pulling me carefully beside him. He propped himself sideways, his back leaning against the web of gnarled roots as I lay along the length of its trunk, nestled between his outstretched legs, my head against his chest.

I held the last grain of melancholy in the palm of my hand, unwilling to let it go, despite knowing its place was with the trillion other grains that sculpted what surrounded us.

Images of my grandmother filled my mind. "Will I

ever see the people I knew?" I asked, afraid to wait in case the memories vanished never to be retrieved.

"Soon you won't remember them," he answered as his fingers softly brushed my hair from my forehead.

"Letting go means losing all of my memories?" I squeezed the last grain a little tighter.

"Not all. There will always be the thinnest of threads for a select few."

"Like Kasey?"

"Like Kasey. But you won't remember him as your child."

The breeze that traveled across the ocean's surface contrasted sharply against the warm air that surrounded us. The light above us faded to a stormy gray. I jumped down to the sand, alarmed at the sudden change and the feeling of dread it brought with it.

Aamon's voice was firm, willing me to stay calm. "You will be okay," he promised, it sounded more like an order than a request.

Staring out across the now churning water, I gasped as an icy-cold splinter the size of a spear pierced my chest. I grabbed at the point of impact, but there was nothing there. Aamon's voice remained controlled somewhere behind me. I wanted to turn toward him, but my feet were cemented to the sand, frozen by a toxic cocktail of fear and pain.

My fingers continued to search for something, the weapon that had inflicted such excruciating agony, the blood that must surely have drenched me, and the organs that must have been hanging from the fissure in my chest. But my trembling hands found nothing.

"Breathe through it," Aamon demanded.

His words reminded me of my labor with Kasey.

How the fuck could he be so composed when I was literally dying in front of him!

"Breathe," he again commanded. I didn't want to, I had never experienced anything like that before, yet I knew regardless that it would hurt, just like when they tell you it's time to push during childbirth. Aamon moved closer, but he didn't touch me, he couldn't. I understood it was something I needed to do alone.

My chest became so constricted I was unable to draw a breath. The world around me started to spin, black spots filled my field of vision, and I fell. I waited to hit the ground, but the ground never came. Instead, a burst of air passed through me, forcing my lungs to contract for what felt like the first time in my life. Somehow, I remained on my feet, the ground beneath me steadied, and my vision cleared. As quickly as it arrived, the pain had disappeared.

The warmth that crept through my body sought out every last tiny frozen particle, long abandoned by the invisible icy armament, each transformed into liquid that evaporated with the warmth of the wind and added to its charge.

Finally, Aamon's arms wrapped around me. I was grateful for his support. Whatever had passed through me had left me feeling weightless. Had he not been holding me, I was sure I'd have floated away.

"What was that?" I croaked.

"He let you go," he whispered as his arms squeezed me a little tighter. Maybe he also worried that I would drift away.

"What?" I choked as panic started to engulf me again.

"Stop," he commanded, his arms holding tight. "Let

go of everything you believed, and focus on just one thing; can you do that for me?"

Unable to answer, I nodded.

"Look deep and tell me how you feel."

"Free," I murmured, surprised by my own response.

"As is he. It's the way it's meant to be. Letting go is the hardest thing, just as holding on is the cruelest."

Aamon leaned back against the driftwood. His arms remained wrapped around me. I placed my empty hand on his forearm. The other hand still clutched the final grain.

"So happy ever after doesn't exist." I sighed. The grain was starting to get warmer.

"Look around. Tell me you truly believe that?"

I wriggled free of his arms and turned to face him. His smile spread from his mouth to his eyes. Even Daeon's beauty took second place in comparison to his. He was the force that made me believe. He was the ever after I didn't dare dream I'd ever have.

He pushed himself from the bleached wood and planted a soft kiss on my forehead. I inhaled, allowing him to feed every need within.

"There is a happy ever after, but only after you let go."

I looked out at the sparking sapphire waters that stretched beyond a curvature. Its horizon met a cloudless sky in an uninterrupted line. Without looking down, I opened my hand. The delicate grain made up of golden hues sat centered in my palm.

As right and necessary as it was, I couldn't watch it go. But I felt its joy as a tiny zephyr that danced from the gentle surf swept it high and carried it away.

The tears that tracked a steady line down my cheek

were for so many things. Contentment and appreciation, for longing and for loss, but most of all for what I had in another life, and for what I loved enough to let go.

You see, there's an ever after for everyone, and within it, there lies a happiness each person has the power to control, as soon as they realize that it starts and ends with them.

From the other side, to the ever after, with love.

A word about the author…

Julia Harrison was born in London and grew up in the Northwest of England. She is a graduate of Liverpool John Moores University and mother to three sons and one daughter. She moved to the USA in 2016 and currently resides in Florida with her younger children and a variety of rescue pets.

Learn more about Julia at
https://juliaharrisonauthor.com/